I0728093

FINDING TREASURE

Also By Pamela Humphrey

In This Series

Finding Claire

Finding Kate

Other Books

The Blue Rebozo: A Novella

Researching Ramirez: On the Trail of the Jesus Ramirez Family

FINDING TREASURE

PAMELA HUMPHREY

Copyright ©2018 Pamela Humphrey

All Rights Reserved

Phrey Press
www.phreypress.com

First Edition

This is a work of fiction. Names, characters, businesses, places, events and incidents are either the products of the author's imagination or used in a fictitious manner. Any resemblance to actual persons, living or dead, or actual events is purely coincidental.

All rights reserved. This book or any portion thereof may not be reproduced or used in any manner whatsoever without the express written permission of the author except for the use of brief quotations in a book review.

978-1-947685-00-0

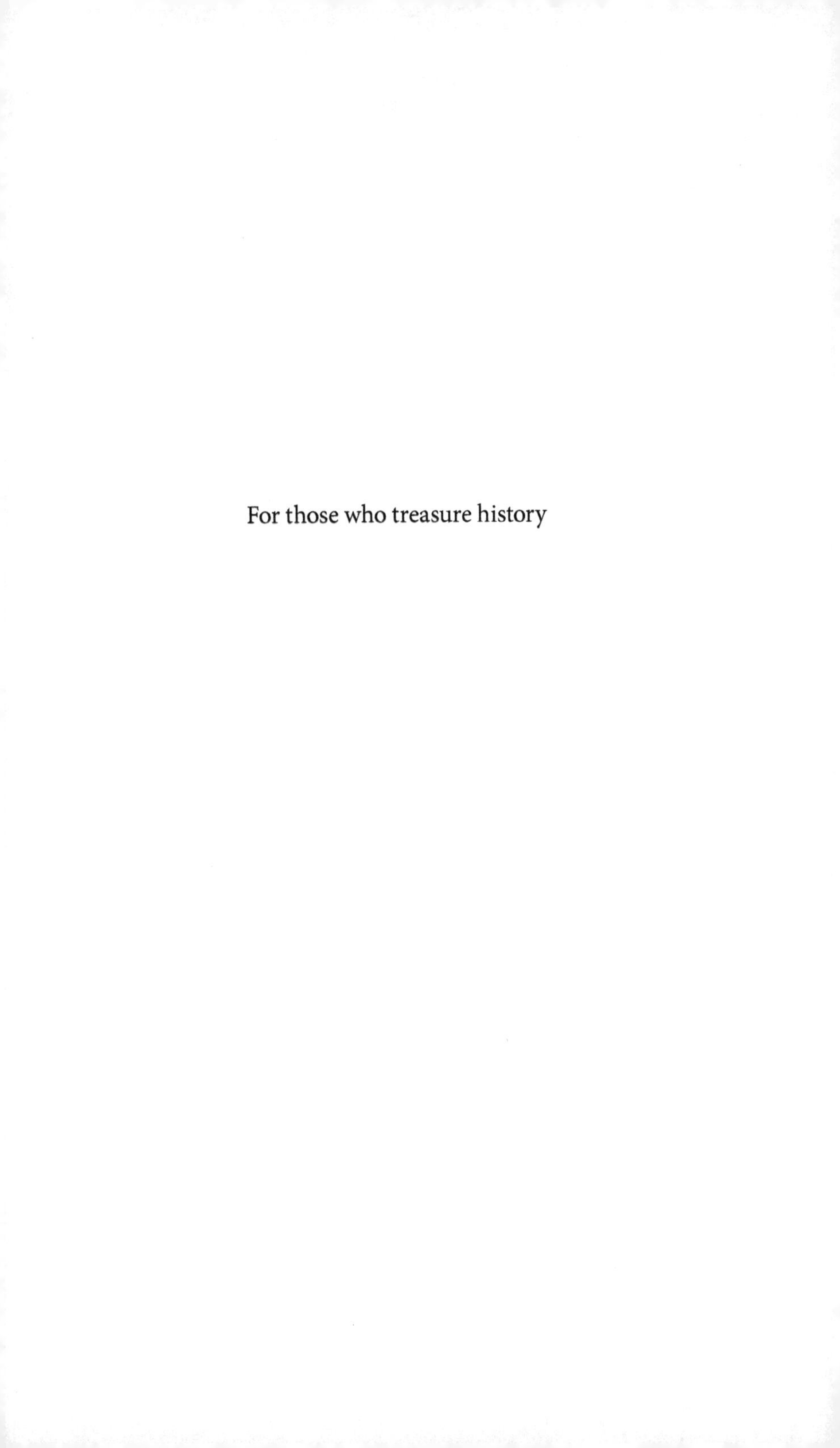

For those who treasure history

CHAPTER ONE

April 4 – 2:15 pm

*A*lmost perfect. Describing life that way made me wary, as if acknowledging it invited the bottom to fall out of my happy, snow-globe-worthy existence.

My hair danced around my head and whipped in my face as I zipped down the highway with the windows rolled down. My red, freshly manicured nails glistened in the sunlight. The ink still wet on the signature, I'd just signed the first client for my new genealogy business.

After my life turned upside down months ago, I started over with a few extras: a new boyfriend, a new dad, a fabulous new house, a large bank account, and a near perfect life. With the recently acquired funds, I had the chance to pursue my dream. My first assignment: to research genealogy as a surprise for a woman's birthday, a gift from her husband.

When Eddie Rabbitt came on the radio singing "I Love a Rainy Night," I christened that day "The Best Monday Ever," and I'd had some pretty good Mondays. That song always prompted a smile because it reminded me of the nickname Alex gave me after we met.

I couldn't wait to tell him about how well the client meeting had gone. Always supportive, he'd encouraged me in my endeavor. After a quick stop by my house, I headed to his cabin.

As I drove out of town, past the overgrown land that lay adjacent to my property, I noticed a brightly colored *For Sale* sign that wasn't there yesterday. Curiosity coaxed me to the side of the road. Behind trees and bushes hid a small wood frame house. I snapped a few pictures. I had no idea how far back the property stretched. Glancing down the length of fence, I spotted an old metal sign. *Kent.*

That wasn't a name I'd heard mentioned around town. I'd have to ask about it the next time I wandered into The Drugstore. Maggie might know something about the old place. *Might? Who am I kidding?* Maggie seemed to know everything about everyone who lived or had ever lived in town. When the blue Victorian went on the market, she talked about it for weeks. The tiny town had an interesting idea of excitement.

Even contemplating the spark of an idea seemed crazy. *I don't need that property.* What would I do with acres and acres? Raising livestock wasn't on my bucket list. I trudged back to my car but allowed myself one last glance. Wildflowers grew beside the caliche road. I wanted the property. I snapped a picture of the sign in case I decided to call about it later.

Back in my car, I headed to Alex's. When I pulled up in front of the cabin, I parked next to a black sedan. Heat still radiated off the hood. *Whose car is that?*

I glanced toward the door and froze. A tall brunette had her arms around Alex. She kissed him. *Only on the cheek.* That's what I tried to tell myself, but it didn't make me feel any better. I watched her curves disappear into the cabin.

My happily-ever-after crumbled before my eyes. Glued to the driver's seat, I debated whether to drive away or go inside. My insecurities taunted me. Although I only saw a glimpse, the woman was beautiful. Taller, trimmer, and younger than me, she seemed completely at ease hugging Alex. My Alex. Tears stung my eyes.

He wouldn't. Would he?

Thoughts, like cats and dogs, chased each other in circles, making me dizzy. The world outside spun. I squeezed my eyes closed.

Don't cry.

I dug around in my center console for a tissue.

Go inside.

Whatever the explanation, it wouldn't be uncovered in a box of tissues.

Don't panic.

The last time I told myself not to panic, only a few moments after, I learned my brother-in-law had been shot. No, the last time was when I was being held captive. I left panic on my list of options, very near the top. Alex didn't expect me for another hour, but he'd given me a key. I closed my eyes, trying to think rationally, but the image of that woman with her arms around my boyfriend danced on the inside of my eyelids.

I turned off the engine and nearly went through the windshield when Alex rapped on the car window. Swallowing back my questions, I opened the door.

He offered his hand to help me out of the car. "You coming in?"

I slipped my hand in his and hoped my trust hadn't been misplaced.

His brows knitted together at the sight of my red, puffy eyes. "What's wrong, Kate? Did your meeting not go well?"

Determined to set my jealousy aside, I cleared my throat and steadied my voice, hoping to sound confident and chipper. "It went great. He hired me." I glanced up, praying my face didn't telegraph my thoughts.

"How long have you been here?" Laugh lines creased near his eyes.

"A few minutes." I studied the laces on his sneakers.

He slid his arms around me and whispered in my ear, "Were you going to leave without coming in to meet her?"

I leaned into him, inhaling the piney scent of his deodorant—or maybe that was the scent of his shampoo. "I hadn't decided."

He kissed the top of my head and tangled his fingers in my hair. "You can trust me, Kate. Always." He held my gaze, his eyes the luscious, vibrant green I loved.

"I want to. That's why I turned off the engine… to go inside." I kissed the cleft in his chin.

"Come meet my sister." His fingertips slid down my arm, and he took my hand.

I didn't budge, even when he started toward the door. "She's going to think I'm crazy." My cheeks grew hot, a sure sign that my face matched my nails.

"Maybe." He winked. A gentle tug pulled me to his side, his warm fingers laced with mine.

I tightened my grip with every step.

"Relax." He opened the door and moved aside for me to enter.

I took a deep breath as I walked inside. His sister, who had those same sparkling green eyes, smiled and hugged me. "I've heard so much about you."

"It's nice to meet you." I'd hoped to make a good first impression with his family, but now my only hope was to salvage what I could during the rest of our meeting.

Alex stood behind me and wrapped his arms around me. He stood a head taller, and I just cleared his chin. We fit together like puzzle pieces.

"Kate Bentley, Marisa Ramirez. Marisa, Kate."

"Bentley? I thought it was Westfall." Marisa looked from me to Alex.

"I changed it a couple months ago."

How much had Alex told her about me?

"Interesting. I'm sorry to pop in unannounced. I decided to surprise my brother, and I hoped I'd get to meet you as well." She tucked a dangling dark strand behind her ear. "You are exactly as he described you."

I pressed back against his chest and wished I could've heard all that he said about me. "Let's sit. We don't have to stand here. He finally bought a couch." Tilting my head back to catch his reaction, I laughed.

Red-cheeked, he rolled his eyes.

"That's how I knew he was truly in love." Marisa grinned at her brother.

Alex's prized recliner had been pushed to the side, and a cushy brown couch faced the fireplace. I kicked off my shoes and dropped onto one end of the sofa. Marisa perched on the edge of the recliner.

"I'll grab drinks." Alex disappeared into the kitchen.

"So, you live in Austin?" I mentally kicked myself for jumping to such a rash conclusion after only a glimpse. If I hadn't been so blinded, I might've seen the resemblance.

"I did, but I recently moved to San Antonio. Alex doesn't know yet." She pulled a strand of hair into the corner of her mouth, chewing at the end.

This was the sibling he was closest to. It seemed more and more apparent that when he said closest, he meant the only one he spoke to on any regular basis.

"Alex doesn't know what?" He handed her a Dr Pepper and dropped onto the couch next to me, offering me a Coke. His gaze stayed fixed on his sister. "What haven't you told me?"

"I got a job in San Antonio and moved in with a friend." Marisa brushed her hair away from her face and smiled at me. "Alex tells me that you're a genealogist, Kate."

"Sort of. Well, yes. Just starting out. I used to work in web design."

"Is it hard to find work in that field here?" A single eyebrow raised, and her voice held a hint of… accusation, maybe. A protective little sister peeked through her grown-up exterior. She probably assumed I sponged off her brother.

"Oh, no. I just haven't looked for those jobs." I could've teased and told her that Alex financed my life, but if Marisa thought I was serious, it wouldn't be the best way to endear me to his family. "I recently came into some money. It's giving me a chance to try something new." Out of the corner of my eye, I glimpsed a smile dancing in Alex's eyes. It still sounded like someone else's life when I talked about my story.

"Marisa, you moved? Why didn't you say anything? When?" His brow furrowed.

"Four months ago. Just before Christmas." She swiped at unseen specks on the toe of her heel. "I didn't tell you because I didn't think you would approve of my friend." She had all the attitude of a younger sister trying to avoid a lecture.

"Before or after we got together to make tamales?"

"Before."

His shoulders sagged. "Wouldn't approve? Marisa, you're an adult. You can choose your own roommates." He leaned forward, his elbows resting on his knees.

I ran my thumb along the tight muscle in his arm. He hadn't quite grasped her meaning, but he would in … three … two … one.

His eyes widened, and his neck muscles tensed. "You mean a guy? Is it serious?"

"Alex,"—I laced my fingers with his—"moving in together is a big step. I'm sure she'll tell you all about her new roommate when she's ready."

I knew the topic made Alex uncomfortable. Born to play the big brother role, he took it seriously, determined to protect his little sister from harm, of any sort. He expected the same restraint he showed in our relationship from anyone who dated his sister.

Marisa sighed and leaned back into the recliner, hopefully convinced I wasn't a horrible match for her brother and maybe even an ally for her. She seemed like a genuinely nice person, and I anticipated getting to know her better.

Alex shifted, still gripping my hand. "Let's grab an early dinner. Does that work for you, Marisa?" He didn't lecture or huff, which amazed me.

"I can't. I need to get back. It's been a delight meeting you, Kate. I haven't seen my brother like this in a long time. It's heartwarming."

My heart jumped up and down, and my cheeks ached from the stretch of my grin. "I'm sorry you have to rush off. I'd love to get together again."

"Are you busy tomorrow? We can meet for lunch if you're free."

"Great. I'm guessing Alex has your number. I'll text you mine, and you can message me the details." I hugged her. Perhaps I'd rescued that first impression after all.

"Sounds good." Marisa stepped into her brother's embrace but didn't linger. "I should go."

As soon as Marisa's black car turned out of view, Alex nuzzled my neck. "She liked you."

"I hope so."

He padded into the kitchen. "What do you say *we* go out for an early dinner?"

"I say yes."

Kibble clattered into Bureau's bowl. "Eat up. We'll be back after while." He stroked black fur as the cat gobbled up yummy crunchies.

After locking the front door, Alex caught my hand, and we strolled out to the truck.

He almost always opened my door and helped me in, but this time he caught me around the waist before reaching for the handle. "Why were you jealous?"

"Jealous? That's silly. She's your sister." I leaned back against the truck and batted my eyelashes.

"But you didn't know that when you were sitting in your car contemplating a retreat." The boyish grin that added sparkle to his eyes spread across his face.

"I guess I was a little surprised." I wasn't getting off the hook for my reaction.

"Jealousy was written all over your face—red eyes, a few tears, a pinched brow." He ran his knuckle along my jawline. "Don't you trust me?"

"Of course I trust you." The words tumbled out without hesitation. I trusted him with my life.

"Then you have no reason to be jealous." His green eyes held my gaze.

To him, it was a simple matter of logic. He didn't understand that my jealousy, in my mind, had little to do with him, and more to do with my own perceived shortcomings and past experiences. I shut down that train of thought as I wrapped my arms around his neck.

He lifted me 'til my toes left the ground. "I love you, Kate."

A thousand butterflies fluttered inside my chest when the L word rolled off his tongue, but I grew concerned that maybe after wading into the relationship pool, he was content to stay in shallow waters. Nearly thirty-two, I wanted more than a dinner-and-a-movie kind of relationship. I wanted a ring. He'd alluded to promises, to our future, but never brought up marriage. Given his past, I figured he needed time, and understandably so. *Better not to rush things.* That's what my head said. My heart stamped its foot, crossed its arms, and refused to listen.

"I love to hear you say that." I glanced down as my feet connected with the dirt.

"And?" He grinned.

"I love you too." Holding fistfuls of his tee shirt, I pulled him closer and met his lips.

He pressed me to the truck and with his fingers tangled in my hair, tilted my head, deepening our kiss.

My bones turned to jelly, and if not for his arm holding me close, I'd have melted into a puddle of desire at his feet. My chest ached for a breath, but, ignoring basic needs, I cradled his face, his stubble rough under my palms.

A hair's breadth from my lips, he whispered, "Only you, Kate."

I pressed a kiss to his neck before burying my face in the muscular curve. I was living my happily-ever-after. Almost.

"Tell me about your meeting. How'd it go?" He opened the passenger door.

"I signed my first client. He hired me to research his wife's family as a surprise birthday gift. Isn't that such a romantic idea?"

"Totally romantic." Alex over-enunciated the words and chuckled.

"Anyway, he waited until the last minute to ask. Her birthday is in less than a month. He gave me all the info he knew, but her mother's side is a complete mystery."

"And now you're on the case."

The waitress waved as Alex and I entered. Most of the staff knew us by name at the restaurant. I tucked into place in our favorite booth, and Alex slid in next to me. Waitresses found it amusing that Alex and I shared the one side.

"So, I'm guessing you are in a hurry to start researching."

"Yes, but it'll keep." I pushed the menu to the side. Every time we came, I ordered the same dish.

Our waitress brought over two glasses of sweet tea. "The usual?"

Alex raised his eyebrows and looked my direction.

"Yes, please." I handed her my menu.

Alex nodded, and the waitress grinned as she hurried away.

"What are you going to name your business?" He coiled the paper from his straw into a tiny circle.

"I'm not sure. Kate's Genealogy Services sounds cold." I drew small hearts in the condensation on my glass. "But I can't think of a name that conveys warmth."

"That's a tough one. Tell me more. What is it you aim to give the client?" In full fix-it mode, he hunched forward, ready to tackle ideas.

"Ideally, I'd give them four to six generations back on both their maternal and paternal lines. I know that won't always be possible. But…"

"But what?"

"It's more than just names. I want to give them a sense of connection to their past. Even if only on one branch, a story, a glimpse of real people from their family set into history."

"Interesting. So use my family tree as an example."

"I haven't gotten very far with yours, I'm afraid. With getting settled in the new house and all the classes and research I did to start the business, I never picked up your research again."

"I wasn't making an accusation, Kate."

"Okay. Well, your great grandfather's family lived east of San Antonio on a rented farm. They were likely sharecroppers, who planted and harvested the cotton, then earned their share when the cotton sold at the gin. Or they could have been tenant farmers, who, for a place to live and a little bit of money, worked the fields."

"The family farmed. That gives me a sense of who they were."

"But putting it into the context of history alters the picture a bit. After the Civil War, landowners sought cheap labor to do the work previously done by slaves. Cotton farming was hard, backbreaking work. Landowners recruited families from Mexico. Entire families lived in small one or two-room shacks. Every member of the family capable of working, regardless of age, worked the fields. Imagine grandmothers lugging a bag of cotton in the July heat, their hands cut and bleeding from the sharp bolls that only begrudgingly released their fluff." I held out my hands as if showing my not-bleeding hands helped make the point.

"Not the idyllic picture of farm life."

"They were hard-working people who left their homes and extended families behind, hoping for opportunity." I touched Alex's arm and wiped the mist from my eyes. "They battled prejudice and ignorance. It wasn't an easy life."

Alex quietly coiled and uncoiled the straw wrapper. "Knowing more about the time period changes the picture a bit. I'm not sure I fully realized how rough they had it." He brushed his thumb over the top of my hand. "I'll think more about a name, but nothing comes to mind right now."

I leaned my head on his shoulder. "When I'm finished with this project, I want to work on your tree some more."

"And what about the Bentley tree?"

"I'm almost afraid to look." Last time I shook the family tree, secrets fell out from places I didn't know to look, secrets that had me tied to a chair, staring at a gun.

Alex sighed. "I get that."

"I will, though. Someday."

The waitress cleared her throat as she stepped up to the table, carrying two plates loaded with shrimp, rice, and roasted veggies. "And here you go. I'll be back to refill your tea. Can I get you anything else?"

"No, thanks. I think we're good."

The topic of genealogy evaporated as we dug into our food. While we ate, we chatted about the parts of our day the other had missed.

"Alex, when you have time, there is a place I want you to see." I wasn't sure how he would react to the idea of buying the property, but his opinion mattered to me.

He eyed me over the rim of his tea glass. "That's vague."

"You know that land behind The Castle?"

"The overgrown land on the other side of your back fence that looks like no one has set foot on it in years?" He laid his credit card on top of the check.

When we went out, he insisted on buying. After the first month, I quit arguing the point.

"It's for sale. Saw the sign today."

His gaze focused on me, he rested his folded arms on the table. "How much?"

"Haven't called the realtor yet. I don't even know how many acres."

"Call Marisa. She's a realtor." He sounded almost excited about the idea.

"You don't think it's crazy?"

"If you want it and can afford it, what's crazy about it?"

I pushed my plate away and shifted to face him. "The wanting it part."

"If you get it, maybe I'll buy you a llama." A soft chuckle rattled in his chest. "Two, actually. They prefer companionship"—he leaned down and planted a kiss on my cheek—"which I totally get."

I dropped my purse near the door as I walked into the cabin. Thunder rumbled in the distance.

"Storm's coming. How about a movie until it blows over?"

I kicked off my shoes. "Sure. What movie?"

"I thought we might watch *The Alamo*. Ever seen it?"

"Nope, but before we start, we need popcorn." I padded into the kitchen, and Alex followed.

He pulled the large metal bowl off the top shelf of the pantry and slid it up to the air popper without me even having to ask. More quiet than usual since we'd left the restaurant, he was bothered by his sister's announcement, at least that's what I guessed. Either that, or he didn't like the idea of me buying the land—not that I would really go through with it. I hadn't even inquired.

I dug out the butter and popcorn kernels. While a stick of butter melted in a saucepan, I dumped a half cup of the kernels into the air popper and flipped the switch. After several seconds, white mini clouds exploded into the large metal bowl. I turned the bowl as it filled. Once the butter foamed and the sizzling died down, I drizzled the golden liquid over the popcorn and added a heavy sprinkling of salt.

"Is this movie part of my Texas education?" I tossed the popcorn to distribute the salty, buttery goodness.

"Something like that." He carried our drinks out to the living room and cued up the movie as I settled on the couch. With the popcorn bowl in his lap and me nestled under his right arm, he pressed play.

Chapter Two

April 4th – 10:30 pm

Alex watched as her tail lights retreated down the driveway and around the bend. He looked down at the app on his phone and watched the blue dot move farther away. When the red lights disappeared completely, he walked back inside. With the phone in his hand, he gathered up the glasses and popcorn bowl and set it all in the kitchen.

In the few months he'd known Kate, trouble had hunted her down more than once. He wanted a way to keep tabs on her when she was driving at night, but after the fiasco with a tracking app on her phone, he wasn't about to suggest she download another one. Coding his own tracking app proved to be the solution. With more safeguards than any other of its kind, the tracker required his fingerprint and a passcode before it displayed her location. Once he showed her how it worked, it didn't take any convincing for her to load it on her phone.

The dot continued away from him. He wandered into the office, sat down at the computer, and checked his inbox.

The last few months had brought such change to his life, and he'd spent a significant amount of time rebuilding relationships set aside after his wife, Ellie, died. He'd finally emailed her parents weeks ago. The Jacobsons had emailed back and gushed about how thrilled they were to hear from him after so long. After a few back and forth emails, they mentioned that their son, Rory, told them about bumping into Alex.

Rory had been pivotal in helping Kate the last time she was in trouble. In the email, Ellie's parents asked about Kate for the first time. Alex had kept his answer short but gave enough information for them to understand that it was a serious relationship. After days without a response, leaving Alex to wonder if they were bothered by the turn of events, a reply popped up in his inbox. He read over their email, glancing at his phone between sentences, checking the dot moving across the map.

Alex read the last line, and the rest of the email faded to the background. They wanted to meet Kate. He in no way wanted to keep her away from them, but having her meet his former in-laws hadn't even occurred to him. *Will that be too weird for her?*

He pressed his thumb to the circle—a requirement to continue tracking after a certain time had elapsed—and focused on the blue dot. When Kate drove home alone at night, he worried about her. A capable, grown woman, she'd demonstrated she could take care of herself, but he worried nonetheless.

Each night, saying goodbye and whispering goodnight into the phone grew more tiresome.

Bureau jumped up, bumping his fuzzy black head on Alex's hand.

"You worry about her, too? I have you to thank. If you hadn't perched in that window, I might never have met her." Alex scratched the cat behind the ears, and Bureau purred his appreciation.

The dot stopped in Schatzenburg. She'd made it home. He clicked her number, the one at the top of his favorites.

"Hello." Shuffling could be heard from her end of the line.

"You inside? Your door locked?" He wandered around the cabin, switching off lights.

She must've held the phone to the door because he heard the lock click.

"Satisfied?" Amusement echoed in her question.

"Thanks for indulging me." He tried to limit his overprotective behavior to when she drove home alone at night. "And for coming over. I had fun tonight."

"Me too. And I'm sorry about, you know."

He laughed. "It's good to know you care."

"I liked your sister."

"I'm glad y'all hit it off." He dropped onto the edge of the bed. "Did she text you about lunch?"

"She did. We're meeting tomorrow."

"Good."

For a second or two, they were both quiet, and he tried to stifle a yawn.

She didn't miss it. "I should let you go. You need sleep."

"I have a lot to get done tomorrow so … yeah."

"Sweet dreams." Her voice soft and low, she smiled as she said it. The rise in her cheekbones changed the tone of her voice.

"Goodnight."

"'Night. Love you." It rolled off her tongue every night without any hint of hesitation.

"Love you too." Every night he said those same words, and every night he meant it more than the night before.

His thoughts drifted to Marisa. He hadn't missed her chewing on her hair, a signal that something bothered her, but forcing his sister to talk about what she didn't want to discuss never worked. Withdrawing after Ellie died had strained his relationship with all his siblings, but especially his baby sister. Their relationship changed in ways Alex feared would never let them return to how things were. In the last few months, he'd tried reaching out, multiple times, but Marisa had been distant, refusing his invitations to get together. Maybe showing up unexpectedly signaled positive change. He thought it signified a problem. But he clung to the glimmer of hope. She'd driven out to his cabin, even if she didn't tell him the real reason.

Worry would keep his brain busy until she spilled the beans about why she really showed up unannounced. Meeting Kate and telling him about the move weren't the reasons.

CHAPTER THREE

April 4th – 11:11 pm

I double-checked the door locks and trotted back to the bedroom. The house at the corner of Fourth and Main was my home. I called the Arts and Crafts-style bungalow my mom loved so much The Castle. She'd called it that in her letters to me, and I saw no need to change it. When my dad—though to his face, I still called him Travis—offered me the house, I jumped at his offer. I'd hadn't seen my mom since I was three, but I hoped that living where she'd lived would help me feel connected to her.

Completely updated and remodeled, it imbued an air of welcome and warmth. The front door opened to a great room. Walls had been knocked out between the living room, dining room, and kitchen. Stained wooden columns and beams offered structure where load-bearing walls once stood. A half wall divided the dining room from the kitchen.

When I moved in, the house only needed fresh paint in a few rooms and new carpet in the den. Travis had financed all of that. He'd insisted. And while I didn't like the idea of accepting a handout, letting him do that seemed like a first step toward a father-daughter relationship, which I wanted. Denying him that moment of being a dad wasn't worth paying for it myself.

After the minor updates, the house felt like it had been designed just for me. I'd been here two and a half months and loved every inch of the space.

In my office nook, I tucked the genealogy papers in the filing cabinet and laid the empty tote bag at the bottom of the staircase in the corner of the den. I hardly ever used the stairs. They led to a bonus room that took up the entire second floor. Only a handful of bean bags occupied the otherwise empty room.

I glanced at the time and made my way down the hall.

Denim colored walls gave my large bedroom a cozy feel. A vividly colored quilt of teals, oranges, and blues covered the large sleigh bed; and more pillows than one person could possibly use adorned the head of the bed. I loved the look.

After a quick shower, I tucked under my covers and typed out a text to Alex: *Wish you were here.* I hesitated before sending it, and after staring at it for a full minute, I deleted the words and sent *Love you* instead. Patience and I didn't coexist well.

A kissing emoji popped up on my screen: *Love you too.*

I closed my eyes. The memory of snuggling up next to him that night months ago would have to do.

I'm not sure how long I'd been asleep when a man's voice yanked me out of my dreams. I sat up in bed, cold sweat beading on my face and arms. Maybe my mind was playing tricks on me.

A raspy whisper outside my window sent shivers of terror through my muscles. "Don't hide from me."

Crap! Frozen in place, I stared at the gap in the curtains. My mind raced too fast to form a thought.

The beam of a flashlight darted past my window.

"Stay right there. I'm coming to get you." The man outside sounded even closer.

Staying was absolutely out of the question. I wanted to be as far away from that bedroom window as I could get. I slid out of bed and crept down the hall, clutching my phone.

After I'd found a place to hide, I'd message for help. Navigating the stairs in the dark proved painful, but I swallowed back my yelps, not wanting the prowler to hear me.

Tucked away upstairs in the bonus room, I texted my Uncle Pat: *Prowler outside my house.*

He happened to be a Deputy Captain in the local sheriff's department and lived on the next street over. He must've slept as light as a feather because a response appeared right away: *On my way.*

Huddled under the bean bags—as if they'd protect me from anything—I waited. While panic used my heart as a trampoline, I tried to remain logical. No one had broken in. Maybe the whisper wasn't directed at me.

Who else were they talking to outside the window? Raccoons?

I forced myself to wait before texting Alex, at least until I'd heard something more. It wasn't fair to cause panic when he was thirty minutes away. I hated that he lived that far away.

Phone clutched to my chest, I almost screamed when it vibrated.

Uncle Pat texted: *Neighbor searching for a runaway puppy. He managed to get the pup home. Sorry he woke you.*

Air filled my lungs. How long had I been holding my breath? Having family nearby was wonderful: *Thanks, Uncle Pat.*

Until my heart stopped racing, there was little hope of sleeping. I tiptoed down the stairs, listening. The normal quiet had returned, so I grabbed my laptop and my notes from the client meeting, nestled into the corner of my red sectional, and rested the laptop on my knees. I needed a lap desk, one of those nice ones with the wrist pillow and space for the mouse, but I wasn't going out to get one in the middle of the night.

Genealogy research would give my brain something else to think about, and then at least my time not sleeping would be productive. I scrawled Grace Cooper Jackson's name at the bottom of a lined, yellow page in my legal pad. The pencil scratched along the paper, sounding loud in the quiet house. I added her parents' names to the pencil-drawn tree. Branches crawled up the left side of the page as I added the paternal grandparents. To confirm the names Bruce had given me, I searched for Grace's birth certificate. It confirmed her 1955 birth to George Cooper and Ruth Whittaker. At least the information I'd gotten from the client matched the records.

The websites with large databases of scanned documents made researching much easier. Instead of travelling from county to county, courthouse to courthouse, state to state, an internet connection and a quick search garnered me much of the desired information. At the other end of the room, my printer spat out two copies of the birth certificate.

Immersed in research, I failed to notice how quickly the time passed as I searched for George Cooper's family. George, stationed in San Antonio with the Air Force, originally lived in a small town on the outskirts of Cincinnati. I searched online records to be sure I had the right paternal grandparents listed. Searching the grandfather's name brought up a birth certificate. That provided another generation on the Cooper line.

After digging up another marriage record, I stretched and yawned, then compared the time on the phone to the clock on the laptop, stunned at how much time had elapsed. *4:30 am.* The hours evaporated when I researched genealogy. Knowing that I'd be useless tomorrow without sleep, I snapped the laptop closed and trudged back to bed.

Hopefully no more puppies would escape into the night.

January 30, 1830

After all us children were in bed, I heard Mother and Father speaking in hushed voices, discussing our future. Father shows much excitement about a great opportunity. Mother is much more hesitant.

I lay in bed with my eyes closed wondering how our life will change. Where is this new place Father wants us to go? Is it anything like our home here in Missouri? Is it a big city like we sometimes hear about from people passing through?

I'm caught between sharing Father's excitement and wondering if Mother is right to be worried.

~*~

February 2, 1830

Every night, Father continues to swamp Mother with reasons we should move. His voice starts low, but as his excitement grows, his voice follows. Land and cattle are the words I hear most often. He is excited by the promise of land and cattle. We have only one milk cow. I can't imagine having a field full.

~*~

February 10, 1830

It is settled. We are headed to Texas. Father told us this evening while we were all at the dinner table. Mother says little of her thoughts on the matter.

Father talks of plains full of buffalo and acres and acres of trees. He has been talking to a man named Green. We find it humorous that a man would be named a color. That is his given name, not his surname. When I hear Father talk, I am excited. When I see Mother's tears, I am scared.

Chapter Four

April 5th – 8:00 am

At 8 am, I woke up, wishing I'd closed my laptop earlier. I slid out of bed and padded down the hall to the coffee pot. Once I flipped the switch and started my morning pot brewing, I grabbed my phone and opened the calendar. Lunch with Marisa filled the middle of the day, but the rest remained wide open, which meant I had hours to work on Grace's family tree.

Before I attempted any researching, I needed food. The refrigerator door hung open as I waited for my stomach to tell me what I wanted to eat. Eggs and toast seemed easy enough.

A few minutes later, I sat at the table with hot food in front of me. I sipped coffee and ate, listening to the birds singing outside my kitchen window. After cleaning up, I pulled open the back door. The morning sun and fresh air begged me to wander outside.

A quick walk will be good for me, maybe wake me up.

Too warm for a sweatshirt, I changed into something resembling workout clothes. Already sporting yoga pants, I pulled on a brightly colored tee shirt before heading out the back door. The barbed wire fence that stretched along the back of my property line reminded me of the *For Sale* sign.

Before traipsing through town, I walked the half mile to the property. When I'd texted with Marisa about lunch, I'd asked her to bring me information. The idea of buying the place wouldn't go away, and Alex encouraged it even more. After a few minutes peeking around the bushes, I hoofed it back into town.

The moving truck parked two doors down surprised me. The big Victorian no longer had a *For Sale* sign in front. *Who bought the place?* Maybe later in the week, I'd have lunch at The Drugstore and get the scoop.

College guys in matching tee shirts carried in box after box. Another guy, without a shirt, waved a tanned, chiseled arm in my direction. *Wowza! Is he the new owner?* I reminded myself not to stare. Light brown hair, dark eyes, perfectly toned abs—the guy looked like someone straight out of Greek mythology.

He smiled as I walked past the house. I returned the greeting and continued down the block, wondering about my new neighbor.

My walks, too slow to be considered exercise, gave me a chance to enjoy my little community. My cousin, Libby, honked and pulled over to the side of the road. Her window slid down, and I anticipated she had a bit of news to share about the newest resident.

"Hiya. I can't stay long because I'm headed to class, but that new guy—did you see him?"

"Just a minute ago. Yeah. Kinda stands out in this town."

Libby giggled. "That's an understatement! In addition to the house, he also bought land out on Fire Creek Road. Rumor has it— he's going to plant a vineyard and start a winery."

"Really? That could be interesting."

"Sounds crazy to me. Can you even imagine that sort of thing in this town?" She glanced at her phone. "Oh! Gotta go. Talk to ya later." After pulling back onto the road, she disappeared around the corner.

Between Libby and Maggie, the town gossip was covered. Maggie might have even more info on my new, shirtless neighbor and hopefully, the property behind my house. Visions of a winery behind The Castle made me want the property even more.

Aunt Beth waved from her porch. "Morning. Beautiful day."

"Sure is. I hope all of April is this nice."

"Me too." She went back to watering her flowers.

In a few short months, the size of my family had more than doubled—because I'd actually met aunts, uncles, and cousins. Not all those meetings were positive experiences.

It didn't take long to walk the few streets. Four blocks wide and three blocks deep, Schatzenburg could be described as tiny and quaint. I smiled as I neared Gram's house. She waved as she pushed open her screen door.

"Morning, Kate! Where's your fella?"

"He's at home." I hoped she understood that I meant his own place, but correcting myself only made it awkward.

"I made y'all some cookies." She motioned me toward the porch.

Gram was the heart of the community. One of the oldest residents, she often hinted she knew more secrets than anyone. She also had a huge sweet spot for Alex, not that I could blame her for that. Her grandson, DJ, must've said some nice things about him.

Heat radiated off the bottom of the tinfoil-covered paper plate she handed me. "I just pulled them out of the oven."

"Thank you. I can't wait to have one, and Alex loves cookies."

"He loves more than cookies, I dare say." Her eyes sparkled in her I-have-a-secret sort of way.

I stuttered, unsure how to reply to Gram's casual but pointed comment. "I, uh, hope so."

"When you have a free night, bring Alex and come have dinner with me." She enjoyed the reaction her words had when they landed. "Hard to believe, but I make wonderful enchiladas."

"Just say when. We'd love that." I watched my feet going down the stairs, side-stepping the creaky spot. Eager for a warm cookie, I hurried back to the house. Ringing started as I unlocked the back door, and I kicked myself for forgetting my phone.

Halfway across the kitchen, I spotted Alex's picture on the screen. Hoping to catch him before he hung up, I ran to grab it. "Hello?"

"Hey, Kate." Alex echoed slightly on his Bluetooth. "Mind if I come work at your place today?"

"Not at all. Gram made you cookies. They're still warm."

"I hoped you'd say yes. And cookies? That's even better. I'm right around the corner." He rarely worked from my place, and I wondered what prompted the surprise.

"Let yourself in. Cookies are on the counter. I'm going to jump in the shower. I've only had one, so don't eat them all."

After a quick shower, I padded down the hall as I twisted my wet hair and pinned it up with a clip. Alex sat at the table, smiling.

"Did you save me any cookies?"

"One or two." He tapped the table. "I have something I need to talk to you about."

Only a slight variation on "we need to talk," that phrase ranked right behind "I love you, but…" on the list of ways not to start a conversation with your girlfriend.

"Okay? Sounds ominous."

"Remember how I emailed Ellie's parents." He stared at the table as he mentioned his late wife's name.

I sat down across from Alex and laid my hand on his. "I remember."

"They want to get together for dinner, and they expressed an interest in meeting you." Hesitation weighed in his voice. "I know that's asking a lot."

Navigating the path that led to our future—and I wasn't sure what that would look like—while being ever-conscious of his past wasn't easy. Without a manual on *How to Deal with Your Boyfriend's Late-wife's Family*, I made it up as I went along. "Do you want me to be there?"

"You know I do, Kate."

"Then I'm happy to meet them."

"Really?" Surprise tinged his question.

I got out of my chair and dropped into his lap, adding to his surprise. Framing his face with my hands, I danced my lips along his stubble. "I knew about this part of your life from the very beginning." I traced the line of his jaw with my fingertip. "Does the idea of meeting them make me nervous? A little."

"Why?"

"A part of me worries that I might be compared to Ellie. I don't want them to think I don't measure up or don't deserve you."

"They'll love you. I know they will."

The sincerity in his eyes made him believable. I met his lips, warm and welcoming. He released my curls and ran his fingers through my hair. When he deepened his kiss, I sighed and leaned into him. I'd been very clear about what I wanted and didn't want in our relationship, but the longer I loved him, the fuzzier those clear lines felt.

When we came up for air, he asked, "What's on your calendar today besides lunch with my sister?"

"As much as I'd like to sit here and do this, I have to work on my first case."

"Well, don't let me distract you." He chuckled as he tugged me close for another kiss.

A few minutes later, I hopped off his lap and grabbed my computer and notebook before heading into the den. "I'm going to be in here. You can set up wherever you want."

For two hours, the click of keyboards and the scratching of my pencil on the notebook filled the quiet. I continued working on the paternal side of the tree. Smooth and straightforward, it probably meant that searching the maternal line would be near impossible.

I was staring at the lopsided family tree when Alex, who had stretched out on the other end of the sectional, brushed his finger up the arch of my foot.

"Ack!" I jerked my foot away from him. "What in the world?"

"I wondered if you were ticklish." A tease played at the corner of his mouth.

"And now you know." I glared at him over the top of my notebook, trying to hide my smile.

"I'll be good, so you can work."

"I'm worried I'll hit a brick wall on the mother's side and not be able to offer her much information. I really want to be able to give Grace something she'll treasure."

"Why do you think you won't find anything?"

"Just nervous, I guess."

"You did it for Travis." Alex raised his eyebrows, daring me to make a counterpoint.

"We'll see. Want me to make you something to eat before I leave?"

"Whatcha cooking?" He started singing Hank William's song, "Hey Good Lookin'."

He only had to ask one little question, and I'd be happy as a bumblebee in a flower garden to cook something up with him.

I wandered into the kitchen with him right behind me. "I'll make some taco meat and you can either have tacos or taco salad." I slipped my colorful, ruffled apron over my head and tied it behind me. I could feel the warmth of Alex's grin before I even turned to face him. "What is it with you and this apron?"

He waggled his eyebrows. "You don't have to cook for me."

"I know, but when I do, you give me that look. And I do like that look." I laughed and tossed the ground beef in a pan.

Alex roared with laughter. "Tacos sound great."

I handed him a tomato and a head of lettuce. "Will you chop?"

"As you wish." He was in quite the mood.

"As soon as I spice this, I'll run and change. I don't want to be late for lunch."

"I really appreciate it, Kate."

"I'm not doing it as a favor to you. I want to have lunch with Marisa. She'll tell me stuff about you that you won't tell me. And she's bringing me info about the land." I kept my back to him as I seasoned the meat, listening for his reaction.

His breath tickled my ear. "I have no secrets."

My shoulders shot up, and I giggled at the ticklish sensation. "Why are you in such a hurry for me to spend time with your sister?"

"Because you're a fabulous person and I think she would thoroughly enjoy your company."

"And the real reason?"

"The whole roommate thing concerns me, and I'm hoping she'll talk to you about it."

"When the timer goes off, it's ready." I started down the hall to change.

"Thank you."

When I walked out of the bedroom, Alex wrapped his arms around me. "You're the best."

"And don't you forget it." I stretched up and gave him a quick peck.

He strolled to the stove and served himself tacos. "I'll clean up and let myself out. Please let me know how it goes."

"If you want to come back tonight, I'll make dinner."

"It's a date." He ran to answer a knock at the front door. "Hey, Becca. What's up? And why do you have Kate's bag?"

Becca walked in, a smile spread across her face and dancing in her brown eyes. She and I had become fast friends. DJ and Becca were Alex's closest friends when I met him, and now they were my friends, too. Hanging out with a married couple added an interesting twist to life.

"Kate and I have a lunch date, and this is my bag. It just looks like hers. Mine is predominantly turquoise. Hers is clearly blue."

Alex shook his head, chuckling. "Of course, they are so different. What was I thinking?"

"Oh, no! I double-booked lunch dates." Embarrassed, I scrambled for my phone. "Come on in, Becca."

I shot off a quick text to Marisa: *Just about to leave. Friend showed up because I forgot we had lunch scheduled. Mind if she joins us?*

She responded quickly: *The more the merrier. See you soon.*

"Becca, how do you feel about driving into town with me and meeting Alex's sister for lunch?"

Becca gaped. "Really?" She turned and raised her eyebrows, studying Alex's expression. "She's serious?"

"Yes, she's serious. Marisa came by the cabin yesterday, and they decided to meet for lunch. Kate can tell you all about it." He winked at me.

"Let's go. I'll tell you about it in the car." I grabbed my purse and the bag of genealogy papers off the counter.

Before I had the car in reverse, Becca brought up the conversation. "DJ and I have never met any of Alex's family."

"Meeting her was unexpected. Marisa was hugging Alex in the doorway as I pulled up to the cabin. I made a *complete* fool of myself."

"What did you do?"

"I didn't get out of the car. I sat there for several minutes and contemplated leaving." I glanced at Becca. "Looking back, it was a stupid, knee-jerk reaction."

She laughed out loud. "I wish I could have been there."

"That's not all. Alex came out to the car and tapped on the window." My cheeks warmed as I continued the story. "I swear thought bubbles show up above my head. Even Alex knew I was jealous."

Becca laughed harder and gripped her sides. "I would give anything to have seen your face."

"It was embarrassing. I'm not sure what I was thinking."

She could hardly breathe because of her laughter.

I rolled my eyes. "It wasn't *that* funny, Becca."

"Sorry." She tried to stifle her giggles. "Are you sure Alex knew you were jealous?"

"He asked me about it."

I drove several miles before Becca caught her breath.

We arrived at the restaurant and waited outside for Marisa. She pulled up a minute later in her black sedan and stepped out looking just as stunning as yesterday.

Becca whispered through her smile. "I'm sorry for laughing so hard."

"Now you understand," I whispered before stepping up to greet Alex's sister. "Marisa, this is my friend Becca. I met her through Alex. Her husband is a good friend of his."

"Yes. Alex mentioned you both." Marisa hugged each of us before pulling open the door to the restaurant. "Thank you for meeting me, Kate. I'm glad Becca could come. I hope you don't mind, but I asked Paul to join us. He's running a little late, though."

"Paul is your *roommate?*"

"Yes." Marisa cast me a knowing look. "The one I didn't mention to my brother until yesterday."

"I'm excited to meet him." I hoped after meeting Marisa's boyfriend, I'd be able to ease Alex's concerns.

We followed the hostess to a table, and our waiter swooped in as soon as we sat down. He sat a basket of chips and a small bowl of salsa on the table. "My name is Tyler, and I'll be your server. What can I get you ladies to drink?"

Once our drink order had been taken, he raced off, and our conversation resumed.

"Becca, Alex mentioned you and your husband during our last conversation. I've learned more about the last three years of Alex's life in our last few phone calls than in the dozen calls before it. My brother was never overly talkative, but these last few years, he was very quiet."

Becca teared up. "I only met him after he moved out to the cabin. DJ went to college with him. He said Alex was different then, more like he is now."

Marisa leaned forward, her eyes reflecting her grin. "DJ? Is he really tall? Light brown hair? Really laid back?"

"That's DJ," Becca and I answered in unison.

"I think I remember him. He lived across the hall from Alex."

Becca laughed. "He did, but that was long before I knew him. I'm surprised you remember."

Marisa blushed. "I was a nine-year-old visiting a college dorm. Most of the guys on Alex's floor treated me like a squirt, which I totally was, but DJ was funny and nice. And he could solve a Rubik's cube, which, at the time, I found quite impressive."

I shook my head and pictured him showing off, his notable grin spread across his face.

Becca giggled. "I want to stop on the way home and buy him a Rubik's cube."

We were still laughing when our waiter sat our drinks on the table. We asked for a few extra minutes and focused on the menus, trying to decide what to order. Marisa read and answered texts while we discussed what looked good.

When we closed our menus, our waiter returned. "What can I get for you, ladies?"

He wrote down what we wanted, and Marisa ordered a plate for the still-not-present Paul.

"Oh. Before I forget. Here's the information you asked about. It sounds like a wonderful property." She handed me a single sheet with details about the land.

"Thank you. I didn't know you were a realtor until yesterday. Alex didn't say a whole lot before that, just that you lived in Austin." I regretted that I'd sat with my back to the door, which made scanning for Paul impossible.

"See, not talkative. I joined a group here. In fact, Paul has a friend who referred me for a job in his office. The working environment is pretty different than where I was in Austin, but I'm liking it, overall."

"I bet you'll do great. San Antonio seems to be doing well in the housing market right now." I peeled the paper off a straw.

"It is. And it helps that I speak Spanish." Her green eyes sparkled when she laughed. "Tell me about the two of you. Becca, what do you do?"

"I stay home. But I make and sell jewelry."

"She makes gorgeous pieces. You should see them sometime." I grew impatient waiting to meet Paul.

"I'd love to see them." Marisa stirred a packet of sugar into her tea. "Kate, tell me about your new venture. Alex sounded excited."

"He told you about it?"

"He talks about you quite a bit." She grinned like she harbored other tidbits she hadn't revealed.

"I just signed my first client. I'm very excited. And your brother is wonderful. He's been very supportive."

"He thinks the world of you, you know."

I smiled stupidly. Words hid behind sheer glee.

Marisa sipped her tea. "My brothers, sister, and I all worried about him. Our family isn't especially close now, but we care about each other. No one liked that he retreated to that cabin after what happened. You brought light into his life again. He is like the Alex I knew before. Thank you." She reached across the table and patted my hand. "You seem perfect for him."

I blinked away tears. "I don't know what to say to that. I love him very much."

"I can tell." She smiled, checked her phone, and replied to a text. "Any questions you want to ask about him?" She winked.

Caught off-guard, I hesitated. "Um, well, give me a second to think."

She laughed. "I promise you, as far as I know, he doesn't have any dark secrets."

"Good to know." I contemplated her original question. "How gawky was he in high school? He still hasn't let me near his yearbooks."

"Very. He was pretty scrawny for a while. It wasn't a good look for him." Marisa looked past me, and her words trailed off.

Becca kicked me under the table, and I whipped around excited to see Marisa's roommate. An older guy stood in the way, and I leaned to see around him. Becca kicked me again. I turned to her, eyebrows raised.

"Hello, Ladies." The older guy stood next to our table, hand extended toward me. "I'm Paul." His hand felt like a dead fish, no firmness in his grip.

I smiled, trying to hide my surprise. "Nice to meet you. I'm Kate. This is my friend, Becca."

He wasn't exactly old, just not at all what I'd expected. I determined to keep an open mind. Ten to fifteen years older than I was, he sported a coral dress shirt. It set off his golden tan, the kind that looked sprayed on. The perfectly coiffed hair and manicured nails contrasted with his deep East Texas accent.

Paul picked up both Becca's bag and mine out of the empty chair and held them out toward Marisa. "Your bags, baby."

"Oh. Sorry. I'll move those." I reached for the bags, then set them on the other side of my chair.

Becca hadn't wanted to leave her jewelry in the car and had grabbed my bag too. I prayed I wouldn't forget it at the restaurant.

Paul rubbed the back of his neck. "Oh, I thought they were hers."

"Tell me, how did the two of you meet?" Becca pulled the question off my lips.

"I wanted to sell my house, and this angel walked through my door." He gazed at Marisa as he answered.

Likely story. You probably saw her picture and requested her as an agent.

Something about Paul didn't sit well with me. I tried not to let my opinion be colored by the rings on every other finger, or the chains hanging around his neck.

Paul eyed Becca. "So, you're dating Marisa's brother?"

She crossed her arms in front of her. "Not me."

Her words hung awkwardly at the table until Marisa piped up. "Kate is dating Alex."

"Forgive me. I got confused."

That happens when you get old. My dislike grew by the minute, but he hadn't really done anything wrong.

He turned to face me. "Marisa says you've made her brother a happy man. You must have *talents* he appreciates."

Becca kicked me a third time where she'd already left a bruise.

Marisa slapped him on the arm. "Stop it, Paul. Be nice."

He laughed but stopped when he noticed Becca and I weren't joining in. "My attempt at humor fell flat. I won't give up my day job." He dropped his hand under the table, and seconds later Marisa stiffened.

Check please.

The waiter brought our food to the table, and I prayed I could maintain my smile until lunch ended. What Marisa saw in this guy bewildered me. Stunning and independent, she didn't seem the type to put up with the likes of Paul.

When we'd finished eating and the plates were cleared, Paul pulled a handful of twenty-dollar bills out of his wallet and tossed four of them on the table. "Please, let me."

Marisa excused herself, and Becca followed suit, leaving me alone with Mr. Unlikeable.

"How did you meet her brother?" The syrup disappeared from his voice.

"It's a complicated story. He helped me when I needed it most." I had no intention of telling him how Alex let me stay at the cabin. Paul would only twist it and make it sound crass.

"We should have dinner soon. I want to meet this brother Marisa admires so much." He sounded almost jealous of her affection for her brother.

"I'll talk to Alex and Marisa to see what we can schedule." Having Paul and Alex meet seemed less and less a good idea every minute I spent near Paul.

"Marisa's a good thing for me. I mean, look at her." He slurped the last drops of Diet Coke from the bottom of his glass.

"What do you do?" I tossed out the first question I could think of, anything to change the subject.

"Last night by candlelight, we—"

"For work."

"I thought it was kind of a personal question." He chuckled, unfazed by the fact that funny didn't describe him or what he'd said. "Give that boyfriend of yours a call. Would tonight work for dinner?" His grin made me want to shower.

Marisa walked up and patted him on the shoulder. "We have tickets for tonight. Remember?"

"How silly of me. But we could go for dessert." He stood up and nuzzled her neck. "And then share our own dessert later."

I braced for Becca to kick me again, but she didn't.

Marisa pushed him back. "Another night would be better, when we are invited."

With promises that we'd all get together again soon, which I had every intention of putting off as long as possible, we said goodbye to Marisa and Paul. Becca made another run to the ladies' room before we headed out the door. While I waited, I bought one of the funny tee shirts the restaurant had for sale.

"Ma'am, here's your card. Please sign here." The cashier slid the folded tee shirt into a bag.

"Thank you." I signed, then tucked the bag under my arm and waited for Becca.

She hurried out, her cross-body purse bouncing as she walked. "Oh, my bag."

We rushed back toward the table and met our smiling waiter halfway across the room.

"I was just coming to find you. Your bags."

I kicked myself for walking away from my research. "Thank you so much."

"All my current projects are in this bag. So glad we remembered." Becca hugged it to her chest. "Why'd you bring your bag?"

"I thought about a quick run by the library, but I'll do that another day." I unlocked the car, and we climbed in.

We made it all the way to the highway before Becca broke the silence. "Lunch was interesting. What are you going to tell Alex?"

"I'm going to tell him that Marisa thinks he's completely in love with me." I glanced over my shoulder as I blended into traffic.

"That's not quite what I meant, but she's right. He's so happy now." Becca started sniffling.

"You okay?" I glanced at her and wondered about her sappiness. Crying at the slightest whim smacked more of me the last few months than Becca.

"Oh, yeah. It's just so sweet." She stopped talking and stared out the window.

"Let's talk about something not sweet."

"I didn't like Paul. He gave off a creepy vibe."

"Uh, yeah. Ewww. I don't get it. Marisa comes across as so level-headed." I opted not to tell Becca about his weirdness when she left me alone at the table with him.

"You probably couldn't see because you were across the table from Marisa, but he had his hands … let's just say there's a reason I didn't finish my lunch."

I laughed at Becca's dramatic eye roll. "No wonder Marisa looked so uncomfortable. What am I going to tell Alex?"

Becca and I stopped at a little antique barn. Rows and rows of little booths housed antiques and collectibles of all sorts. After standing near the front door in awe of the treasures stacked in corners, displayed on shelves, and hanging on the wall, we split up, and she headed for the nearest jewelry booth. I wandered the aisles, paying attention to the uneven floor boards after nearly falling on my face. Somehow, the rough interior made the collectibles inside stand out more. Hoping to find old photos, paintings, or other items that I could use to decorate, I flipped through a box of old signs and photos. The extra room needed décor. I wanted a Texas vibe in there. Denim, vintage prints, and bandanas seemed right for a room whose most frequent guest so far had been Alex.

As I wandered through the cluttered store, I tried to envision different pieces in my house. When I spotted the antique glass cookie jar, I danced a small jig in the aisle. It would be perfect in my kitchen, especially given Alex's deep appreciation of cookies. After brushing off the dust and sneezing as a result, I carried the jar to the register and set it down along with the handful of antique photos I'd picked up. "May I leave these here for a few minutes while I continue shopping?"

The clerk looked over the top of his wire-rimmed glasses and smiled. "Absolutely, young lady."

In the far back corner, I spotted a booth with old jewelry. About to call Becca, I noticed a locket. Silver, with a flower etched in the top, the locket seemed meant for her. She'd love it. Waiting out of sight while she checked out, I tried to figure out how to purchase it without her seeing.

I walked to the front after she checked out and found her staring at an antique baby carriage. More than anything Becca wanted to have a baby, but she didn't talk about it much. I hung back not wanting to interrupt her thoughts.

She glanced up and flashed a wary smile. "I'll meet you outside." She hurried out the door.

My heart broke to see her emotional, but her rushed exit gave me the perfect opportunity to make my purchase. The clerk followed me to the back and opened the glass case. The locket was even more beautiful up close. A small blue stone accented a flower engraved on the top.

At the counter, he tucked the locket in a small box and wrapped my jar. I watched Becca stroll back and forth on the sidewalk, the phone to her ear, as the clerk rang up my finds. I handed him my credit card, and after a quick swipe, he handed it back.

"Thank you for stopping in. Come back and see us."

A bell jingled on my way out. "Thank you. Have a nice day." I waved to the clerk.

"Love you, too. See you later." Becca ended her call as I unlocked the car.

"Need to go home?"

"No. Just talking to DJ. I have my project stuff. If you don't mind, I thought I'd stay at your place for a while."

On the way back to the house, we stopped off and bought the Rubik's Cube Becca wanted. We both looked forward to DJ's reaction.

Disappointment pricked me when I pulled into an empty driveway. Even though Alex mentioned letting himself out, I'd hoped he'd still be there when I returned, but he wasn't. Stepping into the house, I smiled. He'd left the kitchen spotless. *One more reason to love him.*

Becca dropped her bag on the dining room table and showed me a stunning necklace she'd recently finished. She'd removed the pin from the back of a brooch and used the front as the focal piece on a choker. The coral cameo surrounded by pale grey pearls anchored a 15-inch choker strung with vintage grey pearls and light coral glass ovals. A new, but vintage-looking clasp finished it off. She laid out several other of her recent creations.

"Becca, you are a true artist. These are beautiful." I held them up to my neck modeling them.

"Thanks. Go ahead and work on your stuff. I have enough to keep me busy. Go. Research."

"I think I will."

With Becca's stuff spread out on the dining room table, I retreated to the den. The back corner of the den had a round table, a credenza with my printer on top, and a filing cabinet. Very few files resided in the drawers, but I hoped to someday need another one to hold client files.

After picking up pages off the printer, I sorted them into two stacks: my copies and the client's. I double-checked that I had print-outs of all the documentation I'd already found, then dropped onto the floor near the coffee table.

I picked up where I'd left off researching the Cooper line. Many of Ohio's vital records had been digitized, making it possible to search from my couch—or floor as it were. Jumping between genealogy web-sites, I managed to take the Cooper line back another two genera-tions. I also filled in other branches on the paternal side of the tree. The tree grew more and more lopsided. But I continued researching the branches on the paternal side.

When I hit a roadblock on that side, I took it as a sign that it was time to even out the tree. I focused on Grace's maternal side. Her hus-band had told me that her mom, listed as Ruth Whittaker on the birth certificate, died in childbirth. Grace grew up knowing nothing about her mother's family.

A quick search for Ruth's name produced over fifty results. Without more information, I couldn't be sure which Ruth was Grace's mother. Staring at the list of results, I tried to think of her life as a timeline. I couldn't move forward from Grace's birth date, only backward, so I decided to search marriage records. Their marriage license might have recorded where she lived, which might help point me in the right direction to find Ruth's birth certificate.

I searched the database and finally found their marriage record. They were married in Texas, but there was little helpful information on the license besides the county and Ruth's age.

I scrawled her birth year and a note to search for her death record on my yellow pad. The phone rang, startling me out of my thought process. "Hello." I glanced at the clock and realized the time. Becca and I had been quietly involved in our own activities for hours.

"Hey, I'm headed your way." Alex called me from the truck. He sounded just a wee bit different on his Bluetooth.

I glanced at the yellow pad and notes. "Oh no, I didn't realize the time. Becca is here. When you get here, I'll tell you about lunch and my research."

He chuckled. "Be there in a bit."

I hung up and searched for Ruth's death certificate, quickly forgetting about dinner.

Chapter Five

April 5th – 6:32 pm

Forty-five minutes later, Alex walked in the door carrying three large pizzas. "I brought dinner. Hey, Becca!"

"You're a saint!" Kate ran in from the den and threw her arms around him making pizza boxes wobble on his outstretched hand. "How did you know I hadn't made dinner?"

"The 'I didn't realize the time.' was a clue." He dropped the boxes on the counter, pulled her close, and kissed her.

"Three pizzas? What kind? How much do you plan to eat?" She stayed in his arms but tilted her head back to toss questions at him.

"A pepperoni with extra cheese, a sausage with mushrooms, and a supreme pizza. I called DJ. He's on his way over. Apparently, his wife didn't feel like making dinner tonight." He grinned at Becca. "Ben's coming too."

Kate patted his chest. "I'm glad you met Detective Torres. I like him."

Alex had met Ben Torres only days after meeting Kate. He'd been one of the detectives assigned to the San Antonio case related to her disappearance. Genuine and helpful that first week, he jumped in to help again when trouble visited Kate a second time. During those first few encounters, a friendship grew. It cemented the night Alex decided what he wanted after he and Kate had a spat. Ben and DJ had circled round him, kept him company while Alex stewed. Neither asked about what happened. Alex appreciated friends like that.

Becca grabbed plates and napkins and laid them on the kitchen table. "Dining table is covered in my stuff. Need me to move it?"

"Nah." He poked Kate in the arm. "I've been waiting all afternoon for a phone call. How was lunch?"

Becca and Kate exchanged an unmistakable glance. He waited while they chose their words.

"I really like your sister." Kate shuffled the boxes to the table.

"I was glad it worked out for me to go." Becca busied herself with the plates and napkins while she spoke. "They were nice." She choked out the last few words.

"You met this elusive boyfriend?"

Kate nodded. "We did."

"Why won't I like him?" Alex dropped into a chair.

"You might like him. He's *very* nice." Becca grabbed two slices of pizza.

"Nice, huh? I'm not sure that's the reason Marisa didn't want me to know about him."

"He's a little older than I expected. And a bit syrupy when he's not using off-color humor." Kate popped the top on a Coke. "But Marisa likes him."

"How much older?"

"Maybe forty-five." Kate shot Alex a sideways glance, gauging his reaction. "What do you think, Becca?"

"Probably. Maybe he didn't age well. He seems to be fighting it."

Alex breathed in deep but didn't utter a word. He rubbed the cleft in his chin.

Kate stood behind his chair and draped her arms around him. "Don't let it stress you, please."

"I'm trying not to." He reached up and patted her arm.

"Your sister gave us the inside scoop about you." She leaned in close, her cheek pressed against his.

"Okay?" He ran his fingers back and forth along her arm.

"According to your sister, you are completely in love with me, and I brought the light back into your life." She said it quickly, probably so tears or sobs wouldn't interrupt her. "And she said you were never talkative."

He pulled Kate into his lap. "All true."

Happiness danced in her eyes. "She likes me." She slid out of his lap and returned to her chair. "And your siblings clearly care about you quite a bit. They'd been worried about you, until recently."

"At least one of us is liked by the other's family." He winked. His reference to her sister, who had not warmed to the idea of their relationship, came across as humor, but the situation irritated him. Meg irritated him.

"Most of my family likes you." She jumped out of her chair. "Oh! I bought this cookie jar today." She did a Vanna White impression, motioning toward the counter.

"We already finished Gram's cookies. You going to fill it?" He raised his eyebrows, waiting for an answer.

"Sure, when things get stressful." Kate smirked.

"Y'all crack me up. You could've finished an entire pizza already." Becca shook her head.

"Tell me more about my sister's boyfriend." Alex pulled out the chair for Kate.

Becca shot him a look.

"Don't start." He pointed at her. "Marisa's my little sister, and I'm trying to look out for her. I need to know these things."

Kate and Becca elaborated on Paul, mentioning his innuendo-laden humor and sleazy gazes. After a bit of laughter and eye-rolling, Kate seemed eager to leave the conversation behind.

Alex jumped up to answer when someone knocked at the door. "Ben or DJ? Who is it?"

When he pulled open the door, Ben laughed. "If DJ isn't here yet, that means there is still pizza left, right?"

Alex shook his hand. "Come on in."

They all settled at the table and piled slices on their plates.

Kate explained about her new client and about the work she'd done on Grace's family tree. "I've found lots on her father's side. I just started looking at her mother's side. Is it too much to ask that I could type a name into Google and find a link that lays out the entire family line?"

"Yes." Becca laughed. "They wouldn't need you then. Would they?" When a knock sounded at the front door, she jumped up and pointed at her bag. "Put it on the table."

"I'm sure you'll dig something up. Maybe there are family secrets to uncover." Alex added another two slices to his plate, then watched Kate pull a Rubik's Cube out of Becca's bag. She set it, packaging and all, on top of the pizza boxes.

Ben groaned. "Secrets? Maybe you should stop her from doing those genealogy searches."

"Great idea, Ben. I'll just *make her stop.*" Alex squeezed Kate's knee. He had no intention of asking her to stop, not that she'd comply if he did.

Kate acted as if the exchange never happened. "You mean a scandal?" She watched Becca and DJ across the room.

"Ooooh. Did you say scandal?" Becca furrowed her brow in mock disapproval as DJ carried her to the table.

"I see your arm has healed nicely, show-off." Kate watched the two of them, delight sparkling in her eyes.

DJ grinned. "Hey! A Rubik's Cube. I used to be able to solve those things."

Becca buried her face in his neck, giggling.

"What'd I miss?" DJ lowered her into a chair.

"Not sure, but something about the cube is funny." Alex shot Kate a sideways glance.

"We learned over lunch you were a master of the cube in college." Kate squeezed Alex's leg.

"Who did you have lunch with?" DJ dropped his Stetson on the counter and scratched his head.

Alex joined in the chuckle. "They had lunch with my sister."

DJ snagged four slices of pizza. "I remember now." A mischievous twinkle lit up his blue eyes. "She still remembers me, huh?"

Becca elbowed him. "Watch it."

DJ grinned and folded his pizza slice in half before taking a bite.

Alex grabbed DJ a soda. "Have you looked for a death certificate?"

"Found one, but I haven't printed it yet." Kate picked the red onion off her slice of supreme before taking a bite. "How's the police business, Torres?"

Ben often ribbed her for calling him Torres. "You can call me Ben."

"Sorry, habit." She colored a bit.

Conversation continued through dinner, the genealogy talk shoved to the back burner.

When the doorbell rang, Kate jumped up and ran to the door, leaving Alex to wonder who'd shown up at her door at nine at night. Everyone he'd invited sat around the table.

She opened the door, and a man held out a bottle of wine. Kate glanced back into the kitchen. Her face registered every thought that ran through her head. If Alex wasn't so confident of how she felt, he might've been jealous. She clearly found the stranger attractive.

"Hey. I'm Philip Prescott. I just moved in two houses down. Are you free?" His shirt seemed a size or two too tight.

She stepped aside and pointed to the kitchen. "I'm Kate. Come on in."

"I was hoping to meet my neighbors, and you were by far the prettiest. I saw you walking this morning." He flashed her a sleazy, toothy smile. "And I should apologize for waking you in the middle of the night."

Ben kicked Alex under the table, a smirk tugging at his lips. "New neighbor. That's fun."

Alex shot him a warning look, drawing a quiet chuckle. *Waking her up in the middle of the night?*

"I wondered who bought that old house. Did you find your puppy?" She looked at Becca, her eyes wide, and tried to stifle a laugh.

"I did. He's not used to the new place. I'm sorry I scared you."

"Alex, Becca, DJ, Ben, meet Philip. He just moved into that beautiful blue Victorian a couple houses down. Phillip, this is my boyfriend, Alex, and these are our friends, Ben, DJ, and his wife, Becca."

Ben jumped up and shook his hand. "Nice to meet you."

DJ gave a nod and draped his arm around Becca. "Hey."

Alex grabbed a chair from the dining room table. "Have a seat."

Kate accepted the wine and handed it to Alex. "Will you pour me a glass? Anyone else?"

Philip beamed. "Sure, I'll take one. I hope you like Rieslings."

DJ answered quickly. "None for us, thanks."

Ben shook his head, reigning in his smirk. "No thanks."

Alex poured the chilled wine into two glasses and wondered how long the new neighbor had been planning his visit. "Here you go." He handed them to Kate and Philip.

"You aren't having a glass?" She laid her cool fingers on Alex's knee.

"I'll be leaving pretty soon." Alex laid his hand on top of hers.

Awkward silence danced like a circus elephant around the room.

Philip broke the silence, but it made things no less awkward. "I didn't realize you had company. I can come back when you're alone."

Alex moved his hand to Kate's leg and squeezed her knee.

She chewed her bottom lip, hiding a grin. "Oh, no. This is much better." She offered Philip a plate. "Help yourself to pizza."

He picked up a slice of pepperoni. "Thanks."

"What brings you to the small town of Schatzenburg?" She wiped her hands and crisscrossed her legs in the chair, then pulled Alex's hand back to her leg.

Amused, Alex winked just so he could watch her face light up. She didn't disappoint him.

Philip set his pizza back on the plate. "I recently sold off my start-up. Decided this was the perfect place to try my hand at something different and start a winery." He sipped his wine. "Schatzenburg is close enough to San Antonio to enjoy the amenities of a city, but far enough out you can see the stars. So much beauty here. Maybe I'll name a wine after you, Kate."

DJ jumped up from the table, coughing. He'd taken a sip of his Coke just as Philip finished. Ben covered his face with his hand, eyes focused on the table. Alex's friends weren't helping the situation.

"You okay?" Philip stood up.

DJ waved him off. "Just went down the wrong pipe."

Becca rubbed DJ's back, avoiding eye contact with anyone else at the table, likely in an effort to maintain composure.

"Aren't wines named for either their grape variety or the region they were grown in?" Alex kept his gaze focused on Kate's hand as he asked the question.

"Oh, yeah. Maybe I'd just have to name the entire winery after her." Philip raised an eyebrow.

DJ patted the table. "Tell us more about your startup."

Philip spoke in detail about the technical aspect of his business. Alex understood what he described, but it sounded rehearsed. Tempted to ask questions to see if he could punch holes in the story, he opted not to. He preferred to watch and gather information, so he could form an educated opinion about Kate's newest neighbor. Besides, after questioning the wine-naming, he'd only come off as combative. He could always poke holes later.

"I've always loved that old house." Becca fiddled with the Rubik's cube. "Fixed up, I imagine it'll be gorgeous."

"I'm going to restore it. Some of the work has been planned out already." Philip expounded on the old house and his plans for returning it to its former glory. Elaborating on wallpaper appropriate to the age of the house, he dominated the conversation.

He had just launched into an explanation about color fade when Ben scooted his chair back. "I hate to eat and run, but the morning shows up early, and I have a forty-five-minute drive."

Kate hopped up and hugged him, a gesture that always seemed to catch Ben off-guard. "I'm glad you came."

"Need a Dr Pepper for the road?" Alex pointed to the refrigerator.

"I'm good. Goodnight." Ben waved as he slipped out the door.

DJ launched into a new subject before Philip returned to wallpaper explanations. "Y'all notice that the Kent property went up for sale?"

Alex grinned. "Kate's inquiring about it."

"Really?" Becca sat forward, eager for more information.

Kate put her hands up. "I haven't decided anything yet."

Ben hadn't been gone two minutes when someone knocked.

Kate glanced at Alex. "I guess Ben forgot something."

He jumped up and patted her on the shoulder. "Probably so." He pulled open the door. "Back so soon Be—Marisa?" Thanks to Kate and Becca's detailed description, he recognized Paul and his spray on tan right away.

"I'm sorry to show up unannounced twice in one week, but Paul really wanted to meet you. You mentioned Kate lived in this town, so we drove around until I spotted your truck and her car. I sort of guessed you'd be here."

"Come in." Kate slipped in next to Alex and tucked her arm around him. "Can I get y'all some coffee or wine? I'm afraid we've polished off the pizza." She looked up at him, her eyes wide with surprise.

"Paul, it's nice to meet you, finally." Alex shook his hand, then pointed toward the back of the house. "Why don't we all move to the den?"

"Great idea." Kate walked over to the counter and started a pot of coffee.

Alex introduced Marisa and Paul to DJ and Philip, before they all settled in the den. After dragging in a couple extra chairs, Alex wandered back into the kitchen and wrapped his arms around Kate while she poured coffee. "What a surprise."

"Careful. I don't want to burn you."

"Did you know they were coming?"

"He asked me, but she said they had tickets to something. I'm kinda shocked they showed up." She leaned back into his chest and smiled up at him. "You handled it well. Help me carry these mugs, pretty please."

Kate and Alex passed around coffee, then sat while Paul regaled the others with stories from his travels abroad, only interrupted by tales from Philip about his travels. The longer Paul talked, the more Marisa shifted in her chair. If Alex hadn't lost the ability to read his sister, sheer effort held her smile in place. Something was definitely wrong, and Alex hoped Marisa would talk to him soon. She didn't cast admiring glances at Paul; her gaze pleaded with him to stop talking. *Why is she living with this guy?*

After an hour of listening to Paul, Alex needed to leave, as much to get ready for the morning as for his own sanity. He draped his arm around Kate and leaned in close. "I hate to run out on you, but I need to head home."

She gazed back at him with the same wistfulness that preceded every goodbye of late.

He stood and drained the rest of his coffee. "I'm sorry to break up the party, but I have a six thirty Skype meeting in the morning."

A collective groan went up from the group.

Marisa jumped up. "We should be going. I didn't intend to keep y'all so late." She hugged her brother before turning toward Paul. "You ready?"

He pushed himself off the sofa and gripped her hand. "Whenever you are, baby."

Kate walked them to the front door but paused as Paul sauntered through the great room, running his fingers down the dining room table, scanning the walls.

"Beautiful house you have."

"Thank you." She hugged Marisa and kept her voice low. "We should do something again soon."

Marisa glanced at Alex, then whispered to Kate. Alex had a pretty good idea about their exchange. He chuckled inwardly as he walked up and watched his sister pale.

He wrapped his arms around her. "Thanks for introducing me to your *roommate*."

She braved a half-smile and waited for him to offer a follow up comment, which he didn't do.

He stuck out his hand to Paul. "Good to finally meet you."

As Paul and Marisa climbed into a dark sedan, Kate and Alex watched from the porch. The car pulled away, and he wrapped his arms around her. She sighed. "I don't want you to go."

"I'm sorry, but I've gotta get some sleep." He kissed her on the top of the head and pushed open the door.

Becca gathered her jewelry. "We need to get going too."

Kate pointed to the back door, then slipped her hand in Alex's. "I'll be back inside in a minute. I'm just going to say goodbye."

Becca nodded and continued tucking brooches and beads into baggies.

Outside, standing next to the truck, Kate stopped. "What did you think of Paul?"

"I'm not crazy about him, but Marisa likes him, I think, so I'm trying to give him a chance."

"Sorry for the description I gave earlier. I should've been nicer."

"I recognized him right away based on what you'd told me. I might not have been able to stay so calm otherwise."

Before Kate could respond the back door swung open.

"Kate, I need to be heading home." Philip stared at Alex as he spoke. "I hope you don't mind if I come by again some time. This was fun."

Kate spun around and leaned back into Alex. "Sure, we'll see about having dinner one night again."

He smiled his perfectly straight smile, then waved as he sauntered off toward his house. "I'll bring you a different bottle of wine next time, but definitely something sweet. Just like you."

Alex waited until his words couldn't be overheard. "I'm not too sure about your new neighbor." He inhaled and smiled down at Kate. "And what was that about waking you up in the middle of the night?"

She turned back toward him and wrapped her arms around his neck, combing her fingers through the shorts hairs on the back of his head. "Jealous?"

"Should I be?" He pulled her tight.

"Voices close to the house woke me up, and I texted Uncle Pat. He told me it was a neighbor looking for his puppy."

"Glad your uncle is close by." Alex added a little extra passion to his goodbye kiss, enough to hold her over until he saw her again, or maybe it was to hold him over. "Love you, Rainy."

Her dark eyes sparkled in the moonlight. She melted when he used the nickname he'd given her the day after they met. "Love you too. Call me later?"

"Yep."

Alex dropped his keys on the table and filled the cat bowl. "Hey, Bureau. Sorry I left you so long." He shuffled through his mail and wandered into the office.

The cat joined him, seeking attention after he'd filled his belly.

"After my meeting in the morning, I'm headed back to Kate's. Maybe one of these days, I'll just take you with me." He set his laptop bag and his shoes near the front door.

Once he'd tucked in bed, he called Kate. "Did your neighbor show up again with a different bottle of *sweet* wine?"

"I think maybe you *are* jealous." She seemed almost giddy about having the tables turned.

"I thought about heading to your place after my meeting in the morning. If that's okay?"

"Always. And I hope you know that you have no reason to be jealous."

"He's closer, younger, taller, richer, better—"

"Don't you trust me?"

Alex laughed. "Ouch. My own words used against me."

"I love you, Alex, only you. You know that."

"Love you too. Did you lock all the doors?"

"Yes. I even double-checked all the locks, same as every other night. Goodnight." She let the last word ring out like the end of a song.

"'Night, Kate." He ended the call and stared at the phone, wrestling with the urge to gather his laptop and head back to her place.

Who shows up with a chilled bottle of wine to meet the neighbor?

He jumped out of bed and fished a dress shirt and jeans out of the closet, then gathered whatever other clothes he'd need for the morning.

Once the duffle bag was packed and ready, he reconsidered. *Don't be stupid. Go to bed.*

He hung the clothes on the doorknob, dropped the bag near the door, and crawled back in bed.

March 19, 1830

So many of our things are being left behind. It is hard to imagine life without dishes. There is limited room in the wagon, so we must choose wisely about what to take on the journey. I pleaded with Father to allow me paper and ink. He winked and whispered that he would find a place for my treasures.

~*~

March 21, 1830

The wagon is loaded. Mother insisted that she will not leave without her spinning wheel. Father said he would allow her that luxury, but now there is little room for anyone in the back of the wagon.

Today we said goodbye to Granny and Papa. They are scared for us. Even though they smiled, you could see it in their faces.

~*~

March 28, 1830

I miss Granny and Papa. Fourteen years of seeing them almost every day, and now I wonder if I will ever see them again. Several times I have seen something beautiful or fascinating and thought to tell Granny, but I can't.

I'm thankful for the other two families that are traveling with us. On the journey with us are the Kent family and the Smith family. The Smiths have two daughters close to my age, Lucy and Clara. Having other girls around makes the time pass more quickly.

Reuben, though he watches out for me, is not interested in talking about what Texas might be like. Brothers are like that. He spends more time with the Kent's older son, Wesley. They are close to the same age, though Wesley may be nearing twenty. Jeremiah has no desire to talk. He only wants to run in the grasses. With only my brothers, the trip would have seemed much longer.

Chapter Six

April 5th – 11:30 pm

I crawled into bed after the interesting evening. While my new neighbor was delightfully good-looking, I scratched my head at his continued advances. My relationship with Alex wasn't any secret. Anyone around us more than two minutes recognized we were dating, except apparently Philip.

The biggest surprise of the night had been Paul's visit. Marisa spent most of the time at the house tense and apologetic. I made a mental note to call and arrange a lunch for just the two of us. She looked like she needed a friend.

My thoughts quieted to a low murmur, and I drifted off to sleep.

The sun wasn't up yet when the sound of shattering glass woke me. I bolted upright. It sounded close. *Was someone breaking into my car?*

The creak of the back door echoed down the hall like a sound effect in a horror movie.

Someone is in my house!

My limbs refused to work.

I have to hide. But where? Hiding upstairs wouldn't work this time. I ran to my closet. Items I'd stashed, not thinking I'd ever actually use them, pulled my attention to the shelf. I could do more than hide.

My hands shook as I grabbed the wig and stand. I shoved pillows under the quilt and balanced the stand and the brown wig on a feather pillow, facing away from the door. If anyone peeked in the room, it'd look like I slept through the noise. Maybe they'd leave without hunting me down or worse.

Muffled curses in the kitchen rippled a renewed panic through me.

Hide!

The dark closet seemed my best option. I crawled to the back corner behind my dresses and listened. Footsteps and shuffling echoed in the quiet house. Drawers opened and closed in the kitchen. Huddled in the corner behind a suitcase, I tapped out a text to Uncle Pat: *Come quick! Someone is in my house. I'm hiding.*

Then I dialed 911. When the dispatcher answered, I told her in a whisper what was happening. She relayed my situation to the local sheriff's office and kept me on the phone, saying they were en route.

Waiting, I prayed whoever had broken in wouldn't venture into my bedroom.

April 15, 1830

I am tired of walking.

Lucy has told me all that she's heard about Texas. The stories of Indian attacks have me worried. Perhaps that is why Mother never talked of our "adventure"—as Father like to call it.

~*~

April 18, 1830

When I try to sleep, Lucy's tales of Indian attacks play in my head and make sleep difficult. When my eyes close, my mind creates the scenes she described. But I know it is too late to turn back, not that it is my decision. Father is not concerned, or at least that's how it seems.

~*~

April 30, 1830

I was almost asleep when Reuben shook me awake. He'd been listening to the men talking, which he does often.

We won't be going to New Orleans, as I hoped. The stories I'd heard about the city made me want to see it. But it also meant we wouldn't be boarding a ship, and that made me happy. I feared we would all be lost at sea.

Reuben says we will cross the Sabine River, but I can't imagine how we will get the wagons across the river. Do they expect us to swim?

CHAPTER SEVEN

April 6th – 2:22 am

Alex jolted awake and grabbed his phone. "Hello?" He forced his eyelids up. Darkness still encased the cabin. He rubbed sleep from his eyes and tried to read the numbers on the alarm clock. *2:22*

"Alex, I'm on my way to Kate's. Someone broke in." DJ's words punched Alex in the gut.

His feet landed hard on the floor as he jumped out of bed. "Is she okay?"

"I don't know anything else."

Not Kate. Memories from three years ago stirred his gut. Visions of Ellie slumped on the floor threatened to expel dinner. *Please don't let anything happen to Kate.* "How? What?"

"Maddox called me. She texted him that someone broke in and then called 911. Deputies were dispatched to her address. In the text, she said she was hiding."

Alex put DJ on speaker and swallowed back the fear that soured his stomach. "She better be okay." His face burned with anger. Tears stung his eyes. "I'll be there as soon as I can." Flooded with a fear of reliving the past, he tried to shove those memories out of his head. The break-in, too reminiscent of how his wife had died, rattled him. He struggled to push the thoughts aside. He needed to focus on getting to Kate's.

"I'll call when I get there. Have your Bluetooth on." DJ's voice was strained. "Alex, as soon as I see her I'll let you know what's going on, okay?"

"Thanks." Alex hung up and threw his phone. It bounced off the bed, landing somewhere on the other side. He picked up the nearest pair of shorts, pulled them on, and yanked a tee shirt over his head. After grabbing the clothes from the doorknob and his duffle bag, he ran to the living room and pulled on his shoes.

"Bureau, I gotta go check on Kate."

Alex picked up the laptop and made it halfway out the door before remembering his phone. He darted back to the bedroom and searched the bed and floor until he found it.

In the truck, he yelled and cursed while he drove toward the highway. The thought of an intruder in Kate's house made him ill. *She's alone.* He tried to think of places in the house where she might hide, anything to keep his mind off his worst nightmare. He had to picture her hiding somewhere, alive, otherwise he'd go crazy.

The thirty miles between them felt like an ocean he had to swim. Thankful for a seventy-five mile-per-hour speed limit, he took full advantage. He ranted until rage made it hard to focus on the road, then tried to calm himself with assurances. *Kate is smart. She called 911.*

The pavement disappeared into the darkness ahead of him. Occasionally lights from a passing car chased away the inky black. *Please let her be okay.* His headlights reflected off the white lettering on the green highway signs along the side of the road, the only indication that he was closing the distance between them. Each mile marker felt five miles from the next.

If anyone lays a hand on her…

He couldn't think like that.

After fifteen torturous minutes of waiting for DJ's call, the lights of Kerrville in his rearview mirror, he pressed the button on his Bluetooth as soon as his phone made a sound. "DJ, is she okay?"

"She's completely fine, but they didn't catch the guy. He slipped out before the officers arrived."

"I'm ten minutes out. Is she right there?" Alex relaxed his jaw and took a deep breath.

"She's speaking with Maddox right now."

"Tell her I'm on my way."

Alex pulled to a stop behind the patrol cars and slammed the truck door as he bolted toward the house. Philip stood next to Kate on the porch, his shirt conveniently missing. But Kate left little doubt that she wanted Alex. When she saw him, she ran down the front steps and sprinted across the yard.

She didn't wait for him to say anything before cradling his face in her hands. "I'm okay. Whoever broke in never even saw me." She hadn't even been crying.

"Rainy." He pulled her to his chest. The anger and terror that gripped his heart gave way, and his tears fell freely.

She slid her arms around his waist.

He held her, not knowing how he'd ever convince his arms to let go. "I was sick with worry."

Her head buried in his chest, she sighed. "When DJ said he'd called you, I knew you'd be upset. I'm so sorry."

"It's not your fault." He dragged his sleeve across his face, then pulled her close again. "Did they take anything?" He stroked her hair, wondering if her calm exterior would crumble once things quieted down.

"Not that I can tell. He dug through the filing cabinet in the den. Some of the kitchen drawers were hanging open. My purse and tote bag were dumped out onto the dining room table."

"He?"

"Sounded like a man."

"Did he go into your room?"

"Not that I saw. He left moments before the dispatcher said that officers had arrived." Kate tightened her grip on him. "Thank you for rushing over."

Alex kissed the top of her head. "I wonder what he wanted."

"It was almost as if he was looking for something specific. You think they wanted information from Bruce's file?"

"Can't imagine why it would be important to anyone." He didn't want to let go of her. "If anything had happened to you …"

Philip stepped off the porch and took a few steps toward them. Alex shot DJ a silent plea. Whatever the shirtless neighbor wanted to say could wait. Preferably, he could write it down and mail it … from Oklahoma or Siberia.

DJ called out to Philip. "Captain Maddox would like to ask you a few questions."

"I don't know if I'll be any help, but sure." He hurried into the house.

Alex met DJ's gaze and thanked him with a slight nod. Kate inched up on her tiptoes and touched Alex's face. He looked down at her.

"Alex, I'm not hurt, only a little shaken up." She nestled against his chest. "Just hold me, please."

It wasn't hard to oblige her. Resting his chin on her head, he ran his fingers through her hair. "I can't lose you, Kate."

They still stood wrapped in each other's arms when DJ and Maddox stepped off the porch.

"Ahem." DJ lifted his Stetson and smoothed his hair. "Could we talk a minute?"

One arm still draped around Kate, Alex shook DJ's hand. "Thanks for calling me." He extended a hand to Maddox. "I'm glad you're here."

"Sorry we didn't get here sooner. I wasn't home when I got her text. I'll have the guys ask around tomorrow to see who else might've seen something, but I think we are all done here for tonight." Maddox hugged Kate, shedding the part of Deputy Captain and stepping into the role of uncle. "If you remember any other details, just call. Your Aunt Beth was worried sick. Please call if you need anything at all."

"Thanks, Uncle Pat." Kate nodded. "If I remember more, I'll call."

"You'll get me the last name of your other guest?" He looked up from his phone as he stepped away.

"Yes. I'll call tomorrow and find out."

"Thanks." Maddox sauntered off, talking to the dispatcher as he climbed into his SUV.

DJ rubbed the back of his neck. "Kate, I sent your very attentive neighbor home. You want me to park in front until morning?"

Alex shook his head. "Go home to Becca. I'm staying."

"Call if you need anything. Can I talk to you alone just a minute, Alex?"

Kate squeezed Alex's arm. "I'll wait for you inside." She turned toward DJ. "Thanks for coming, for everything. Tell Becca I'll call her in the morning."

Alex watched Kate walk inside before giving DJ his attention.

"Are you okay? I hated to call before I knew she was safe, but you wouldn't have forgiven me if I'd waited." DJ rocked back on his heels.

"You're right about that." Alex rubbed his face. "I'm just glad she's okay."

"And if he returns?"

"I'm not a vigilante." He shoved his hands in his pockets and kicked at a rock on the ground. "I don't care about getting even. I only care about keeping her safe."

"They dusted for prints. Not sure what they found. Kate gave them a list of everyone here tonight, so they can do elimination prints if they have to." DJ patted him on the shoulder before walking away. "Get some sleep before your meeting."

Alex moved his truck into the driveway and walked in through the back door. A board covered the broken pane. Kate stood at the counter wiping her face, her eyes red. Finally, she'd let herself cry.

He hated to see her scared and upset. "You aren't going to start baking now, are you?" Humor seemed a necessity.

She offered him a faint smile. "No. I'll wait until after we sleep. I have a lot to clean up first." She looked around at the fingerprint powder. "You have a meeting in three hours. There are clean sheets on the bed in the extra room. Go sleep."

"In a minute." He pulled her close. His face buried in her hair, he inhaled the lavender scent of her shampoo. Slow, deep breaths did little to calm his heart rate but stirred a passion deep inside him.

Fear dissolved into desire. He tasted the tears on her cheeks as his lips sought hers. His mouth pressed to hers; he tangled his fingers in her hair. The thought that he might never again have held her, kissed her, compelled him to hold her tighter, kiss her more deeply. She needed to know how much he loved her, and words seemed insufficient. But they'd set clear boundaries. She'd made her feelings known.

Moaning, she grabbed his shirt in her fist. He lifted his head, letting her breathe, but she closed the gap within a second. The non-negotiable boundary loomed closer. Alex backed her against the wall. His hands trailed down her sides, and he fingered the hem of her sweatshirt. He wanted her, wanted to feel her, touch her. His fingers slipped under the layers of fabric, searching out her skin.

Instead of tensing at his touch, she leaned in closer.

Call a halt. You're pushing it too far. Alex pulled away.

Breathing heavily, she fell toward him, but he caught her by the shoulders.

"If you need anything, you know where to find me." He gently stood her up and stepped back, out of reach.

Kate dropped into a chair. Tears glistened on her eyelashes. Plodding through wet cement would have been easier than walking away from her. He glanced back over his shoulder. She sat in a kitchen chair, hugging her knees to her chest.

Much earlier than he wanted to be awake, Alex was Skyping with his client when he heard clanking and shuffling in the kitchen. He'd felt like a zombie when he woke up, but a quick shower had him looking presentable and awake. No one on the other end of his internet connection was any wiser about what he'd been through hours before. After more than an hour of pitching himself, answering questions, sorting through details, and figuring out a delivery schedule, he accepted the job.

"I'll send the contract within the hour, which will include all that we've discussed. You can reply with any additional information." Alex ended the call and wasted no time typing up the contract. Once he walked into the kitchen, he wouldn't get much work done.

His laptop allowed him to work from Kate's place instead of being tied to the office in his cabin, and he'd never been more grateful he bought that computer. As he typed, he listened to Kate jostle about the kitchen.

Just as he finished typing up the email, she called Becca.

"Hey, hope it's not too early. . . . I'm fine. . . . No, really. . . . I woke to the sound of breaking glass. I slipped out of bed trying to figure out what to do. . . . For a second, I was tempted to check it out, but I was too chicken. . . . Exactly. Remember how this house was? All kinds of stuff piled in the extra room when I moved in. . . . Well, it proved helpful. Wait 'til you hear what I did."

Alex tilted his head back and listened.

Pans clinked. Then she continued, "Anyway, I haven't gotten rid of all that stuff, but that's not important. There was a wig on a head stand in one of the boxes and when I saw it, I stuck it in my closet. I guess it belonged to my Grandma Betty. . . . Yep, that's what I did. I laid that wig on my pillow and used pillows under the quilt for my body. . . . Oh, yeah. I hid in the closet with the door open the tiniest bit."

Based on the wonderful smells wafting from the kitchen, Kate was preparing breakfast as she rehashed the night's events. "When the deputies arrived, I said goodbye to the dispatcher, and as soon as I hung up, I grabbed other clothes to throw on. I wasn't about to let everyone see me in what I slept in . . . I know, right? That's all I need in this little town."

Alex loved to hear how her mind worked. She surprised him by doing what he'd never think to do. He couldn't help but smile as he wondered what she wore before she pulled on the sweatshirt and yoga pants.

After clicking send on the email, he tiptoed into the kitchen in his stocking feet. Kate still chatted away with Becca, but the subject had moved on to the kiss and his retreat. More open with Becca than he'd expected, Kate had mistaken his abrupt departure as a sign of continued uneasiness about the break-in. For now, he was content to let her think that.

He leaned back against the counter and watched her. Brown curls bounced as she reached from the counter to the pan, then checked the oven. When she wasn't using her free hand to cook, she used it to illustrate her story. Her other hand kept still only because it held the phone to her ear. She turned around, and her eyes brightened with delight. He loved the smile that lit up her face when she looked at him, a different smile than the one she flashed at everyone else.

"Hey Becca. I'll talk to you later. Alex is done with work." Kate laid her phone on the counter. "Breakfast is just about done."

"Smells good. How did you sleep the rest of the night?" He held open his arms, and she nestled against him.

"Like a rock. Thanks for staying." Brown eyes smiled up at him from under her dark lashes.

"My meeting went well. They hired me."

"They'd be foolish not to. I'm glad it went well in spite of the eventful night." She kissed him on the cheek and stepped back to the stove.

"I heard you telling Becca about it. I'm glad you didn't go investigate."

She pulled a pan of biscuits out of the oven. "I am much braver with my online searches than in real life."

He grabbed the platter of sausage she held out and set it on the table. "And I couldn't be more pleased."

While she stacked the biscuits in a fabric-lined basket and filled a bowl with creamy sausage gravy, he poured them each a cup of coffee.

"You used a wig to create a body double? That was pretty quick thinking."

"Don't you ever have those 'what would I do if…' conversations with yourself? When I moved in and saw that wig, that was my first thought, which is why it was in my closet."

Alex shook his head and grinned. The more she talked, the more he loved her.

"By the amusement on your face, I guess only one of us thinks through those types of scenarios without provocation."

"It was clever. If they saw you asleep, they wouldn't look for you or wonder if you'd seen them."

"That's what I hoped anyway." She stirred sugar into her coffee before taking a sip. "Oh, I never asked. How did you find out about the break-in? I don't even know how DJ found out."

"DJ called me. He heard about it from Maddox."

"I was going to call you but decided 911 was a better option."

"I'm glad."

"I stayed on the phone with them until the deputies arrived, then I answered questions. When DJ walked up, he said you were on your way. I'd only finished talking with them moments before you got here."

"It seems your new neighbor is also very interested in your well-being but doesn't own many shirts." He ran his last bite of biscuit through the gravy on his plate. "Kate, it was the longest thirty miles I've ever driven." He didn't look up as he said it.

"Einstein had an entire theory about that. Relative time differences." She ignored the reference to Philip.

Alex shook his head and served himself a fourth biscuit and smothered it in gravy. "You're funny."

"After breakfast, go sleep a while. I'm going to continue researching Grace's tree. I need to think about something other than a stranger digging through my things."

"So you are going to dig through someone else's history?"

"Exactly."

"Let me help you get this cleaned up, then I'll sleep. I'm pretty beat." He carried the dishes to the sink.

"Just sit those on the counter. I'll take care of it."

He planted a quick kiss on her cheek and headed down the hall. "See you in a couple hours."

May 20, 1830

There is very little to say about our journey beyond that it is long and tiresome. Father says we may arrive at our new home in a month. I ache at the thought of traveling that much longer.

I think Mother has a secret. Given her condition, I understand why she shed tears about coming to Texas.

~*~

June 2, 1830

We crossed the river into Texas on a ferry. I was glad I didn't have to swim. The weather is exceedingly warm, and I am ready to be in our new home.

Chapter Eight

April 6th – 8:37 am

I gathered the rest of the dishes as Alex trudged down the hall. The squeaky spring in the mattress yelped as he stretched out. Last night had dredged up horrible remembrances for him. He worried about me, but it was more than that. Heart-wrenching memories flooded back when he heard about my break-in. Hopefully, a full stomach and more sleep would help him feel better because forgetting wasn't possible.

After cleaning up after breakfast, I planted myself on my red sectional, legs crossed. My beautiful new piece of furniture could comfortably seat five, more if you didn't care about comfort. The cherry red was a beautiful accent against the pale turquoise walls in my den. After pulling out my notes and yellow pad, I rested the laptop on my thighs. Navigating to one of my favorite genealogy websites, I pulled up the death certificate for Ruth Cooper and printed two copies. It listed Ruth's parents as Samuel Whittaker and Susanna. *Unknown* was written in place of the surname of her mother.

A search for the name Samuel Whittaker resulted in pages of possibilities. I allowed myself a groan before looking over Ruth's death certificate again, hoping to find information to narrow the search. It listed Samuel's birthplace as *Penn*, so I changed the search. That shrank the list of results, and after going through the list, I found a Samuel who matched on a census record.

Within a couple hours, I had two more generations on the Whittaker line filled in and most of the related documentation printed. I sent off a few emails, requesting certificates. Online, I'd found enough to confirm my findings as accurate, but hoped I could get copies of other documents, which hadn't yet been digitized, before I presented the information to Grace. The more success I had researching the maternal side, the more unfounded my dread of failure seemed.

I yawned and contemplated a short nap, but each record I found kept me staring at the screen even though my eyes wanted to close. Finally, I gave up and snapped the laptop closed. As I tiptoed past the extra room, a knock sounded at the front door.

I'd just gotten a text from Becca, so I knew it wasn't her. Not wanting the visitor to wake Alex, I hurried over, then groaned inwardly as I guessed at who it might be. Although extremely handsome and well-built, Philip irritated me. I pasted on a smile and opened the door.

He held out a bouquet. "Something to brighten your day after the events of last night." He stepped close to me, and I backed up, which he took as an invitation to come inside.

"Thank you." I pointed to the kitchen. "Would you like a Coke?"

"Oh, no thanks. I stay clear of those. They are like poison." He smiled that don't-you-just-love-me smile. "But a glass of water would be great."

I filled a glass and handed it to him, without even offering ice. "Thankfully, only a window was damaged last night. I'm fine." I snipped the ends off the stems and arranged the flowers in a vase. Reminded of the break-in, my mind ran through the possibilities of what the intruder might have wanted.

In the extra bedroom, the mattress spring creaked.

"Excuse me just a moment." I left Philip sitting in the kitchen and ran down the hall.

Shirtless, Alex stood next to the bed, rubbing his eyes and looking around. Treated to a view I rarely saw, I lingered in the doorway an extra moment.

"Mmm." I picked up his tee shirt, which had fallen to the floor. "Looking for this?"

He took the shirt, and a sleepy smile disappeared behind the soft cotton fabric as he pulled it over his head.

"Philip's here. He stopped by to check on me."

Alex raised an eyebrow. "I think he needs me to explain things to him." He swept me into his arms, and a grin spread across his face.

Giggling at his surprise maneuver, I wrapped my arms around his neck. "You'll be nice, right?"

A soft chuckle rumbled in his chest.

My lips brushing his ear, I whispered, "Alex Ramirez, behave."

"Philip! How are you? Thanks for checking on *my* Kate." He shot me a sideways look, a smirk tugging at one side of his mouth. "She gave me quite the scare last night." Alex, all warmth and manners, put me down and shook hands with Philip.

"Oh, Alex. I didn't realize you were here." The smile fell from Philip's face and landed with a thud on the floor.

I hurried to the counter, trying to stifle a laugh. "He's here a lot." After getting a pot of coffee brewing, I pulled a dozen cinnamon muffins out of the freezer. I set the microwave to defrost and took a seat next to Alex.

"What woke you last night? How did you know about all the commotion over here?" He draped an arm around me.

"The weather has been so nice that I've been sleeping with my windows open. I heard Kate's voice and thought for a little while that I was just dreaming. Turns out, I really heard her."

Alex ignored the implication. "Did you see or hear anything else?"

"No, but I rushed down because I thought she might want someone to make her feel safe. Since she lives here *alone*." Philip found the red button and pushed it like a toddler holding the television remote.

Alex stared at the table.

I jumped up. "The coffee is ready." After filling a mug, I looked over at Philip. "Coffee?"

"Yes, please. Just black."

When I handed Alex his coffee, I purposefully made eye contact. The sparkle still shown in his green eyes, and I relaxed a little. After setting a mug in front of Philip, I set out plates and silverware, then loaded the warm muffins in a basket and put them on the table with the butter dish. "Help yourself."

Alex dug in without hesitation, and Philip followed suit.

He was halfway through a muffin when he put it back down on his plate. "These are delicious. Where do you buy them?"

"They're not *bought*. Kate *bakes* them. She's fabulous in the kitchen. I'm lucky to have a girlfriend that cooks and bakes." Lines near Alex's eyes crinkled, though Alex managed not to laugh out loud.

Philip grinned at me. "Another plus to having her as a neighbor."

"She's pretty fabulous." Alex winked at me as Philip buttered another muffin.

"I'll have to pop in over here more often." Philip stuck out his hand like he wanted me to grab it. He withdrew it quickly when I stood up and gave him my back as I poured myself another cup of coffee.

Alex caught my free hand as I sat down again. "Anytime you see the truck here, you are welcome to knock. We may or may not answer."

"So, Kate, do you like the flowers? I tried to imagine which ones seemed most like you. How'd I do?"

"They're nice." If I'd recorded the exchange, a nature show would've wanted the footage. The narration in my head made me want to snort. *The dominant male stands his ground as the roving male from another pride tries to impede on the hunting ground.*

Alex glanced at the vase on the counter.

Philip wore a smug smile and crossed his arms in front of him, his biceps stretching the sleeves on his shirt. "I thought those might brighten her day. A reminder that I was close by." He thought he had the upper hand because he was richer and by magazine standards, better looking. He seemed to expect women to fawn over him when he flashed his bright, white smile.

I glanced at Alex. He winked and brushed his thumb along the side of my hand. I loved everything about him, and he knew it. Philip wasn't my type. He came across as arrogant and self-absorbed.

"I'll let you guys visit. I'm going to get back to work." I kissed Alex on the cheek, reminded him in a whisper to be nice, and retreated into the den. From my spot on the floor, right in front of the sofa, I couldn't see them, but I could hear almost every word.

"Need more coffee?" Alex's chair scuffed against the wood floor.

"Nah, one cup is plenty for now. Tell me, Alex, what do you do?"

"Programmer. I work remotely. Contract work."

"Cool. I had no idea you were a computer geek."

"Yep. Winery is a big change from a software business."

"It's something different." Philip mumbled something else that I couldn't quite hear.

I strained but couldn't make out the next few comments from either of them. I thought about relocating to my office corner, hoping I could hear more clearly when Alex's voice could be heard again.

"It's a nice little town. People here look out for each other."

"Well, I do appreciate you guys being so nice and inviting me in for pizza. Meeting people is hard for me." Philip, the former head of a company, obviously had a lot of money, and yet he sat in my kitchen bemoaning the difficulty of making real friends. "I think maybe I come on too strong. Try too hard."

Their voices dropped again. I caught myself leaning toward the door.

"Kate is single, *not married*, right?" Based on his question, Philip must've thought that until I had a ring on my finger, he still had a chance.

Alex answered in a whisper, and even though I tried with everything in me, his response was too quiet to be heard. Whatever he said wrapped up the visit. A minute later Philip called out "goodbye" as Alex showed him to the door.

I shuffled papers as footsteps approached. Alex stretched as he walked toward the couch. His shirt lifted, and I was ever so tempted to run over and tickle him. *I don't even know if he's ticklish.* I opted to wait for another opportunity to indulge in the fun of discovering the answer.

"You done searching already? You found everybody?" He knew full well I'd only been listening.

"I put it away for now. Thought you might need some attention."

"Need?" He smirked and dropped onto the sectional.

"Philip left in a hurry. What did you say to him?"

"He needed to go. I was nice, just like you asked." He leaned forward, his cheek next to mine. "You know the whole bit about you baking and such, I was joking."

"You aren't lucky? I'm not *your* Kate?"

"So you did know. Good."

"You have work stuff to get done?"

"I wrapped up everything yesterday in preparation for today's meeting." He tousled my curls, which I loved.

I hopped off the floor and walked around behind him. He sat up. I pressed my fingers into his tight muscles, massaging.

He sighed and rolled his neck side to side as I kneaded along his shoulders. His muscles relaxed under my touch.

"You're all mine?"

"Uh huh." He dropped his shoulders as I circled my thumbs along his neck. He patted the couch next to him, and I gave up my job as masseuse. "Come sit. I want to chat with you about something."

"Is this one of those 'We need to talk' conversations?"

"I just want to talk to you." He leaned forward, his elbows on his knees.

I dropped onto the couch.

"You don't have to sit so far away."

I snuggled up next to him. "I'm listening."

"Do you like living here?"

"Yes." I answered quickly but scrambled in my head wondering about the question behind the question. I assumed what he asked and what he meant differed.

"You prefer small town life to living in town?"

"Are you asking because of the break-in?"

He shrugged.

"I like living here. I'd probably like living in San Antonio if I lived there. If your next question is 'Where do you see yourself in five years?' don't bother asking. I hate those types of questions."

"Where do you see yourself in *three* years?" He patted me on the leg, smiling.

With you, anywhere. I leaned my head on his shoulder. "What do you really want to know?"

"I think I already know the answer. You love this place." The words barely out of his mouth, a knock sounded at the door. "You expecting someone?"

"Your sister said she'd try to get by here today to show me the land. Do you have time to look at it with me?"

"Absolutely." Alex popped up off the sofa and answered the door. "Marisa. Come on in."

"Alex, it's such a surprise to find you here." His little sister liked to tease. "Hey, Kate."

I jumped up and hugged her. "Thanks for coming."

She jingled keys. "Want to take a look? I can get us onto the property but not into the house. I don't have the keys to that yet."

Turning around, I grabbed Alex's hand. "We should probably take the truck, right?"

"Probably best. I'm guessing the roads there need work?"

"Most definitely." Marisa answered a text, then looked up. "The last resident moved out several years ago. Based on the pictures, I don't think anyone has set foot on the property since then, except the realtor that listed it."

We all piled in the truck and drove the half-mile to the gate. Marisa unlocked it, and Alex drove through and stopped, waiting for her to climb back in.

"It's probably a good thing we brought the truck. These caliche roads are in desperate need of repair." He glanced back over his shoulder at Marisa as she buckled in. "Where to?"

"Just follow the road until you can't, I guess. I want Kate to be able to see what the land looks like. We can also get out and walk if y'all want."

We bumped along the road, winding between scrub oaks, mesquite trees, and overgrown juniper bushes. We passed the wood frame house, which looked much more dilapidated up close.

"Somewhere on the property are the remains of an old, *old* dog run house. Mostly just a footprint. But as I said, no one has lived on the property for years." Marisa pointed at the house. "And it's a bit obvious."

Alex drove at a snail's pace, while she pointed out features mentioned in the information. "There is a creek and a barn, but they advised not to go inside. It needs to be torn down."

Weathered red peeked through the overgrowth farther down another branch of the caliche road.

"Headstones!" I rolled down the window, and juniper-scented Hill Country air filled the cab. "Mind if we go look?"

Alex slowed, scanning for the path to the family plot. "She likes to see dead people."

I shook my head. "He thinks he's funny."

Marisa rolled her eyes.

He found the overgrown remains of a road, and we made our way to the cluster of large trees, where headstones dotted the ground near the base, surrounded by an ancient-looking wrought-iron fence. Alex parked outside the black iron gate, and we all climbed out. A small sign dangled from the gate, creaking as the wind blew, the name on it lost to time and weather.

The headstones were simple and old, but they were fairly well-preserved. Under the branches of a mighty oak, they'd missed the worst of the blazing sun and pounding rains.

"The stories they could tell." I paused at each grave trying to make out the names.

"If anyone—other than either of you two—says a word, I'm outta here." Alex winked at me.

"You know what I mean. Marisa, was there any history about this place in the info?"

"Not really. I'll see what I can find out for you, though."

I tugged Alex to the far edge of the family plot. "What do you think?"

"It's beautiful land. And after driving past the house, it's clear that the land is the reason you want it."

"I've read over the information Marisa gave me. I can afford it."

He wrapped his arms around my waist and pulled me close. "If it were just you, no one else to consider, what would you do?"

I wasn't quite sure what to make of his question. "It isn't just me, and I want your opinion."

"They aren't making more land. I think it's a worthwhile investment that won't depreciate. And"—he kissed me—"I love you too."

"Let's drive a bit more, but I think I want it."

For another half hour, we poked along, discussing the landscape and telling Marisa about the break-in.

When we returned to the house, she hopped out in a hurry. "When I get the keys to the house, we can go through it."

"Marisa, start working up the paperwork. I want to buy the place."

Her green eyes widened, sparkling below perfectly shaped eyebrows. "Absolutely. We'll make them an offer and see what they come back with. I'm sorry I can't stay longer, but I have an appointment. After that, I'll call, and we can discuss numbers."

"Thanks!" I waved as I pushed open the back door. Inside, I caught Alex's hand. "Let me make you some lunch."

"Come here for a sec." He led me to the couch. Holding my hand, he touched my red nails one at a time. "I never worried about you being in the house alone . . . until last night."

"Alex, I'm really okay." I didn't mention that thoughts of someone prowling through my house haunted me almost constantly.

"I need to run home and feed Bureau. I also have something else I need to take care of in town. If you want, I can come back over. Even stay the night in the extra room if you'd feel safer." He stared at my nails, waiting for an answer.

Yes. Yes. Yes. I would feel so much safer if you stayed. That's what reverberated in my head, but that's not what poured out of my mouth. "Come for dinner. I'll cook. But don't feel like you have to spend the night. I'll be fine."

He nodded and walked into the kitchen.

I wrapped my arms around his waist. "Last night scared me, and I know it stirred up unpleasant memories for you. But I'll be okay here by myself."

He held me tight and inhaled as if he was going to respond, but he didn't, at least not with words. He tilted my face and softly, sweetly brushed his lips across mine. My anticipation grew as I waited to feel the force of a deep passionate kiss, but instead I only heard a whisper.

"I'll be back for dinner." He slipped out the back door.

I didn't even get my goodbye kiss. *Wasn't he tired of the wading pool already?*

With a few hours before Alex would return for dinner, I turned on the television and opened my laptop to hunt for more information about Susanna, Ruth Whittaker's mother. I searched marriage records in Texas. On the second page, I found what I wanted, a last name. Susanna Kimble married Samuel Whittaker in 1918. They married many years before Ruth was born. As I searched the birth records, I compiled a list of children. Ruth was the youngest of eight—six boys and two girls. The printer spat out multiple pages.

I wanted to find out more about Susanna. A death certificate would hopefully provide information. I pulled up the website with images of some Texas death records available online. I entered her married name and added Texas as her place of death, venturing a guess that she'd died in the state. Up popped her death certificate at the top of the result list. Susanna K. Whittaker died in 1960. Her death certificate listed her parents as John Kimble and Louisa Wilson, both born in Texas.

The Kimble line proved easy to trace as others had done extensive research. As I read through family stories and other histories posted about the family, I jotted notes and bookmarked pages. Maybe that was the connection I could give my client. But Louisa's name transfixed me. Somehow that felt like the connection, maybe not her, but her line.

I poked around a bit more. After navigating to Ancestry, I searched for Louisa Wilson. I entered an educated guess for the birth year and typed in her husband's name. At the top of the list of results was a matching person from another family tree. I clicked the link. On Louisa's profile, it listed her parents as Charlie Wilson and Madeline Kent. Accepting others' information without documentation was a common error when people researched genealogy, and I determined not to make it. I jotted down the names, circled them, and added a large question mark next to the circle.

Farther down in the list of results, I found a marriage record for Louisa and John Kimble. The information in that record narrowed her birth year. I sent all that I'd found to the printer, two copies of each, then ran and sorted the papers into two stacks. I tucked my copies in the file cabinet and the other copies into a folder on the table. After shuffling papers, I sat down with the laptop again, hoping to find more about Louisa. Another tree also had her listed, but her mother's name was different. Madeline Hughes. I scratched my head. It was too much to hope it would be straight forward.

Keys jingled as the back door opened. "Hello?" Alex's voice sounded … different, robust but tinged with emotion.

"Coming. I lost track of time. I haven't even started coo—" I stopped as soon as I rounded the corner. My heart fluttered.

Dressed in black slacks, a crisp white dress shirt, and a tie, he revved the pitter patter of my heart into overdrive. And the shiny black cowboy boots were a nice addition.

I leaned against the counter and fanned myself. I rarely saw him dressed up, but I liked it. I liked it a lot. "Wow."

He grinned his boyish grin, and flowers appeared from behind his back, a bouquet twice as big as the one I'd received from the neighbor. "For you."

I laughed. "They're beautiful! Thank you." I hugged Alex, careful not to crush the flowers.

"I thought they might look nice in front of those others." He laughed at his own punchline.

I stretched up, but I only received a peck on the cheek. Turning away, I pulled the kitchen shears from the knife block. "I'll get these in a vase."

As I snipped the ends and arranged the flowers, he leaned on the counter next to me, and his demeanor sobered. "When I woke up, I was … what's that word you like to use? Brooding? Anyway, last night did send me reeling. If the outcome had been different, I don't know what I would've done. But I can't live in the what-ifs. I should have learned that long ago. I guess we can thank Philip for helping me shake my brooding."

His words and attitude were loving and intimate, but physically he'd pulled away. It left me confused and a bit frustrated.

"You definitely rose to the occasion." I pulled chicken out of the refrigerator and plunked it in a pan to simmer.

Alex sat down at the table.

"Want a beer?" I slid my apron over my head and tied the strings behind me.

"Sure." He kicked his feet up into the chair across from him.

I poured myself a glass of Moscato and popped the top off a locally brewed brown ale. While we talked and waited for the chicken to cook, I aimlessly wrapped a twist tie around my finger, my ring finger. I wasn't trying to drop hints, but subconsciously, maybe I was. Hint or not, I convinced myself it was unintentional.

When the timer beeped, I tossed the twisted circle on the table and jumped up. The chicken shredded easily using two forks. I added seasonings, tomato sauce, and a little bit of water before returning it to the burner. While that bubbled on the stove, I chopped tomatoes and lettuce.

My phone rang just as I put down the knife. "Hello."

"Kate, thank you. What you bought me is stunning. I found it in my jewelry bag just now."

I haven't given her the locket yet. "Becca, I didn't put anything in your bag, but I can pretend and take the credit. You bought it and forgot maybe?"

"No way. Wait until you see this thing. It looks vintage. Maybe DJ picked it up somewhere. I'll ask him about it when he gets home."

"You free tomorrow?"

"Call me. Sorry to interrupt your dinner. I just found it and wanted to call before I forgot."

Alex warmed tortillas and served himself a plate. "Everything okay?"

"Yeah. Becca called to ask if I gave her a piece of jewelry. She found one in her bag. But I didn't put it there. Maybe DJ wanted to surprise her."

We carried our food and drinks to the den and set everything on the coffee table. Alex took off his tie, and I slid my pile of genealogy information out of the way.

After we ate, our empty plates stayed on the coffee table while we snuggled on the couch, and I told Alex about what I'd been able to dig up.

"I found conflicting information for one person, which just goes to show that you can't take people's word for it. Finding a source is important. I'll have to dig to figure out her real name." I continued, telling him all that I'd found about the Whittaker and Kimble lines.

Alex rubbed my neck while I talked, his hands warm as always. "What will you search next?" He massaged from the base of my skull down to my shoulders, moving his thumb and fingers in small circles.

Staying on topic required concentration. "I want to find out about Louisa's family. I feel like that's where the connection will be—the story I want to give Grace."

"Sounds like the families were in Texas a long time."

"They have been. I need to read more about early Texas history. Watching *The Alamo* helped."

"You light up when you talk about genealogy." Alex's green eyes intimated his approval.

"What do you think that man wanted?" I figured he'd understand that the break-in was never far from my thoughts.

He tensed. "I wish I knew."

I stopped short of asking if he thought it could happen again.

At 11 pm, he stretched. "I should go."

"Thanks for hanging out with me and letting me ramble."

He brushed his fingers along my cheek and kissed me on the forehead. "I love to listen to you."

"That's what all guys say when they're dating."

He winked and draped his tie over his shoulder as he sauntered toward the back door. "Goodnight."

I stood by the door wondering what happened to my goodbye kiss.

I'd told Alex I was fine by myself, but I'd chosen my words carefully. I didn't say I felt safe because that would've been a lie. The break-in rattled me. My perfect little house didn't feel like a fairytale castle anymore. After Alex drove away, I bolted both doors and checked the latches on all the windows. Satisfied that every door and window had been secured, I switched on lights all over the house, except upstairs. I refused to climb into the dark bonus room without anyone with me.

I had plenty to keep me busy, and I could sleep tomorrow. I flipped through my spiral and stared at Louisa's name. I added her parents' names, Charlie Wilson and Madeline, to the tree. I underlined where the mother's last name should be, leaving an empty space.

Hughes or Kent? Unsure of her last name, I started my search with Charlie, hoping to find a marriage record. Charlie Wilson married Madeline Kent in 1856. The marriage certificate listed her age as twenty. I searched for a birth record for a Madeline Kent, knowing she was born about 1836. I didn't find it listed in the Births and Christenings.

I popped back to Ancestry.com and compared the trees where I'd seen her listed. In both trees, it listed her mother as Tabitha Miller. One tree had her father as Wesley Kent, the other as Nathaniel Hughes.

Alex's recent film choice came to mind as I stared at Madeline's birth year. If her family was, in any way, tied to the revolution that would make an interesting story for Grace to learn about her family.

I jumped when the phone rang. "Hello."

"I'm home. Just called to say goodnight. You sure you're okay?" Weariness reverberated in his voice.

"Oh yeah. I have every light on, but I'll be okay." I loved that he cared but didn't want him worried about me.

"Call me in the morning."

"I will. Love you."

"I love you too, Kate." His voice made me think of warm chocolate drizzled on strawberries.

I hung up the phone and padded into the kitchen. Pans rattled as I yanked them out of the drawer below the oven. I really needed to search, but flour, sugar, and eggs had been calling to me since Alex walked out the door. Thinking of warm chocolate was the tipping point.

With all the ingredients measured out around me, I creamed the sugars, butter, and eggs with a fork and watched the sugar dissolve into a golden paste. After a splash of vanilla and oil, I mixed in the dry ingredients a half-cup at a time. Wooden spoon in hand, I stirred and stirred until the cookie dough was combined and firm. I dumped in an extra-large bag of chocolate chips, ignoring the fact that the recipe called for less. I wanted chocolate. Lots of chocolate.

Forcing my fingers into the dough, I kneaded in the morsels. I scooped out a small amount, and after rolling it between my palms, a round ball of dough formed. I dropped it onto a parchment-lined cookie sheet, then repeated the process. Neat rows with enough room for each cookie to spread out without bumping its neighbor filled the pan. When I'd crowded the cookie sheet with all that could fit, I slid it into the oven and set a timer.

I pulled out strawberries and melted the small handful of chocolate morsels I'd set aside. While the cookies baked, I snacked on my treat and focused on Grace's tree. I searched for Madeline, entering only her first name, then adding her mother's name. I set a ten-year range for the birth year, hoping that would turn up something, anything to find more information. Before I hit the search button, the timer beeped.

I swapped trays, but as I was shuffling the cookies to the cooling rack, an idea popped into my head. As soon as the cookies had been moved, I ran back to the laptop and opened a new tab. A quick Google search listed the early Texas counties. When I added Miller to the search terms, two promising links popped up: The Gonzales Memorial Museum and The Miller House. Both were in Gonzales County. The Memorial museum housed information about the Texas Revolution. The Miller House was staged to represent a time period close to the time of Madeline's life. I wanted to visit both, even if it didn't generate any new genealogy information.

Having so many leads to follow excited me. I continued reading about Gonzales County and the timeline of the Texas Revolution.

Though time travel wasn't possible, time warping seemed to be, but only when I searched genealogy records. Three hours had vanished, and all I had were scribbles, notes, and six dozen chocolate chip cookies. I made sure the oven was off, grabbed a Coke, and returned to my hunt.

By 6 am, I couldn't focus my eyes any longer. Leaving all the lights ablaze, I closed the laptop and wandered down the hall to my bedroom. In bed, I pulled the covers up to my chin and let sleep pull me under.

Chapter Nine

April 7th – 9:03 am

The bright sun permeated my eyelids, creating a red glow. A buzzing near my head repeated over and over. After swatting at whatever insect dared disturb my sleep, I buried my head under a pillow and returned to my dreams.

Hours later, I awoke to the smell of coffee. I bolted upright, pulling the covers up to my chin. *I live alone. Why does my house smell like coffee?*

Reigning in the stampeding thoughts—none of them good—I swung my legs out from under the covers.

As if a bad guy would break in and make coffee.

Perched on the side of my bed, I avoided looking at my reflection in the mirror. I didn't need it to see it to know how horrid I looked.

I'd only given out three keys to The Castle. My dad had a key. DJ and Becca had a key, and Alex had a key. He'd never shown up unannounced before, and I couldn't imagine my dad or Becca coming over and letting themselves in without calling first or at least knocking before entering. I looked down at what I'd slept in and decided whoever had made coffee didn't need to see me like that. I pulled on yoga pants and a sweatshirt and trudged down the hall.

Alex sat at the breakfast table with a cup of coffee, a stack of cookies, and the local paper. "Good afternoon."

"Afternoon? To what do I owe this pleasure?" I yawned and shuffled toward the table.

"I called. Five times. You didn't answer. I may have been concerned enough to drive over and let myself in."

I gathered my tousled mess of curls into a hair tie. "You spied on me while I slept?"

"Only long enough to determine that you weren't a wig and pillows." He poured me a cup of coffee and added three teaspoons of sugar. "You look like you could use this?"

"That bad, huh?"

He laughed instead of answering the question. "Becca called me. She was worried when you didn't answer. She wants to come over when you're awake."

"I wonder what else I missed. What time is it, anyway?"

"Eighteen minutes past noon. How late were you up?"

"Very late. I think I heard the neighbor leave for work." I stood next to the table, still trying to shake my haze.

Alex waited until I set my coffee down and pulled me into his lap. "I'm sorry I woke you. And to me, you are always beautiful."

I relaxed into his arms and laid my head on his shoulder. "I think I'll doze here for a few minutes." I might have too if he hadn't tested my ticklishness. Again. Squirming and giggling, I maneuvered my way out of his arms. "I need some breakfast."

He jumped up and opened the oven. "I brought you tacos."

"One of the many reasons I love you."

I shot off a text to Becca: *I'm awake. Come whenever.*

Her response appeared almost instantaneously: *Be there soon.*

"Now that you know I'm alive, you heading home or are you going to work from here?" I pulled the tacos out of the oven.

"You want me to stay?" He raised an eyebrow and grinned.

I dropped back into his lap and dotted his face with kisses. "All the time." That wasn't a lie. I didn't have to give a second's thought to that question. Popping up out of his lap, I plopped down in my own chair and between bites, told him about last night's finds. I grabbed my laptop. "I discovered two museums I want to visit." I flipped open my laptop and waited impatiently as it booted. Clicking keys, I hastily pulled up the schedule for the Texana room at the library. "And, if I drive into San Antonio, I think I can find more information at the downtown library."

"Maybe you can meet Marisa for lunch again."

I hadn't mentioned to Alex that I planned to do that but hoped she didn't drag along her boyfriend. "Why are you so worried about her?"

"I don't know. It's not just because I don't like Paul. She seemed … different."

"I'll be sure and call her when I go." While I ate, I told him about the museums in Gonzales.

Someone knocked, and I ran to the door, thinking it was Becca. Pulling it open, I found myself face to face with a stunning blue cameo surrounded with silver filigree.

"That's gorgeous. And it does look really old." I stepped back for her to come in.

"Where would I get a genuine piece like this? Seriously? Can you imagine its value if this wasn't a well-done replica? It drives me crazy that I don't know when or where I got it. I'd go get more." She took two steps inside and stopped.

"Come on in. Alex is in the kitchen."

"Is he just over here all the time now?" Becca raised both eyebrows and waited for an answer.

"Pretty much." I shot her a look, ending that line of questioning.

Judging from the grin Alex wore, he'd heard our conversation. "I'm going to hide and get some work done. I'll be in the den." He disappeared around the corner, out of the way but close enough to hear us talk. He won points for planning on that one.

I poured Becca a cup of coffee. "What are you going to make out of that fabulous brooch?"

"Not sure yet. I'll wait for inspiration to hit. How's the genealogy search?"

"If they are open, I want to drive into San Antonio tomorrow and visit the downtown library."

"I think I'm free tomorrow. I'll go with you, if you want." Becca glanced at her phone. "I can't stay long. I'm meeting DJ for lunch. Today is the anniversary of when what's-her-name and I got pulled over."

"Aww. You met DJ five years ago?"

"Yep. We celebrate it each year at the steakhouse. It's silly." Becca's grin said that to her it was anything but silly. "Did you call about that land? I saw Marisa give you the information."

"Yes. I'm very interested, but what do I need with forty-five acres?"

"You don't have to do anything with it. But buying it guarantees that you won't have a weirdo building something behind your house."

"You mean like a winery?"

"Exactly."

"In answer to your other question, the search has gone well so far." I filled her in on my progress and told her about the museums that might have more information.

June 14, 1830

We are almost to the DeWitt colony. Father has been whistling most of the day.

~*~

June 15, 1830

We have arrived, but there is little here, only a small town with huts. Many do not even have windows.

We were assigned a lot in town. Land will be assigned later. But we have no house. Father says it will be easy to build one quickly. There is ample wood available from the surrounding trees.

Lucy, Clara, and their family say they will build a house here in town. The Kents plan to live in town only until their land is granted. Mr. Kent wants to live outside of town.

~*~

June 16, 1830

Five other families arrived today. They routed through New Orleans and came across the water. I listened carefully to the stories they told. When they were picking dewberries along the coast, they saw Indians looking down at them from the bluff. I am glad we came a different route.

Mother smiled today. The new families are from Missouri also, so perhaps she doesn't feel alone out here anymore.

CHAPTER TEN

April 7th – 1:28 pm

Alex tried to focus on work, but his unsettled mind played through the events of the last few days. After Becca left for her lunch with DJ, Kate nestled on the couch, determined to find every possible ancestor she could find for her client. He stared at his script, but the commands and syntax seemed like a foreign language. He gave up and closed his laptop.

He sauntered across the room and flopped on the opposite length of the sectional. "I was thinking that we should get out of here."

"I'm open to suggestions." Kate set her laptop on the coffee table.

He stretched out on the couch and tucked his hands behind his head. "How late is that museum open?"

"Seriously?"

"Yes. Gonzales is a drive, but it would be fun."

"Let me look." Kate googled The Gonzales Memorial Museum. "It's open until six."

"If we leave now, we can make it."

"Give me five minutes to make myself presentable." She hopped up and bent over him.

Passion bubbled inside him. As she leaned in for a kiss, he turned his head, and she planted a kiss on his cheek. She pulled back, and questions shaped like tears threatened to escape.

"While you get dressed, I'll pack some snacks." He jumped up and rested a hand on her shoulder before walking away. On the trip, he needed to talk to her, to be honest.

She hurried down the hall.

He tossed chips and cookies in a bag and threw drinks and ice packs in the soft-sided cooler. After deciding what he wanted, he thought only of her. Keeping secrets from her proved more difficult than he imagined, and the doubt in her eyes just now would keep him up at night. But he would hug that line as much as possible to give her the memorable moment she deserved. After all, she'd only turn thirty-two once.

When Kate padded down the hall, her eyes red, she smiled. "I'm ready. Did you pack some cookies?"

"Sure did. Got your notes?"

"Oh, thanks for reminding me." She ran into the den.

He met her in the doorway as she darted back toward the kitchen. Focused on her bag, she jumped when he wrapped her in an embrace.

"I love you, Kate."

She relaxed into his arms. "I know."

"And I owe you an explanation."

Running her finger down the front of his tee shirt, she lifted her head and met his gaze. "You want to talk here or on the way?"

"Let's talk in the truck." He gathered the cooler and snacks.

Kate stopped near the truck, watching leaf cutter ants parade across the driveway. Alex's habit was to open her door and help her in, so she waited for him. After tossing the food in the back seat, he pulled her close again and slowly pressed his mouth to her bright red lips, giving her the kiss that she'd expected in the den.

"Are you teasing me?"

"I promise I'm not." He opened her door and helped her into the passenger seat.

"You do have some explaining to do." She winked and buckled her seatbelt.

Chapter Eleven

April 7th – 1:43 pm

It took all my restraint not to bombard him with questions as soon he started the engine. The silence in the cab of the truck felt like a heavy mist, the kind that settles when the early morning air deposits dew just before sunrise. But even with the uncertainty of dodged kisses, I felt safe with Alex. Always. I thought of a hundred conversations to start but forced my tongue to silence and waited until Alex started his explanation.

As a distraction, I focused on the patches of wildflowers that colored the landscape.

After multiple glances in the rearview mirror, Alex cleared his throat. "Using your side mirror, without turning around, tell me if you see a cream-colored car coming up in the next lane."

"I see it. Why?"

"I think maybe we're being followed. Let me try this." He changed lanes, slowing in the outside lane to 60mph.

"It's still behind us."

"Maybe I'm just being paranoid after the break-in, but just in case…" He exited and drove into a gas station.

I watched for the car as he jumped out and pumped gas. "I didn't see the car exit."

"He stayed on the highway."

After filling the tank, we pulled back onto the highway and continued to the museum. As we crossed under Loop 410 on our way through San Antonio, Alex combed his fingers through his hair. "When I see your eyes red and know that I'm the reason, it breaks my heart." He stayed focused on the cars ahead. "I know you've noticed that I haven't really kissed you since the night of the break-in."

"You mean except for right before climbing in the truck? Because I'd label that as a kiss, a good one too."

He chuckled. "Not counting that."

"I noticed."

"Don't think it's because you aren't desirable or because my feelings have changed. Neither of those are true."

I stared out the window not wanting him to see my expression. He'd snatched the reasons out of my thoughts like a magician plucking quarters out of my ears.

"We talked about waiting." He took a deep breath and shifted his grip on the steering wheel. "Until marriage." The last word pirouetted like a dancing elephant.

I held my breath waiting to hear what would follow.

"Am I wrong in thinking that's where this is headed?" He looked at me and quickly added one more word. "Eventually?"

"I hope so."

He clearly said the word "eventually," but I heard "not for a really long time." If he wasn't going to kiss me anymore until then, it would be a really long wait.

"Our conversation left things very clear. You didn't want to sleep together." He shot me a sideways glance. "And I was—am fine with that."

I nodded.

"That, for me, is reason enough, and I give you my word that I won't cross that li—"

The truck lurched as he stomped hard on the brake. He stopped.

Tires behind us squealed, and we both held our breath, waiting for impact. But the minivan stopped with seemingly only inches to spare. We inched along with traffic funneled to one lane. Alex stayed quiet, watching the brake lights in front of him.

I wished for the prancing pachyderm to tiptoe its way back into the conversation. On and off, the brake lights flashed, and we crept forward. He passed policemen moving flares out of the roadway, and cars spread out into all three lanes.

He glanced at me, honesty burning in his eyes. "I have every intention of keeping that promise, but I need your help."

His words yanked on the light bulb string in my head. I'd used the passion of his kisses and the closeness of his embrace as a measuring stick, but his restraint was the true measure. Every peck on the cheek and quick hug before slipping out the door read like a sonnet conveying desire.

"Kate?"

"I didn't know."

Alex reached for my hand. "I thought it was obvious I wanted you. Apparently not."

I wiped my tears and smiled, his words circling my brain like an airplane dragging a banner. "I sorta thought what you said not to think."

"I guessed that when I saw your reaction earlier." He set the cruise control and relaxed his shoulders. "Walking away from you that night after the break-in took every ounce of will power in me."

Let's circle back around to the M word.

Alex exited the highway in Gonzales, and I scanned my notes. I wasn't sure what I'd learn at the museum, but it would at least give me a visual of the life Madeleine might have lived.

I leaned forward when Alex pulled up in front of the dog-run style house. "I wonder when this was built. It's amazing."

We slid out of the truck and headed up the walkway.

"The house was built in 1845." He pointed to the Texas historical marker plaque. "On the original site of the home belonging to Jeremiah and Abigail Miller."

"I wonder if and how they were related to Tabitha, Madeline's mother." I slipped my hand into his palm and smiled as his fingers tangled with mine.

We peered in the Plexiglas-covered windows and doors. Alex pressed a button and a recording of the history of the house and its owners played over a speaker. I snapped picture after picture as I listened to the mellow voice drifting from the box mounted on the wall.

"When we're finished here, let's go across the street to that other museum." I jotted notes as I listened to the history.

"Sounds good."

After we'd heard the recorded history twice, we strolled down the sidewalk and across the street to the other museum. We slipped into the Gonzales Memorial Museum only a half-hour before they closed. It held display cases full of treasures from the past. Old dresses, antique china, and kitchen gadgets caught my interest. Alex read about old farming apparatus and buffalo skulls found nearby.

"Alex, look at this. A couple of these brooches look similar to the one Becca has. I wonder if it really is old."

"Could be."

We crossed to the other side of the museum and a friendly gentleman greeted us. "Welcome to the Museum. Have a look around. If you have any questions, let me know." He pointed at a rack of brochures. "Those give more information about the area and historical events that happened in and around Gonzales."

"Thank you." I glanced around at the cases and noticed the chronological arrangement of the room.

Alex stood transfixed in front of a cannon. "Is this *the* cannon?"

I had no idea what he meant, but the attendant obviously did.

He grinned. "The very same. Would you like to hear its history?"

"Absolutely. I know bits and pieces about it but had no idea it still existed." Alex stood near the counter as the man behind it recounted his tale.

I worked my way around the room, reading about early Texas, then the revolution. Overhearing the attendant's story, I learned about the famous cannon at the center of the disagreement between the Mexicans and the colonists. When I spotted the list of local men that fought in the battle for independence, I yanked out my notebook and jotted down the list, gleeful that I recognized some names. Much of the information on display, Alex and I had dug up in our research, but this museum contained a few tidbits and stories not found online.

The trip hadn't added any branches to my tree, but I had images to give to my client to help paint a picture of the way her ancestors lived. That excited me.

Before heading home, we stopped for dinner at a little BBQ joint in the town square and had some of the best sausage I'd ever tasted. On the drive back to my house, I hoped he'd bring up the conversation from earlier and maybe provide a timetable.

He didn't.

We talked about the displays we'd seen and the history of Texas. Darkness cloaked the highway as we made our way home. I loved Schatzenburg for many reasons; although, the stars alone would be enough. The cluttered sky sparkled more than any other place I'd lived, at least it seemed that way to me.

Alex pulled into my driveway and came around to open my door. "I'll grab stuff while you unlock the house."

I shivered as I slid the key in the lock and laughed at myself. My blood thinned a little more each day I lived in Texas. I switched on the kitchen light, and Alex dropped the cooler and leftovers on the table.

I watched as he walked, his shoulders tight. He put away the cooler and dropped snacks on the pantry shelf. Snuggling up behind him, I wrapped my arms around his middle and nestled my face in his back.

"Can I tempt you with a cup of coffee on the porch swing?" I tried to offer a creative alternative to snuggling on the couch. I'd had the swing installed two weeks before but had only used it alone for coffee in the morning a couple of times.

"That sounds wonderful." He squeezed my hand before I stepped away.

The coffee pot sputtered and grumbled as the water heated. I set the kettle on the stove to boil water for my hot cocoa. "I'll be right out. I'm going to throw on some sweats because it's a bit chilly out."

A low rumble of a laugh bubbled out of Alex. "However did you manage to live in Denver?"

I laughed as I hurried down the hall. Minutes later, wearing sweats and fuzzy socks, I wrapped my fingers around the mug of cocoa he offered me. Mini marshmallows bobbed on the top. "I was cold all the time."

The screen door squeaked as Alex pushed it open. "The swing is perfect for this porch."

I tucked my feet underneath me and leaned my head on his shoulder. "I thought so. It's the first time I've sat out here at night."

"Are we okay, Kate?"

"Uh huh. Thank you for…" I wasn't sure how to finish the sentence.

"Talking about my feelings?" He winked. "I'm trying." He stilled and put his finger to his lips.

I glanced around and saw Philip running on the opposite side of the street. I cupped a hand over my mouth. He was the last person I wanted on the porch right then.

When Philip ran out of earshot, I smiled up at Alex. "He didn't stop by today." I interlaced my fingers with his.

He kissed my hand. "What a shame."

The soft creak of the chain and the shuffle of Alex's boots on the porch echoed in the quiet as we enjoyed togetherness on the swing. If I squinted my eyes just right, the eventually didn't seem so far away.

June 20, 1830

I met Naomi today. There are a handful of other girls my age. Although life seems bleak, the promise of friendship gives me hope.

Raids by the Comanche are more commonplace, especially among the families that settled on the outskirts of the colony. I try not to think about it, but reports of attacks occur weekly.

July 15, 1830

We are living in the shabbiest of huts. There are no windows, just holes in the walls. I would never be so cruel in my description if Father or Reuben could see or hear because they worked so hard to build it. The floor is dirt and we don't even have a table. The only sign of civilization is Mother's spinning wheel.

August 9, 1830

There are no churches. On Sundays Father reads to us from the Bible, but I miss the gathering of people.

I see Naomi almost daily. She lives a short walk from our place. Not all the families live in town like us. Others live even farther, so I see them rarely but worry for them often.

Mother's secret is no longer a secret. Even in her layered dresses, her condition is obvious. Father hopes for another son.

Chapter Twelve

April 8th – 8:12 am

Alex slid out of the truck and grinned at the sight of Kate in her apron standing in the doorway. "Good morning, Beautiful."

"You're here bright and early."

"You said you were making breakfast."

"I just put the casserole in the oven. It won't be ready for about an hour. Want to join me for a walk?"

"Will you wear your apron?"

"No."

"Pretty please."

"I will not." Kate laughed as she untied the strings. "You don't have to come."

"I want to, but I really like your apron." He dropped his stuff in the den before joining her in the kitchen. "Let's walk and be neighborly."

She pulled on her tennis shoes and grabbed her sunglasses off the counter. As they stepped off the porch, she pointed toward Gram's. "Let's go that way."

Hand in hand, they strolled toward the hub of town.

Gram called to them from her porch. "Mornin'. Y'all have time for a cup of coffee?"

"Absolutely." Kate grinned as Alex squeezed her hand.

He followed her onto the porch. "For you, Gram, we always have time."

"Have a seat here. I'll bring everything out." Gram's wrap-around porch resembled a magazine spread. Furnished with a quaint table and antique metal chairs, it invited conversation. Potted flowers added color and warmth.

Gram hurried out with a tray of assorted fruits, a carafe of coffee, and everything else they needed to enjoy it. "I'm so glad I caught you. I heard about what happened the other night. Did they catch the man that broke in?"

"No. He slipped out before the police arrived." Kate stirred sugar into her coffee.

"Such an odd happening. I'm not sure anyone's ever had a break-in here in town." Gram poked at a spear of cantaloupe.

"Leave it to me to be the first." Kate shook her head. "Sorry about bringing crime to your little town."

"Oh, this town has seen its share of crime, but it's been a long while."

Gram's wistful stare made Alex wonder about her comment.

"There was an odd car parked farther down the road that night. Didn't notice what kind, a light color." She pointed with her fork to the road that led past Kate's house and out of town.

Alex refilled his coffee cup. "Did you tell the police about it?"

"I did. But not sure it was enough for them to do anything with." She smoothed the fly-away hairs that snuck out of her bun and danced in the breeze. "Alex, I told Kate I wanted to have the two of you over to dinner one night."

"That sounds wonderful." He sipped his coffee but didn't eat, wanting to save room for the breakfast casserole. "We'd love that."

"Tomorrow night?" The glint in her eyes made her look like she had secrets hidden in her pockets.

"That's great. What time? And what can I bring?" Kate crossed her arms as a breeze blew across the porch.

"Six o'clock. No need to bring anything." Gram's smile promised mischief.

After hearing the town news, Kate and Alex helped her carry the dishes back inside, then strolled home. They didn't get very far on their walk but made it home just before the timer went off.

Alex slid the casserole out of the oven and sat it on the stovetop. "What's in this? It smells amazing."

"Sausage, egg, cheese, and tater tots."

"Yum. I haven't had tater tots for breakfast since college." He brewed a fresh pot of coffee while Kate sliced tomatoes.

"Bring me your plate." Kate cut the casserole into rectangles. "One or two?"

"I'll start with two." Alex held his plate steady as Kate heaped two large portions onto it. "Thanks for making breakfast."

"My pleasure. What's on your agenda for today?" Kate watched as he took his first bite.

He made sure to give her a reaction. "Delicious. I love this." He took another couple of bites before offering a suggestion. "What do you say we call Travis and see if he wants to come for an early dinner? I'll throw steaks on the grill. We can invite your sister and Tom, too."

"I think it's a great idea. Meg and Tom are out of town, and I'm not sure she'd come anyway. She only rarely answers my calls or responds to my texts. What made you think of Travis?" Kate jumped out of her chair and reached for her cell phone.

"Call Travis, and then I'll explain." He continued eating while she walked away to talk to her dad.

Five minutes later, she walked back into the kitchen. "He's coming. I told him four o'clock." She dropped back into her chair and looked at Alex, waiting to hear the explanation.

Alex served himself another piece. "Travis looked for you for nearly thirty years. He wants time with you, and I feel like maybe I get in the way of that."

Tears puddled in her eyes. "You are never in the way." As she blinked, drops escaped down her cheeks. "It's still hard. With Meg unwilling to meet him, I feel guilty, like I'm somehow betraying her. After I'm around Travis, I want to be angry with my … Scott. But …"

Alex had guessed that she harbored mixed emotions given all she'd learned about her family. "Katie, you can love someone and still be mad at them." He reached out and grabbed her hand. "You changed your name to Bentley. That was a pretty big clue to Travis that you care."

The surprised look in her eye had him replay what he'd said in his head. *Katie? You've never called her Katie before.*

"Thank you." She yanked a tissue from the box and dabbed her eyes. "After we finish breakfast, I'll get stuff for dinner. I'm going to make a run to Fredericksburg and shop there. How does a dessert from that marvelous bakery sound?"

"It sounds like your life is too calm if you are buying your baked goods." He winked.

"Whatever. I just baked several dozen. You haven't been shorted on cookies."

"I'll ride along with you."

Kate shook her head. "You don't have to go everywhere with me just because of the break-in. Stay here and relax."

An hour later, Kate bounded toward the door. "You have the tracking app, so you'll know where I am and won't worry about me."

"Be safe." Alex stretched out on the couch and thought about her, thought about the smile that showed up just for him, the way she felt in his arms, how life seemed brighter and more complete with her around. He loved her. He liked having her near, not always to snuggle or kiss, just the companionship of having her close. At the rate he'd been driving back and forth the last three months, he would put thousands of miles on his truck this year, without leaving the state. More than ever, the distance between them felt like an expanse. As he pondered, the gears in his mind wound to a halt, and he snored on the couch.

He jolted awake at the sound of a repetitive shrill squawking and grabbed his phone. "Hello?"

Kate whimpered before she spoke. "Someone is following me. A light-colored car."

"Where are you?" He jumped off the couch, yanked on his boots, and ran out the back door, grabbing his keys as he went.

"One of the back roads between Schatzenburg and Fredericksburg. I don't know the name of the road." Her voice drenched in fear, her words came out shrill and stuttered. "Oh no, he's speeding up. I think he's going to hit me."

"I'm on my way." Alex climbed in his truck, still holding the phone to his ear. "I'm in the truck. Stay on the line." He put it on speaker, so he could have both hands on the wheel. The way he planned to drive necessitated using two hands. "You still there?"

"Yes. He gets up right on my bumper and then backs off just a little. I don't know what to do."

"Just keep a steady pace. Do you see anything around you?"

"There's nothing out here."

He tried to hide the panic in his voice. "Stay calm."

Her voice cracked. "Alex, I'm really scared."

"I'm coming." He rolled through a stop sign. "Just hang on, Katie. I'm on my way." His knuckles were white, his face hot. "Do you recognize the car?"

"It looks lik—" Squealing brakes drowned out her scream, then a loud crash punctuated the noise.

"Rainy? KATE!" He pushed the accelerator to the floor.

You have to figure out where she is.

He slowed down and pulled over long enough to open the app that mapped Kate's phone. He entered the code and touched his thumb to the sensor. The blue dot flashed on his screen. He had a destination.

There was little traffic which allowed him to fly along the country roads. He grabbed his Bluetooth and called DJ, the map with the blue dot still on the screen. Bouncing over a cattle guard, he slowed his speed. He knew better than to rush through an open grazing area. Thankfully, there were no sheep asleep on the pavement.

"DJ, I think someone ran Kate off the road. We were on the phone when I heard a crash."

"Slow down. What? Is she okay?"

"I don't know. I'm using the tracking app to find her. She's on one of the back roads."

"Where? I'll head that way."

Alex gave the directions and promised to call again with an update. After hanging up, he called 911.

"What is your emergency?"

After spewing a quick explanation, he gave the same directions to the operator. "I'm on my way there now."

"Stay on the line with me. I've dispatched an ambulance and have a trooper on the way."

Please be okay, Katie, please. He rounded a bend and the dot on the map drew near. Kate wasn't far away. *Or at least her phone isn't.* He put the brakes on that train of thought.

As he crested the top of a hill and crossed another cattle guard, he saw her little blue car smashed against a tree. Tail lights disappeared over the next hill. *They didn't stop?*

"She hit a tree." Describing the situation to the dispatcher, he jumped out of the truck, left the door wide open, and darted toward the car. Steam billowed out of the hood, the front end crumpled frighteningly.

Kate stirred as he neared the car, and hope exploded in his chest. The deployed airbag lay in her lap; the front corner of the car had pushed into the passenger seat.

"Kate! Kate? Are you okay?" He yanked open her door and leaned in close. "She's breathing, and she's conscious." He relayed information to the dispatcher.

"Good. An ambulance is on the way." The woman on the other end of the line remained calm even when he struggled to do the same. The tapping of keys echoed through the phone.

Kate's eyes fluttered. Her lips twisted into a pained smile. "Alex, you found me."

"I'm here, Katie. Can you tell me where it hurts?"

"Everywhere. My right leg hurts the most. Where's the man?"

"What man?"

"A man reached into my car. He had something over his head. But I remember him opening my door. He was just here."

Alex glanced around. "There's no one here now." Seeing her phone on the floorboard, he picked it up and shot off a text to DJ: *Kate's alive, but injured. Will call when ambulance arrives.*

DJ responded: *Only minutes away. Already called Maddox.*

Alex stroked Kate's hair. "Do you remember anything about the man?"

"No, well, maybe." She cried out as she shifted in her seat.

"Stay still. Don't move. An ambulance will be here soon." Still on the line with the dispatcher, he focused solely on Kate.

"I couldn't stop, but I jerked the wheel at the last minute." She winced.

Alex laid his hand on her shoulder. "Always thinking."

"He shoved me toward the tree. There must be damage to his car."

"We can talk about it later. Just relax but don't go to sleep. You need to stay awake."

"I think my leg might be broken."

"The ambulance should be here any minute." He looked down the road then back to Kate. Besides a few scratches and gashes, there appeared to be little blood. He squatted next to her and held her hand.

In the distance, a whining siren blared. She smiled and let her eyelids fall closed.

"Open your eyes, Katie. Keep them open for me."

She turned her head toward him, eyes only half open.

"Look at me. Let me see your eyes."

Tears hovered at the edge of her lashes. "It hurts."

He kissed her hand. "I'm sorry. They're almost here. Hear the siren?" When the emergency lights crested the ridge, he ended the call with the dispatcher.

As soon as the ambulance rolled to a stop, both paramedics jumped out, and Alex stepped aside, giving them access to Kate.

"I'm only a couple steps away," he called out as he dialed DJ.

Leaning on a fence post, Alex stared at the crumpled metal. *Who would do such a thing? Why?*

DJ answered after one ring. "Is she okay?"

Alex paced next to the barbed-wire fence, phone to his ear. Worried and stressed, he ran his fingers through his hair over and over. "She's alive and talking. I don't know the extent of her injuries." He watched the paramedics work. "Her car is totaled. I don't like this DJ.

First the break-in and now this. I have a sick feeling in the pit of my stomach."

While he talked with DJ, Captain Maddox stepped out of his SUV. He listened and scribbled notes as Alex relayed the happenings to DJ.

"We are almost there." DJ kept calm, but anger played at the edges of his words.

"I want to ride with her to the hospital, but my truck."

"Becca is with me. We'll take your truck to the hospital. You ride with Kate."

"Thanks." Alex hung up and shook hands with Maddox. "You have to find who did this."

He nodded slowly. "We will. She okay?"

"I think so. She was talking to me."

"DJ called me. I came to secure the scene, but a state trooper is on the way. They'll handle the investigation."

While the paramedics lifted Kate out of the car and put her on a stretcher, Alex explained what happened. "She called me to say that someone was following her."

"Did she say who?"

"No. Light-colored car. She started to tell me more when she crashed. I saw tail lights as I crested the hill. Someone either left the scene or drove right past."

"Tell me about that car."

"I only caught a glimpse. Mid-size car, white or tan, maybe."

"And right after that break-in."

"Seems too coincidental." Alex saw the paramedics rolling Kate toward the ambulance.

"Yeah. Especially after Gram mentioned seeing a light-colored car that night." Maddox held out his hand. "I'll give DJ your keys and let the trooper know what you've told me. They'll be calling you."

"Thanks. Oh, Kate said a man opened her car door. But I didn't know that before I pulled it open." Alex handed over his keys. "I'll call you when I know more about her condition."

"You want me to call Travis?"

Alex shook his head. "I'll call him."

Maddox pointed toward the road. "I think that's DJ now."

DJ's Tahoe pulled off the road. Becca jumped out and ran toward them. She stopped near the car and clapped her hand over her mouth to catch her sobs.

DJ rushed up next to her and put an arm around her. He nodded toward Alex. "We'll meet you at the hospital."

Alex fibbed to the paramedic, hoping Maddox was out of earshot. "I'm her fiancé. Can I ride along?"

"You can ride in front." The paramedic motioned toward the passenger side door.

September 10, 1830

Boredom.

For Father and Reuben, this is a grand adventure. They hunt, chop wood, and are always occupied with some task. Jeremiah is the happiest of us all. He runs and plays.

Mother and I sit at home. There is little to do. I write sparingly because when my paper and ink are used up, I fear I won't be able to get anymore.

A recent raid near Plum Creek means that I am staying close to the house. Rumors that they take women and children captive has Mother in fear for our lives or worse.

~*~

September 18, 1830

Father and Reuben have been building a more permanent house. It is near completion. It looks so much like our house in Missouri. I miss our old homestead.

~*~

November 18, 1830

Today I helped Mother bring a baby into the world. It was quite the experience. He is beautiful. Father says we will name him Amos. Mother looks well.

Chapter Thirteen

April 8th – 7:18 pm

I opened my eyes, and Alex teleported across the hospital room. His green eyes sparkled like emeralds.

I admired the stubble on his face and wondered how long I'd been asleep. "Hi."

"Hey, we've been waiting for you to wake up. How do you feel?"

"I've been better."

"Your uncle wants to ask you a few questions."

Glimpses of the accident filtered through my brain fog, and I struggled to remember all that happened. I tried to sit up, but pain erupted from every nerve ending.

"Don't sit up." Alex kissed my forehead.

It felt like I was swimming in syrup. "I'm in the hospital?"

"Yes. Do you remember what happened?" Uncle Pat stood next to the bed, concern etched in his brow.

I blinked, trying to clear the haze. "That car and the tree."

"When did you first notice the car?"

"Right before I called Alex. I didn't think much of the car at first, but then it started getting up right on my bumper, then backing off, only to speed up again. It was as if he was intentionally trying to scare me."

He exchanged a look with Alex. "You said he came to your car? Did he do or say anything?"

"He opened my car door. I don't remember if he said anything. It's all a bit fuzzy."

Alex squeezed my hand. "The man left a note in your car."

"What? What did it say?"

Uncle Pat held up his phone and showed me a picture of a note written in blue ink.

I will get it back, even if I have to hurt people. Keeping it will only bring pain.

"Does that mean anything to you?" He tucked the phone away and pulled out his notebook.

"Get what back?" I looked at Alex, wanting answers I knew he didn't have. "I don't know what he wants."

Alex pulled a chair close to the bed. "We are thinking the same guy that ran you off the road, broke into your house looking for whatever he thinks you have."

"I'm almost sure they are related, but whoever broke in, avoided contact with you. The car incident was a scare tactic it seems." Anger clipped Uncle Pat's words.

A blue blur crossed the room. I turned my head too quickly, and the room continued spinning even after I stopped moving.

The blue blur checked the monitors and wrote numbers on my chart. "Hello, Miss Bentley. How are you feeling?" The nurse stood still and came into focus.

"Like a tree ran into me."

Uncle Pat stepped away from the bed. "I'm going to let you get some rest. If you think of anything else, have Alex call me." He shook hands with Alex before disappearing from the room.

"From zero to ten, what's your pain level?" The woman in blue patted my hand.

"Twelve."

"I can give you something." The nurse injected something into the IV. "That'll help, but it'll make you pretty sleepy." She whisked back out the door as fast as she'd entered.

Alex sat down next to the bed and took my hand. "You rest. I'll be right here."

"Travis!" My words escaped louder than I intended.

"I called him. Don't worry." Alex stroked my hair.

"I see him. Hi, Dad." *Had I ever called him Dad before?* Pain meds made it hard to think.

Alex turned and smiled. "Oh, I didn't hear you come in. Have a seat." He stood up and pointed to his chair.

"You stay right there. Holding her hand is an important job." Travis walked around to my other side. "How are you?"

"Sore and loopy, but otherwise I'm fine."

"Are they giving you some good stuff for the pain?" He leaned over the bed, his blue eyes dark with worry.

"I'm sorry about dinner. I never made it to the store."

He patted my hand. "Don't worry about dinner."

"Alex told a fib." I smiled like a Cheshire cat. Pain meds rendered me unable to keep my mouth shut even though I didn't want to tell the story.

Alex squeezed my hand, and I turned to face him. The pale color of my tanned Latin fella made me giggle.

I tried to wink but only blinked. "Shhh. It's a secret."

Travis spoke up and saved me from my prattling tongue. "I'm glad Alex found you so quickly."

"He used the app."

Travis looked at Alex, his eyebrows raised.

"I wrote an app, so I can track her phone, but it requires a password and thumbprint. When she drives home alone at night, I feel better seeing the dot arrive at its destination."

"Good thinking." Travis smiled. "You found a good one, Kate."

I grinned at Alex. "Dad likes you too."

Travis chuckled, then turned to Alex, his tone sobering. "Have you told Meg about what happened?"

"Not yet. I need to call her." Alex rubbed his thumb through the cleft in his chin.

Travis slipped his phone out of his pocket. "Let me. If I can just get the number from Kate's phone."

Alex gave him the number, and Travis created a contact. He stepped into the hall to make the call.

"I left a message." He strolled back into the room. "I'll leave you two alone. I just wanted to check on Kate. You'll call me if anything changes?" He patted my foot through the blanket but directed his question to Alex.

"Of course, sir." Alex stood.

Travis moved toward the door. "Kate, heal quickly. Whatever you need, have Alex call me, okay?"

"Thanks, Dad. Is it okay if I call you Dad?"

Back at my bedside in a second, he clutched my hand. "Nothing would make me happier. Even if it's only until the pain meds wear off."

We all laughed, but Travis wiped his eyes, then he hugged Alex. I don't know if they knew I was watching and listening.

"Thanks for taking care of my girl." Travis patted Alex's shoulder.

"Sir, if you have time to stay, I'd appreciate the company. Kate will be asleep soon, and we can talk about her." Alex glanced over his shoulder and winked at me.

"Hey!" I'd been too obvious about eavesdropping on their conversation.

They laughed, but my eyes refused to stay open. Laughter and words floated far away as whatever that nurse had given me eased my pain and eliminated my ability to stay awake.

The eyes of the man who reached into my car bored into me from somewhere inside my brain. As my mind filed through data, the cover on his face seemed about to peel away. Just as pieces floated together into a recognizable form, Becca's voice pulled me out of my dream. Desperate to know the face, my mind's eye sought the picture, which dissipated into fractured thoughts.

I gave up and opened my eyes. "Hey, Becca."

"I needed to know you were okay."

"Is DJ here?" I glanced around, trying to limit my movement.

"Yes. He's talking with Alex." She pointed toward the door. "I brought your purse from the car."

"Alex is mad, isn't he?" I reached for her hand.

"He's not mad at you." She took my hand in both of hers and squeezed it gently.

"Not at me. At the man. The man that shoved me off the road and left me a warning."

"Someone did this to you?" Becca spun to face DJ. "Did *you* know?"

"Alex told me." DJ circled his shoulders, tense and irritated.

"Who would do that?" Anger flashed in Becca's brown eyes.

Alex teleported again. Maybe he didn't really do that exactly, but he started far from me, way on the other side of the room, then boom, he held my hand. "Welcome back."

"How long did I sleep?" Pain prohibited me from throwing my arms around his neck, but I wanted to.

My phone rang, and he picked it up.

I shifted to a sitting position, biting back yelps of pain. "Let me answer it."

He handed it to me, a mix of concern and amusement crinkling near his eyes. Becca and DJ exchanged one of those 'Uh oh' glances. They all thought I would say something goofy on the phone because of my pain meds, a definite possibility given my history.

"Hello?"

"Hi, it's Marisa. You busy? Can I come over?"

"Whoa, slow down. I'm in the hospital. Can I call you when I go home?"

"The hospital? What happened?"

"A car ran into me. Shoved me into a tree. On purpose."

She didn't respond. There was only silence at her end.

"Marisa?"

Her voice cracked. "Are you okay?"

"Yep. Mostly. My leg is in a cast, and I'm really sore. Otherwise I'm wonderful. Your brother is taking good care of me. Oh, I forgot to call you. I wanted to know Paul's last name." After a minute of quiet, the phone clicked.

"That was Marisa?" Alex took the phone and laid it on the bedside table.

"She wanted to come over."

"Did she say why?"

"She didn't say. But I told her—you heard what I told her." My thoughts came in connected strings, a sure sign the drugs were wearing off, which meant enduring pain. "Becca, make Alex go home to rest. He looks so tired."

Alex shook his head and pulled the chair closer to the bed.

"Kate, I know you've only known him three months so let me explain it to you. You don't *make* Alex do anything. He won't leave the hospital until you leave with him."

I didn't see the point in arguing with her or Alex. "Did Travis leave? How long did he stay?"

He brushed the hair out of my face. "He left about a half-hour ago."

"Did you talk about me?" I pulled his fingers to my lips.

"You are the one thing we have in common." His eyes twinkled, and he flashed that boyish grin.

"So, what did the doctor say? I'm guessing from the cast that my leg is broken."

"Amazingly, you had no broken bones." He tucked the blankets around me. "You have a severely sprained ankle, which required a cast. The doctor said two or three weeks."

"That's what hurts the most."

"You had minor cuts and scratches, but no concussion."

"The doctor told me all this, didn't he?"

"Yes. He came in earlier and talked to you."

"I only remember a little. And that Trooper came?"

"Yes. Trooper Smith asked you about what happened. If you don't remember, blame the pain meds."

"Honestly, so much of today is a blur. It's still today, right?" I pressed his hand to my cheek. The warmth soothed me and lessened the disconnected feeling.

"Yes, but you left for Fredericksburg hours ago."

"Have you even eaten?"

"DJ ran to get me food. I'll eat soon."

"I want to talk to you, but everything hurts."

"I know. Let the nurse give you something."

"It stops the pain, but then I'll go back to sleep." I could feel tears springing up.

He leaned down and tenderly kissed me, letting his lips linger. "You sleep. I'll be here while you sleep and when you wake up."

Becca poked her head out the door, and the nurse came in and gave me another dose of whatever made me forget about the pain.

I drifted off to sleep, envisioning my curls fanned across the pillow, a serene expression on my face. Pain meds were wonderful things.

April 21, 1830

We were officially assigned our parcel of land today. Since Father is building the place in town, I hope he does not suggest that we move to the acreage.

Mother is smiling more. I hope her optimism is contagious.

~*~

November 5, 1830

Finally, the weather has cooled. We are settled in the new house.

I still miss the luxuries of life in Missouri, but life now is better than our first few months. We have planted a few winter vegetables, and Father purchased some livestock. Since Mother cares for the baby, I do many of the chores about the house. It is better than boredom.

~*~

April 2, 1831

This is my last entry until I can acquire more paper. Without schools, Mother is teaching Jeremiah to read. It is my job to help him with his studies while she tends to the baby.

I will miss writing.

The town now has a cannon. The bronze cannon is mounted in one of the blockhouses. Father says it will be a deterrent to the Comanche raids. I pray that he is right.

CHAPTER FOURTEEN

April 9th – 2:44 pm

The next afternoon, the doctor cleared Kate to go home, definitely a good thing. She'd rest better at home, and so would Alex—at her home, not his. The hospital stayed too busy and noisy. Machines beeped. Voices paged doctors over the loudspeaker. Nurses ran in and out of her room every hour. He'd managed snippets of sleep in an armchair within reach of Kate, and the nurses had brought him a pillow, a blanket, and a snack.

When the nurse came into the room with discharge papers, she handed Kate a prescription for pain pills, which she promptly buried in the bottom of her purse. Taking them made her leery. She worried about what thoughts escaped her lips unchecked. When she took pain medication, her tongue loosened. He found it amusing. She found it alarming. It would require convincing to get her to fill the prescription.

Kate sat staring at her leg, in a cast from knee to toes, and chewed her bottom lip.

"Ready to go home?" He slung the duffle bag over his shoulder.

"How can I? The doctor said to try and keep weight off it for the next three days. What am I going to do?"

He sat the duffle bag in a chair. "Kate, really?" He stood next to the bed and held her hands. "I thought maybe I'd come take care of you. If you'd rather I not stay in the extra room, Gram offered me a place to stay. You know, so the neighbors won't whisper. *Much.*"

"That was sweet of her."

"Which would you prefer?"

"I want you to stay with me." She squeezed his hand. "What about Bureau?"

"He's part of the package deal. DJ and Becca will take him over to your place."

"You're the best, Alex."

"I'm glad you think so."

On the way to the house, Alex insisted she fill the prescription, which was the wrong approach, a completely unproductive way to start the conversation. After a lengthy discussion and a lot of begging, she finally agreed, and they stopped at the pharmacy. She hobbled beside him, trying to get the hang of her crutches. With her purse tucked under his arm, he watched her every step, ready to catch her if she slipped.

He guided her to one of the few chairs near the pharmacy counter. "Have a seat. While we wait for them to fill it, I'll grab some snacks. Anything you want?"

"Chocolate, lots of chocolate. And potato chips." She scratched at the cast. "French onion dip, M&M's, peanuts, pretzels, some of that Chex Mix, and sour gummy worms."

"It's not a grocery store, but I'll see what I can find." He shook his head and tried not to laugh as he went to grab a cart.

Twenty minutes later, with five grocery bags full of snacks in the back-seat, Alex pulled out of the lot and headed to Schatzenburg. Kate quietly gazed out the window, more subdued than normal.

"How are you feeling? Are you in a lot of pain?"

"Uh huh. I just want to go home."

"You were due for your meds thirty minutes ago. Please take them." He tapped the cap of her Cherry Coke. "You've got a drink right here."

"Maybe. Did I say anything embarrassing?"

"No." He opted not to bring up the moment she started to tell Travis about the fib. Hopefully, she'd forgotten about it. "Mostly, you slept."

"I promise to take them when I get home." She stayed quiet the rest of the drive.

He parked in the driveway near the back door. After unlocking the house, he helped her inside. "Do you want to go to bed?"

"I want to be next to you."

He steered her to the den. "I'll grab the stuff and be back in a few."

"And I want cookies. Will you bring me cookies?"

After shuffling snacks and bags from the truck, he carried a tray into the den. "Cookies and milk. Sound good?"

"Yep. Thanks."

"And a cup of water so you can take your pills."

"Yes, sir." She moaned. "Now come sit by me."

He complied. All he wanted to do was hold her, suspended outside time. "Your uncle will be by in a little while. He has a few more questions."

She burrowed into his side. "Why would anyone do this?"

"I don't know." He ran his fingers through her hair. "I've wracked my brain, but I can't think of anyone that would want to hurt you."

When a knock sounded, Alex kissed her on the forehead and stood up. "That must be Maddox." He dashed to the front door and pulled it open. "Come in."

"How's Kate feeling?" Maddox dropped his hat on the couch in the front room.

"Very sore. She's in the den."

"You hear any more from Trooper Smith?"

"Not since the hospital." Alex lingered near the front door. "Any leads?"

Maddox shook his head. "Not that I've heard."

"Is he investigating, or are you?"

"It's his investigation."

"But you're here asking questions." Alex smiled, satisfied that Maddox was still on the case, officially or not.

Maddox pointed to the den. "Is it okay to talk with her?"

"Yeah. Come on back."

Maddox sat at the far edge of the sectional.

Kate shifted to an upright position. "You told Aunt Beth I was okay, right?"

"I did. She'll stop by when you feel better. Just let her know when."

"I will. I'm going to need distractions to keep weight off this leg."

Maddox pulled a notebook out of his pocket. "I wanted to see if you remembered anything else."

"I only vaguely remember speaking to you at the hospital."

"Not surprising. Mind telling me the whole thing from the beginning?"

"Sure." She explained about dinner and driving to Fredericksburg. "Anyway, I noticed a car behind me. Every time I turned, he turned."

"Was he following you from the time you left the house?" Maddox glanced at Alex.

"I'm not sure. I only noticed him about five minutes from here. At first, I wasn't sure he was even following me."

"So what made you…?" Alex stopped pacing and dropped onto the couch next to her.

"When we got on that country road with no other cars around, it became really clear, really fast. He'd get close, wouldn't pass, and then back off."

Maddox tapped his pen against the notebook. "What do you remember about the vehicle?"

"It was a car. Light-colored. I'm not good at noticing types or brands."

"Anything you can tell me about the size? Or the license plate? Two doors? Four doors?"

"I never saw the plates. It was a medium-sized car, not sure how many doors, maybe four." She rubbed her face, then jerked her head up. "He had greyish hair. Salt and pepper."

"You'd told me he had something over his head."

"He did when he came to the car. Before that, when he was driving, he got right behind me. I wish I could remember his face." Color washed out of her cheeks; her eyes glassed over. "It's just there in the back of my brain, behind a curtain."

Alex gripped her hand.

"I'm almost sure I've seen him somewhere else, but I just can't remember."

Maddox jotted notes as she talked. "Anything else that stood out?"

"When he opened the door, he looked at me. His eyes were full of anger."

"What color eyes?" He held his pen at the ready.

"I don't remember."

"That's okay. We'll find who did this, Kate. You heal quickly." Her uncle slipped the notebook back into his pocket. "Alex, call me—no matter the time—if you need anything. Hear me?"

"I will."

"You staying here with her?"

"I am." Alex met Maddox's gaze, watching for a reaction.

"Good. She doesn't need to be by herself." Maddox sauntered toward the front door and set his Stetson atop his head. "Y'all have a good afternoon."

Alex tucked a pillow under Kate's head and draped his grandmother's quilt over her.

"I *love* you, Alex." Since Maddox's exit, she'd said the same thing at least fifteen times, no doubt prompted by her deep passion and possibly influenced by the narcotics.

Responding the same way he did the fourteen times before, he kissed her forehead and squeezed her hand. "I love you too, Katie."

"Katie is like Kate and Rainy smushed together."

"I guess it is. Go ahead and sleep for a while." He pushed the coffee table out of the way and dropped onto the floor by the couch. "I'll be right here." He smiled as she caressed the curve of his neck with her cool fingers.

"Think we'll be safe?" Her words sounded more curious than fearful.

"Hired security will be parked outside round the clock." The last time they'd hired security, they'd been disappointed in the result, so

Alex planned to have a second set of eyes watching Kate's place if he needed to leave.

"And I can text you if I need you."

"Anytime you want me."

His phone beeped, and she giggled.

Chapter Fifteen

April 10th – 9:15 am

I opened my eyes and looked around. I remembered falling asleep in the den, but now, tucked snuggly under my covers, my bedroom surrounded me. The house smelled of coffee and spices. *What is he cooking?*

Alex appeared at the door. "Good morning."

"Hi." I swung my legs over the side of the bed and reached for my crutches. "Whatever you're cooking smells good."

"Chorizo and egg. For breakfast tacos."

"I don't even know what that is."

He laughed. "It's a Mexican sausage. Come and eat." He held out his hand and steadied me as I balanced on my crutches.

After a couple tacos and a much-needed cup of coffee, I skipped my pain meds in favor of something over-the-counter that wouldn't render me useless. After a second cup of coffee, I shook off my haze and planned to resume my research. And though I wanted to visit the Texana room at the library, I decided to wait before bringing it up.

After breakfast, I settled in the den with my laptop. I read through my notes and studied the tree to get myself back up to speed, then resumed my hunt for Grace's ancestors.

After hours of research, antsy and cooped up, I forgot my decision to wait and mentioned the idea of a library trip to Alex. "I need to research the early Texas families at the downtown library. If you're busy tomorrow, Becca can drive me." I stroked a sleeping Bureau, who purred in my lap.

Alex snapped his laptop closed and shot me a look. "I'll take you."

"Did I say something wrong?"

He set the laptop on the coffee table and scooted closer to me. "Someone wants something that you either don't have or don't know you have. Until we figure out what's at the root of this, please don't leave the house without me." He sought my gaze. "Please, Kate."

"I'm sorry, Alex. I wasn't even thinking about it like that." I'd done my best to block out all thoughts of the masked man. My shoulders fell as the realization chilled me. Someone wanted to hurt me. I buried my face in his shirt as fear bubbled to the surface.

He wrapped an arm around me and stroked my hair. "I don't want to scare you. I am just trying to keep you out of harm's way."

I wiped my eyes.

He brushed tears off my cheek and tucked a strand of hair behind my ear. "I'll do whatever I have to do to keep you safe. You know that, don't you?"

"Here you are again swooping in to rescue me."

"You do know that the depth of my feelings for you is the same even when you aren't in danger? This 'getting into trouble bit' isn't necessary to keep me around."

I turned and stretched my legs across his lap, displacing a perturbed kitty. "I'll try and remember that."

He ran his hand along my leg. "How long 'til you can put weight on it?"

I shrugged. "Doctor said two or three days to let the swelling go down, then I can walk on it." I wiggled my piggies, which stuck out of the end of the purple cast. "I hope I last that long." Intense itching near my ankle had me teetering on the brink of insanity.

"When I came over that hill…" His green eyes bore holes into the opposite wall.

I trailed my fingers down his arm.

He blinked multiple times and smiled at me. "I'm just glad you're okay."

I rested my head on the couch cushion. "You're amazingly calm and relaxed. I expected more…" I let a shrug finish off my sentence.

"Brooding?"

I nodded.

"I'm not really calm. I'm just controlled for now."

"My poor car."

"Tell me about Grace's family. If I'm going to be around, I might even help if I can."

"You are trying to distract me from talking about my car?" When the air condition kicked on, the smell of flowers filled the air. I craned my neck looking for the source of the scent.

"I expect it will be totaled, and you'll be shopping for a new one once this is off." He rapped on my cast. "What are you looking for?"

"I smell flowers."

"Philip has stopped by three times. There are lots of flowers around here."

"He's crazy about me." I grinned. "You ran interference?" I scratched at the outside of my cast trying to trick my brain.

"He came by a couple of times when you were sleeping. Once when you were awake, but I shooed him off."

"Trying to keep him away from me?" I smirked, waiting for his reaction to my teasing.

He didn't even flinch at my question. "You going to tell me about your genealogy project?" He didn't have to ask me twice. Well, technically, he had asked twice.

I gave him all the information I'd been able to dig up. Eighteen minutes later, I took a breath.

"Madeline was born in Texas in 1836? But you aren't sure who her father is yet?" He seemed genuinely interested.

"Both men that were listed as her father fought in the revolution, the battle for independence. I saw both names on the list of Gonzales men that served."

"We should learn more about that time period."

I flipped open the laptop. Tapping away at the keys, I logged in and pulled up a search page. "Great idea."

"We'll have a second Texas history lesson."

I told him what I knew, and we spent the next hour searching and reading. Using notes in my spiral, what I remembered, and my laptop, we uncovered land records and information about Tabitha and Wesley. A knock at the door interrupted our detective work.

"Are you expecting anyone? Please tell me it's not Philip bringing flowers again."

"DJ and Becca are bringing pizza rolls. I happened to mention that they were your favorite."

"My favorite? You are the one crazy for them!"

He winked as he slid my legs off his lap. "Whatever you say, dear."

September 12, 1835

Nathaniel Hughes came to dinner again this evening. He and Father talked for over an hour, but I was not allowed to eavesdrop. Mother said I would know all in good time the topic of their conversation.

While Mother spun cotton on her wheel, I tried to mend a pair of Jeremiah's trousers. I cannot say I did an acceptable job, as I was distracted from my task by curiosity.

When Father and Nathaniel returned to the house, Father nodded, and Nathaniel handed me a small bundle of blank paper tied with a ribbon. "Happy Birthday" was all he said. Mr. Hughes knows my heart, and his thoughtful gift has captured it.

September 15, 1835

Nathaniel asked for my hand in marriage. Only Texas could produce such a man. When I looked at Father, he nodded. His blessing granted, we won't want to wait long before marrying.

October 7, 1835

Today I became Mrs. Nathaniel Hughes.

Chapter Sixteen

April 11th – 6:30 am

Alex rolled over and tried to force his eyes open when the alarm beeped. He wanted to be up before Kate. In the kitchen, he brewed a pot of coffee, and grabbed the paper off the porch. A man parked in a dark-colored car gave a quick nod, and Alex nodded back. As he turned to step inside, he heard footsteps.

"Good morning." Gram's chipper greeting reminded him of DJ, only in a higher pitch. "I brought you some breakfast."

He smiled and glanced inside. "Come on in. Kate's still asleep." He followed her in and smiled as her slippers made a soft scraping sound on the wood floors. "Whatever you've made smells delicious."

"Awful thing that happened to Kate." She set two tin-foil covered plates on the counter and pointed to the front porch. "Cup of coffee on the porch so we don't wake her?"

"Great idea." He filled two mugs and handed her one.

On the front porch, he leaned against the rail, and she sat in the swing.

"I'm sorry we had to postpone dinner. Kate and I were really looking forward to it."

"Never you mind about that. We can do that once she's healed. You focus on keeping her safe and getting her better."

"I will." Alex inhaled deeply and studied the wooden porch post as he exhaled. "I have to keep her safe."

"I don't know if either of you know how excited everyone around here is to have Kate back. Half of them still call her Claire, though."

"I bet folks clamored to hear the story from you."

"Don't you know it. The most often asked question, 'When did you know?' Well, that's a hard one to answer."

He drained the last of his coffee and waited for her to continue.

"I had an inkling when the two of you came to visit, but I didn't *know* until she told me."

"She really loves this place." Alex set his empty mug on the rail.

"You love her. That's obvious."

"Very much."

"I'd love to attend the wedding." Gram stood and handed Alex her cup. "Tell her I hope she feels better soon."

Silent, Alex watched her shuffle back to her own house.

As he turned to go inside, he heard Kate bumping around. Pushing open the door, he called out, "I'm coming. Let me help you."

He found her sitting on the kitchen floor, her crutches laying out of her reach.

"Are you okay? Did you fall?" He set the mugs on the counter and rushed to her side.

"I'm fine, but I'm tired of help. No offense."

"You need to let me help you. I get that it's no fun." He stuck out his hand to help her off the floor.

Her long lashes hooded big brown eyes as she lifted her gaze to his face. She reached for his hand. "I know you're right, but I still hate it. I feel cooped up and helpless."

"Let's eat, then we'll drive into San Antonio and go to that library."

"I wasn't hinting at that. I just wanted to get my own breakfast without bothering you." She grabbed the edge of the kitchen table and steadied herself.

"You are not a bother." He stepped close and leaned down, his face inches from hers. He slid his arms around her waist and whispered, "I want—"

The doorbell interrupted him.

Kate grabbed at his shirt. "They'll go away. What do you want?"

Alex helped her into a chair and chuckled as he trotted to the door. "I can only think of one other person that would show up this early." He opened the front door. "Hey, come on in."

"Can I see her now?" Philip was the last person Kate wanted to see at the moment, especially given the timing of his interruption.

Alex had put off a visit so many times, he gave in and pointed to the kitchen.

Philip didn't hesitate.

Alex followed him. "But only for a minute."

Philip dropped to one knee in front of Kate. "I'm so sorry you were hurt. You got my flowers?"

"Yes, thank you." She tried to sound polite, but her voice didn't ooze its normal warmth. Out of sorts and interrupted, she clipped her words and crossed her arms in front of her.

He laid a massive box of chocolates on the table. "I brought you these. Do you like chocolate?"

"Thank you. Alex is helping me while I heal." She didn't even tell him how much she liked chocolate.

"If you need anything, call me. If Alex is gone and you need someone, I can be here in an instant." He pulled a marker out of his pocket and wrote his phone number on her cast.

Kate stared at him as if he had wildflowers growing out of his ears. Surprisingly, she didn't whack him with her crutch.

Alex bit back a laugh. "Thanks for stopping by, but we should cut it short because Kate isn't feeling up to company right now." He kicked at a small bead, and it skittered across the floor.

"What was that?" Philip dropped onto his hands and knees.

"Just one of Becca's beads." Alex pointed to the front door. "Why don't I call you later, and we can get together another time for a longer visit."

"Sounds great. Anytime. I'll bring dinner." Philip waved as he walked out. "You have my number."

Alex bolted the front door and walked back into the kitchen. He squatted down in front of her chair. "Where were we?"

She stood on one foot, holding on to his shirt, and pulled his hands around her waist. "Like this, and you were saying 'I want'."

He kissed her on the tip of the nose and then leaned in close to her ear. "I want—"

The phone rang, and Kate jumped. "Just ignore it. What do you want? Please tell me what you want."

"It'll keep." He grinned as he answered the phone. "Hello."

"Is Kate okay? Travis, I mean, Uncle Travis called me. I just got the message." Meg sobbed between phrases.

"Hi. Yes. She's right here. I answered her phone without thinking." He handed the phone to Kate. "Your sister."

"Hey, Meg. How was your trip?"

Alex pulled out a chair, and Kate sat, expecting a long conversation. He ducked into the den and opened his laptop. It whirred as the discs spooled up. The phone call could barely be heard over the tapping as he pounded out a reply to an email. Meg irritated him for a hundred reasons, and he had no desire to listen. Kate would be upset when she hung up, and he'd listen to her talk out her frustration. How the two of those women had grown up under the same roof, he could not fathom.

He logged in remotely to a server at the cabin and checked results of his latest script. The test run had been successful. Somehow, he'd found time to work in the midst of the recent craziness. Once his current project was complete, he'd be free of work projects, at least for a few days.

A chair scuffed against the floor, and Alex made his way toward the kitchen.

"Goodbye. … Okay, see ya then." Kate's voice had all the lightheartedness of thunder clouds before a summer storm.

He poked his head around the corner. "You okay?"

"Why do I have such a hard time talking to her?"

He sat down at the table. "How much did you tell her?"

"Enough. She asked if we were living together. Can you believe that? Oh, and she doesn't like you. She actually said that."

The words stung, but he let Kate rant. The fact that Meg didn't like him didn't surprise him, not that he much cared what Meg thought, but he deeply cared that the rift bothered Kate.

"She wants me to be who I was before I met you. I don't know that person anymore. She thinks you are trying to keep me from being that person."

He didn't like to see Kate upset and had little patience for those that caused it. Tired of hearing about Meg's opinion of him, he steered the conversation in a different direction. "She called Travis *Uncle Travis*. That sounded positive."

"She asked if I was sure he was telling the truth. I know she doesn't want to believe that our dad could've done what he did."

Alex walked around behind Kate and deposited warm gentle kisses along the back of her neck. "I'm listening."

It always worked, his secret weapon. Even at her most agitated, it soothed her.

"And she asked me not to call him Scott. As if?" Kate pulled her hair to the side.

"When is she coming over?" He let his breath tickle her neck as he asked his question.

"Tomorrow." She relaxed her shoulders and sighed. "Can you do that while she's here? It's extremely pleasant."

"That wouldn't be weird at all."

"Back to what you started to say earlier. About what you wanted."

Alex laughed. "I want to eat breakfast. It's already cold." He pulled off the tinfoil, popped the plates in the microwave, and watched them rotate until it dinged.

Two hours later, Alex held the door open as Kate pushed herself along on her crutches into the downtown library. They stopped at the map of the building and searched until they located their destination. "You going to make it to the sixth floor?"

"Of course." She shuffled her way onto an elevator with him beside her, every step.

In the Texana room, Kate surveyed the rows and rows of shelves.

The librarian looked up from her computer and smiled. "Good morning. How can I help you?"

"I'm searching for information about early Texas families. Kent, Hughes, Miller, and Wilson." Kate leaned on the counter.

"What year, hun?"

"1836 and maybe earlier." She also mentioned which county would most likely have records based on what she'd uncovered.

"Give me a moment." The lady's fingers fluttered across the keyboard. "Okay. Just over that way are all the records for that county. You might also want to read about the DeWitt colony."

"Thanks." Kate shifted her weight.

The clerk smiled as Alex steadied Kate, his hand on her elbow. "Let me know if you have questions."

With her purse tucked under his arm, he followed behind her as she navigated to a table. She rested her crutches against the wall and, using the shelves for balance, limped down the row. She stopped at the section for Gonzales County and scanned the books. "Several of these look promising." She pulled several titles off the shelf.

Alex held out his hands. "Let me hold them for you."

After a few minutes, they retreated to the table, his arms loaded with books. A slight thud sounded when he set them down.

"Where do we start?" Caught up in the quest, he grinned and waited for her answer. He understood the fun of the chase, even though when he'd had to search without her, it was to save her, and the thrill of the hunt didn't come into play.

Kate handed him half the stack. "Look for any references to Kent, Hughes, Miller, or Wilson. We can jot notes or make copies if necessary. Also, any references to the DeWitt colony." She set a pack of colorful tabs on the table. "For marking pages."

For two hours, they buried themselves in early Texas history. Alex made several trips to the copier, and Kate's spiral filled with notes.

"Anything else you want to check on while we're here?"

"No. This is a lot of information. We can continue our history lesson at home." Her smile didn't reach her eyes.

He started to ask if she was in pain but stopped himself. The answer was written in the creases in her brow. "Let's get you home." Alex gathered the papers and spiral into her bag and held out his arm for her to stand. Once she balanced on her crutches, he followed her out the door.

Getting Kate into the truck was a sight to see. Once the passenger side door swung open, she balanced using the door handle while Alex laid her crutches in the back seat, then he grabbed her around the waist and lifted her onto the seat. With all her limbs tucked safely inside the door, he closed it and ran around to the driver's side. She could've climbed in on her own, possibly, but he preferred their method, whole-heartedly.

"I forgot to call Marisa. It's a little past lunchtime, but I should still give her a call." Kate pulled out her cell.

He reached over and tapped her hand. "You don't have to. It's obvious you're sore and tired."

"I want to. Really." She dialed.

Marisa answered on the first ring. "Kate, are you okay?"

"Yes. And I'm in town. Is it too late to meet for lunch?"

"Not at all. Same place as last time?"

"Sure. See you there in twenty minutes."

"You didn't mention that I was with you." Alex smirked as he pulled the gear shift into drive.

"Didn't I? Oops. She suggested the same restaurant as last time."

"But I wasn't there so you need to tell me which one." He looked at Kate and winked, waiting for the name of the restaurant.

"You read my mind about so many other things."

When they walked into the restaurant, Marisa waved and jumped up. "Oh, Kate. Look at you. Does it hurt?" She waited until Kate balanced herself before hugging her.

The hostess gathered menus. "Right this way. Booth or table?"

"Booth, please." Alex wanted Kate to be able to stretch out that leg and keep it up.

Marisa slid into one side. "Alejo, I didn't know you were coming."

He leaned the crutches against the wall. "It's nice to see you, too."

Marisa rolled her eyes, then turned her attention back to Kate. "Have they figured out who did it?"

Kate slid into the booth. "No. But the fool left me a note. He wants something back—I don't know what—and is trying to scare me into giving it up." Looking at Alex, Kate raised an eyebrow. "Alejo?"

"It was what my mom called me growing up. Nobody calls me that now." He shot his sister a look.

Marisa paled. "A note?"

"Unfortunately, I didn't see his face."

"I think it was the same person that broke into her house," Alex said without looking up from his menu.

Marisa leaned forward in her seat. "I hope they catch whoever did this and put them away for a long time."

"You and me both." Kate smiled as the waitress walked up to the table.

Marisa picked up a phone that wasn't ringing. "I need to go. I forgot I had a thing."

She clearly didn't have a thing. Alex stood up and gave her a quick hug. "Are you sure everything is okay?"

She answered, "I'm fine." But there were tears in her eyes.

"Marisa?" He kept his hand on her arm. "You can talk to me."

She shook her head. "I need to go."

Kate reached out her hand. "Sorry you couldn't stay for lunch. You should come out to the house again one night soon."

"Sure. Maybe. That would be great. Bye." Marisa knocked over a chair in her rush to get out of the restaurant.

Alex slid into the booth opposite Kate. "Put your foot up on my knee."

"What do you think is going on with your sister? She's clearly not fine." Kate drew circles in the condensation on her glass.

"I agree, but I don't know." He rubbed his thumb through the stubble in the cleft of his chin. "Something's definitely wrong."

They spent lunch talking about early Texas history, avoiding any mention of Marisa or the accident. When the waitress dropped off the check, Kate tossed her credit card on the table and raised an eyebrow, daring Alex to argue with her. He just smiled.

Once the bill was settled, she hobbled out to the truck. He shuffled next to her ready to catch her if she fell. The sound of glass under his shoe brought him to a full stop. Kate wobbled when the rubber ends of the crutches landed on the small pieces scattered on the ground. Alex caught her just as she lost her balance. His arm wrapped around her, he stared at his obliterated driver's side window.

"What the…?" Alex followed that with a few other choice words he rarely uttered.

"Someone is following us?" Kate looked over her shoulder.

He helped her to the tailgate and lifted her up after putting it down. "I don't know what's going on."

Shattered fragments crunched under his feet as he stepped closer to look inside. Glass covered the driver's seat. The papers from Kate's bag were strewn across the backseat and floorboard. Other than that—and a shattered window—nothing appeared disturbed.

He called Maddox. "Someone broke into my truck. I haven't touched anything except the tailgate, but it doesn't look like anything has been stolen. Kate's research is the only thing disturbed."

"Where are you?"

"In San Antonio."

"Did you call the police?"

"I haven't. Nothing is missing."

"Text me the address. I'll be there soon. I'll call it in. I want to have it dusted for prints."

"Thanks."

"What do they want?" Kate's legs dangled off the tailgate.

"I wish I knew." He rubbed his face in frustration. "I'm just glad no one got hurt this time."

Kate stared at the ground as she whispered, "What happens the next time?"

Alex stood between her knees and pulled her head to his chest. "I don't know, Kate."

For hours, they waited—waited on Maddox and the police, waited while they dusted for prints, waited for any clue about who caused all the trouble.

Maddox scratched his head. "There were no prints. None. We expect to see at least the owner's prints. The guy wiped it clean."

"Figures. Just like the break-in." Alex shook his head.

Maddox dropped his voice to a whisper. "Are you still staying with Kate?"

"Yeah, and we have private security parked out front." When Maddox raised an eyebrow, Alex added, "A different company, and if I have to leave, I'll be sure and call someone else to be there too."

"Good. I'm happy to take a watch." He flipped the cover of his notebook open and closed. "I'm glad you called me. Even though we don't have much to go on, I'm trying to sort all this out."

Alex nodded and pulled open his door. "The threat of hurting someone has me unnerved."

"Me too." Maddox glanced at Kate. "Let Kate ride with me, and I'll follow you to where you can clean out the inside and cover that window."

"Thanks."

Covered in clear plastic, the window was an eyesore, but he hoped it would hold until they reached Kate's house. He climbed into the truck and waved at Maddox. As Alex reached for the gear shift, Kate touched his hand. She ran her thumb along the side of his palm. He watched as her red nail moved back and forth, light dancing off the polish.

Her voice quivered as she spoke. "I'm trying not to fall apart. Thank you for being calm."

"You referring to my colorful tirade?"

"Not that. Just in general. He must have followed us, but you don't seem ... I don't know."

"I'm not calm, Kate. I'm so mad I can't—" Alex pounded the steering wheel. "All of these incidents and no leads. It's frustrating. I know your uncle has little to go on, but ..."

"You're not going to investigate on your own, are you?"

"We'll see." He wasn't ready to say no. He wanted the person responsible behind bars, far away from Kate, whatever it took.

CHAPTER SEVENTEEN

April 11th – 3:10 pm

The plastic flapping on the window made for a noisy ride home. I didn't even try to engage Alex in conversation. Though he navigated traffic with ease, his thoughts had him elsewhere.

My phone rang as we neared the house. "Hello?"

"Hi, it's Travis, um, Dad. Mind if I bring dinner tonight? I wanted to check in, and thought Alex might want a break from cooking."

"That would be good, actually." I tried to keep my voice even.

"Kate,"—Travis hesitated slightly—"are you with Alex?"

"Uh-huh, he's driving. Why?"

"Based on the sound of your voice, something's wrong."

I hated that I was such an open book. "While we were at lunch in San Antonio, someone broke into his truck." I gave Travis—Dad, rather—a brief update.

"I'll be there in about an hour or so." He sounded worried.

The security guard waved as we turned into the driveway, and I sighed with relief.

Getting out of the truck was easier than getting in, but I still liked Alex's help.

"What time is Travis coming?" Alex walked beside me as I hobbled toward the back door.

"He said an hour." I balanced while he unlocked the door. "What did I do to deserve you?"

"You knocked."

Despite all my insecurities, Alex acted as if I was the prize.

I beelined for the den, desperate to put my foot up. He handed me pillows, and I nestled on the couch.

He brought me ibuprofen and a glass of water, then laid the laptop on the coffee table in front of me. "Need anything else?"

I shook my head as I popped the caplets in my mouth, then spilled water down my chin.

He laughed as he sat down next to me. "Drinking problem?"

I wiped off the dribbles and swung my legs into his lap. "It's good to hear you laugh."

He shrugged, and his smile fell away. "We didn't tell anyone where we were headed to lunch. You didn't text anyone about it, right?"

"I didn't tell anyone."

"Let's look through the research. It'll help take our mind off stuff." He pulled the pages out of my tote bag and flipped through them. Together we poured through the information. I highlighted lines from the copied pages. He searched the internet for more information and jotted notes in the spiral. We shared interesting tidbits we came across. Bureau sensed us snuggling without him and wandered into the den. He jumped up on the couch and tried to lay down on the keyboard. Miffed that we shooed him away, he flicked his tail, then stretched out next to Alex.

"When was Madeline born?"

"1836"

He ran his hand along my bare leg. "When did Tabitha and Wesley marry?"

"1836. Let me look at what month." I flipped through my spiral until I found the dates. "Madeline was born in August 1836. Tabitha and Wesley married in October 1836."

"Interesting. What do you know about the Hughes guy?"

"Not much. I looked to see if there was a marriage record, thinking perhaps Tabitha married twice, but I didn't find one. But Wesley was married before. I don't know what happened to his wife, but he married in 1834."

"Whatever the story, it happened when Texas declared its independence." He handed me the laptop.

"Yep. Don't you wonder about the stories they could tell?" I opened a new browser window and brought up Ancestry.com. "I wonder how long they'd been in Texas."

"Was the museum worth the trip?" Alex leaned back, tossed a mint in his mouth, and dropped his feet onto the coffee table. The scent of peppermint wafted through the room.

"Absolutely. When I close my eyes, I can almost imagine Tabitha or her daughters mending clothing or stoking the fire." I searched for more records. The clickety-clack of the laptop keys and the soft whoosh of Alex's breathing brought comfort after the craziness of the day. I felt tucked away, safe. Results popped up on the screen. I scanned and searched, sending several documents to the printer.

"Need me to grab those for you?" Alex leaned forward like he was going to get up.

"No. I'll get them later." I stared at him, admiring the cut of his jaw and those green eyes. "When my car barreled toward that tree, I heard you scream my name as the phone flew out of my hand. I thought I might never see you again." I hadn't intended to take the conversation in an entirely new direction, but the words bubbled out.

The laptop lid clicked as Alex pushed it closed. I heard him set it on the coffee table, but my focus stayed riveted to his face. Laying back onto the couch, I sent kitty running when I bumped him with my cast. Alex hovered over me, and I brushed my fingers along his jawline.

Peppermint surrounded me. His eyes spoke volumes in a language I didn't understand. The air around me tingled like a sheet right out of the dryer, charged with static electricity. Sliding my hand onto the side of his neck, I felt the pounding of his heart. I closed my eyes as his lips found mine.

Then someone knocked.

It had to be Travis. *Do dads have some sort of magical radar?* Even at thirty-one, I felt like I'd been caught.

Alex jumped up to answer the door and winked as he walked away. "Probably a good idea to sit up." He'd never kissed me quite like that.

The smell of Chinese take-out preceded his return to the den. Travis held white, paper containers, and Alex carried paper plates and drinks.

I shuffled my papers into a stack. "Hi, Dad. Thanks for bringing dinner." Calling him Dad was easier after my hospital stay, and his blue eyes danced every time I said it.

"You're welcome. They broke the truck window?" Travis sat down on the sectional, leaving room for Alex to sit next to me. The awkwardness between them had disappeared. It made me wonder what they discussed in that hospital room while I slept.

"Yeah. But from what we could tell, they didn't take anything." Alex piled food on a plate and handed it to me. "We aren't sure what they are after."

It was after eleven when Alex and I said goodbye to Travis. I trudged back to the den, and Alex wandered into the kitchen. A few minutes later, he handed me a mug of hot cocoa.

He sipped his coffee. "I like your dad."

"He likes you too, which makes me happy." I leaned my head on his shoulder. "I know why he likes you, I think."

"Because I'm a nice guy? Charming? Intelligent? Interesting to talk to?" He chuckled.

"Yes, all those things, but those aren't what I was thinking."

"Do tell."

"It's because you treat me so well. He was really nice to you tonight, even more than usual."

Alex shrugged. "Maybe. Tomorrow, if it is okay with you and if Becca is free, I'm going out for a while. But only if she can be here to help you. And I'll have to see if Ben, DJ, or Maddox is available to keep watch."

"I don't mind. Are you leaving because Meg is coming?"

"No, Katie. I have something else I need to take care of."

"Like what? Bureau is here. Does it have to do with Marisa?"

Bureau came trotting into the den at the sound of his name. He almost always came when we talked about him, but rarely when we called him.

Alex nuzzled my neck. "You ask a lot of questions."

"When is Becca's birthday?"

"I'd have to ask DJ. Late summer maybe? Why?"

"I bought her a locket, and I'm trying to decide when to give it to her."

Alex sat his mug on the table. "When did you buy it?"

"When we stopped at the antiques place on our way back from lunch with Marisa."

"The day of the break-in?"

I kicked myself for not thinking of it before. "Yeah. Do you think? The clerk said that it had just recently been brought in."

"Where is it?"

"In my bedroom."

"Keep it tucked away for now. I'll let Maddox know."

"Are you going to tell me what you want? We got interrupted earlier. Twice."

He brushed his lips on mine. "I want…" A sigh and smile lingered in the space words didn't fill. He jumped up and scooped me off the couch. Carrying me down the hall, he whispered, "I want to take you to bed."

Words bounced around in my head like rubber balls. "Alex, I, uh…No," I stammered. The memory of the kiss on the couch dominated my thoughts.

Laugh lines crinkled near his eyes. "I'm teasing, but I am ready to go to bed, my own bed. I'd feel better if you were in yours." He laid me in bed and set my pajamas next to me. "Is that okay?"

"I thought—you know what I thought. Yeah. I'm pretty tired."

"Goodnight. Text or holler if you need me. You know where I'll be."

"Alex." I grabbed the hem of his shirt.

"Yes, my dear?" He pretended to fall back onto the bed. Sitting on the edge, he leaned over. "What do you need?"

"This." I sat up and kissed him. "'Night." I switched on the lamp near my bed, and he turned off the overhead light.

"Love you, Katie." He disappeared into the hall.

My heart still beat a hundred miles a minute, and curiosity about what he didn't say earlier consumed me. I didn't handle unanswered questions well.

Finding something else to think about, I imagined Grace learning about her early Texas heritage. She'd be so surprised to hear the story of her family.

Oct 9, 1835

Rumors of unrest are widespread. Father heard that the Mexicans were coming to take our cannon. The men of the town will not hear of it. Nathaniel, Father, and Reuben are with the other men to defend the cannon. It is buried in a peach orchard.

Rebekah (Reuben's wife), Mother, Jeremiah, and Amos all hid in the "old fort" along the riverbank. Mother sent me with thread to find Naomi. She and her mother ripped apart Naomi's wedding dress and are making a flag for the men defending the cannon. I found them as they painted a black star and cannon on the unbleached fabric.

The dress had been so beautiful, but even in a second life, it is used for something important.

Chapter Eighteen

April 12 – 8:30 am

I awoke to the sound of Alex on the phone. I strained to make out what he was saying. So, yes, technically I eavesdropped. But try as I might, I couldn't make out what he said. I pulled on a sweatshirt and hopped to the bathroom. One-legged transportation was sometimes easier than three-legged. When I walked out of the bathroom, Alex stood in my doorway with his back to me.

"Morning. You decent?"

"Yup."

"Want a piggy back ride down the hall?"

I laughed before I realized it was a serious offer. "Are you feeling okay?"

"Never better. Hop on." He squatted down next to the bed where I'd plopped down. "Leave your crutches. I'll come back for them."

I wrapped my arms around his neck and let him grab me around the thighs. Giggling, I held on tight as he straightened. "I have a bad feeling about this."

"I find your lack of faith disturbing."

"You know what I mean." I hugged him tighter. "I haven't had a piggy back ride since I was like five."

"That's a real shame." He was as giddy as I'd ever seen him.

Lingering at the end of the hall, he nodded toward the table. "You made breakfast."

"I did." He gently put me down in a chair.

"What time is your stuff today? Meg is coming early afternoon."

"I'll leave here about two thirty. So, I'll be here to say hello to your sister." Alex set a platter of pancakes and bacon on the table. "And while I'm gone today, Ben is going to park outside."

"Because you don't trust the security guy?"

"Do you blame me?" He set a small pitcher of warm syrup on the table. "I'm trying to be extra safe. Becca will be in here to help you. Ben will be outside to make sure nothing crazy happens."

"What's with the big breakfast and piggyback ride?"

"What? I can't be nice to my girlfriend when she's hurt?"

"Now I'm really worried." Said in jest, I hoped my concern wasn't evident.

When I ruminated on the fabulous breakfast, the playful piggyback ride, and the mysterious appointment, fear nibbled at me. After all the secrets uncovered a few months ago, withheld information made me uncomfortable. Desperately wanting my heart to take cues from my brain, I convinced myself to trust him.

After consuming more pancakes than I should have, I shifted back from the table. "Thanks for breakfast."

Alex jumped up. "Let me get you situated in the den, then I'll clean up. Don't want the place a mess when Meg comes around."

"I'm sorry she's so rotten to you."

"I care about your opinion, not hers. Don't sweat it. I'm glad she's coming to see you." He scooped me into his arms. Turning so my cast wouldn't knock against the walls or door frames, he navigated a path to the sofa and put me down.

I clicked on the TV. "I guess I'll watch something."

"Need your laptop?"

"I can't focus right now. Researching will have to wait." Frustrated, I hid my tears, not wanting him to see me upset.

He'd worked too hard to make it a perfect morning.

Alex tapped away on his laptop, stretched out on the other side of the sectional. "Need anything?"

"Nope." I wanted to tell him how perfect it was to have him around all the time, how much I liked the quiet hours when he worked next to me, his thoughts buried in code. "I love you, Alex." That was all I managed to say.

His laptop snapped shut. "I'm glad."

"What do you want?" I hadn't forgotten the unfinished sentence.

He shifted closer. The look that glinted in his eye last night returned. Grazing his knuckle along my cheek, he tucked a few unruly strands of hair behind my ear. He leaned in, and I closed my eyes, anticipating the feel of his lips. But, as common in our relationship, we were interrupted by a knock at the door.

"Ignoring it would be rude, right?"

"Depends on who it is, but we won't know until we answer." He kissed the tip of my nose. "Love you too."

I turned off the TV. It had to be Meg, and I wasn't hopeful we'd have a pleasant visit.

The door squeaked as Alex tugged it open. "Hi. Come in."

"It's your fault, isn't it? Ever since Kate met you it's been one kind of trouble after another." Meg slashed at people with her sharp tongue, not caring if her facts were correct.

"Kate's in the den. Can I get you anything to drink?"

"No. I'm just here to make sure she's okay." She clicked through the great room.

Behind her, Alex stopped in the doorway. Stormy green eyes focused on me. "Can I get you anything?"

"Something to drink and a few cookies would be wonderful."

"Coming right up." He disappeared around the corner, undoubtedly happy to be away from my sister.

"Have a seat, Meg."

Tears brimmed in her eyes, and she stared at my cast. "Oh, Kate."

I loved Meg, but she fussed too much. I wanted to avoid questions about the accident, so I pasted on the happiest smile I could muster and took a deep breath as she perched on the end of the couch. "I'm okay."

"Does it hurt? How did this happen?"

"I ran into a tree on a country road." Technically not a lie. I buried the truth.

Alex shook his head as he carried my snack across the room.

"I worry about you living out here, Kate. Why don't you move back into the city? You can live with us until you find a place." Meg's red-rimmed eyes scanned the room, a slight curl showing on her lip. She and I had very different tastes in décor—and in men.

"I like it here. This is my home."

She crossed her arms, and silence settled in the room. A knock at the door broke the quiet.

"I'll get it." Alex jumped at the chance to leave the room.

"I don't like him. He's not good for you, Kate." She had no idea how close she skated to getting kicked with a cast.

Becca saved Meg from her fate. "Kate! Hey, Meg." Becca's casual tone helped change the mood in the room. "Meg, didn't you and Tom just get back from Colorado? I bet it's beautiful there."

"Yes. We had a great time. Kate and I grew up in Colorado, you know." Meg went on and on about how much prettier the mountains were than the little hills in Texas.

Alex hovered in the doorway, waiting until Meg finished. "I'm headed back to get ready to go."

"Okay." Curiosity burned in my brain.

The conversation limped along with Meg upset that reality differed from the life she'd known. I tried to be kind, truly I did. At times during the stilted conversation, I almost wished Philip would stop by. Meg probably would've thought he was the cat's meow, perfect for me.

When she ran out of small digs and complaints about how I lived so far away from her, Becca jumped in to rescue the conversation. She updated me on recent jewelry orders, and I told her about my first genealogy client and about Travis's visit. What I didn't mention was the exchange with Alex on the couch. That would wait until both he and Meg were far away from the house.

Meg rolled her eyes. "Genealogy? Really? What happened to your tech job?"

That time, Alex saved her from getting kicked. He stepped into the den all dressed up. He looked sharp. The 8½ Souvenirs version of "Sharp Dressed Man" played in my head.

Becca noticed my smile and whipped around. "You clean up nice."

Alex laughed and leaned down over the back of the couch. After a quick peck on the cheek, he said, "I'll be here until Ben arrives, but I'll let y'all talk."

He wasn't even out of earshot before Meg started up again. "I can't believe he's just going to leave you here. He probably has someone else on the side. Why else would he be all dressed up in the middle of the day."

"I think I need a nap." I pushed up off the sofa. "Thanks for coming by, Meg."

Stunned, she gaped as I hobbled out of the den on my crutches. My timing was good because before I made it to the hall, Torres walked through the front door. I dropped my crutches and clunked over to him.

While I chatted with him, Meg slipped out the back door. I didn't even bother to say goodbye.

"Torres, I packed you snacks for your stake-out." I handed him the small cooler.

He shook his head. "It's not a stake-out. And why do you still call me Torres?"

"Sorry, *Ben*." I knew his name, but when I opened my mouth "Torres" popped out. I needed to be more intentional about using his first name.

"Text if you need anything." He waved as my help for the day peeked out of the den. "Hey, Becca."

Alex stopped before following Torres out the door. "Kate, would you wait to search until I get back?"

"I'll wait. Where are you going?"

"Bye!" Alex closed the door behind him.

"You don't know where he's headed?" Becca handed me my crutches.

"No, do you? Maybe he's going to get the truck window fixed, but that doesn't explain his outfit."

"Nope. He was very cryptic." Becca filled a glass with ice and water.

I must have looked ashen because Becca's expression changed.

"I don't think you need to worry or anything." She smiled. "It's Alex."

"You sure? This is the second time he's been all dressed up, and he won't tell me where he's going. What if he …?" Seeds my sister planted sprouted in my head. It was easier to mistrust than to admit the real reason for my reaction. *What if he found someone better?*

"You going to finish that question? Do you really think he would …?" Becca reacted as if I thought Alex had shortcomings.

"No. Not Alex." I leaned forward, trying to see out the window. "He's gone, right?"

"Yep." Becca hurried through the kitchen. The back door creaked as she pulled it open. "See."

That was my cue. I shuffled back to the den. "He was different last night. Really different. This morning too. If DJ told you anything, you would say something, wouldn't you?"

"Different how? And no, I probably wouldn't tell you."

"Seriously, Becca? I thought we were friends."

"We are, so I will tell you straight up that DJ has said nothing. *Nothing.* If Alex had talked to him, DJ would've mentioned it."

I stared at my Coke can, trying not to cry. I'd hoped for too much.

"Kate, it'll just take him a while. You know how he turns things over and over in his mind. He loves you, but it's too soon for him. Don't you have a birthday soon?"

"Yeah, I do. That's probably what this is all about." The whole trying not to cry wasn't working out too well. "Entertain me, Becca. What do you want to do?" I downed the last of my soda.

"We could watch a movie." She wiped a tear, but her voice sounded upbeat, almost perky.

"A costume drama sound good?" I tried to find my inner perky, though I wasn't sure I had such a thing.

"I'm always game for a good costume drama. Shall we see what Netflix has? Austen or Bronte?"

"Hmm. Bronte. Jane Eyre." I made myself comfortable on the couch and propped up my cast with pillows.

She settled at the other end of the sectional and started the movie. For the next while, I lost myself in Bronte's novel played out before me. We passed tissues back and forth and wiped tears when [SPOILER ALERT] Mr. Rochester declared his love and again when Jane left. Even the happy ending left us near sobbing.

Becca stood with her hands on her hips. "You chose this because the wife comes between them!"

I'd seen that stance before. "Maybe. So what if I did?"

"Kate, be happy with what you have now. Don't miss a happy today, wishing for the next thing."

"Isn't there anything you rea—" I had meant it innocently as way of explaining my feelings, but knew I'd said the wrong thing as soon as the words left my lips. Of course there was something Becca really wanted. "I'm so sorry Becca. I didn't mean it like that."

She broke down and sobbed.

Horrified, I apologized over and over.

She swallowed her sobs and sat down again. "I'm okay."

"Want to watch another movie?" I didn't want her to break down in tears again, so I skipped the second and third rounds of apologies.

"I need to eat something."

I settled at the table while she dug food out of the refrigerator.

The microwave beeped, and Becca pulled out a plate of leftover Chinese food. "Here ya go."

"Thanks. I'm sorry about Meg. I know it's hard for her, but I didn't think it would be this hard." I twisted my fork in the noodles.

"Don't worry about it. She'll come around." Becca served herself a plate and waited as the microwave worked its magic. "I have an idea for that brooch. Now I just need to wait until I have the nerve to touch it again. Any leads on the guy that caused your accident?"

"No."

"Hopefully they figure it out soon."

"I'm afraid Alex is going to start his own investigation." As I said it, an uneasiness settled on me. "Maybe that's where he's been going? He wouldn't want me to know if he was snooping around."

"If he is, he definitely wouldn't mention it to DJ or anyone else.

Investigating isn't a bad idea, though. What do we know? Maybe if we write down information about all three incidents, we can find commonalities." She jumped up and grabbed a notepad off the counter.

"Uncle Pat, I mean Captain Maddox, is treating them as related incidents, but he doesn't have much to go on. But seriously, Becca. Investigating? DJ would not approve."

"I'm only suggesting we write a list."

"Okay then. The break-in happened on a Tuesday night. Whatever they were looking for, they thought I had it by then."

"Tuesday night we were all over here. Nothing unusual, right?"

"Philip showed up with his chilled bottle of wine, saying 'Oh, sorry, I can come back when you're alone.' I'd call that unusual." I glanced down at what she wrote. "Are you listing events or suspects?"

"Suspects. We might as well make it easy for the investigators."

"Are you going to give the list to DJ?" I asked in an accusatory tone, but caught up in the puzzle of figuring it out, we continued. "Tuesday we had lunch with Marisa and stopped at the antique store. Oh, and Marisa and Paul showed up unannounced that night, too."

Becca scribbled on the yellow pad. "Go on."

"You cannot put Marisa on the suspect list."

"That didn't even occur to me. I did add Paul, though, just in case. Do you suspect her?"

"No, but Alex is worried that something is wrong. Never mind." I rubbed my forehead and tried to remember. "On Monday, I met with Bruce Jackson, and then went to the cabin."

Becca laughed. "That was when you thought Marisa was the other woman."

Ignoring her comment, I continued listing my activities. "Before meeting Bruce Jackson, I got my nails done."

"Should I list the nail tech as a suspect?"

"She doesn't even know where I live."

"What about Bruce Jackson?"

"It doesn't make sense."

"Maybe we need to focus only on people that know where you live. And that brings us back to Philip."

"My brain hurts, let's talk about something else. But speaking of Philip, will you grab that box of chocolates off the table?"

October 25, 1835

Come and Take it. That was the cry of the men until the Mexican forces retreated, avoiding a full battle. Nathaniel says that it is a victory for the Texians. Reuben talks of serving with General Austin. With all the chaos of war, for it seems we are truly at war with the Mexicans, I worry for our future.

I clung to Nathaniel as he slept. He leaves in two days to fight with General Houston. Hurry back to me, Nathaniel.

~*~

December 25, 1835

There wasn't much celebrating this Christmas. Many of the men are still away, fighting or preparing to fight.

I have not heard from my Nathaniel, but I continue to pray.

Chapter Nineteen

April 12th – 5:45 pm

Alex pulled into the driveway, eager to see Kate, but that would have to wait. He didn't want to worry her, given all the recent happenings, but whatever was going on with his sister concerned him quite a bit. He wanted Ben's advice on what to do.

He climbed into Ben's passenger seat after parking the truck. "I can't thank you enough for doing this."

Ben waved it off. "Kate just stumbled to your door?"

Alex chuckled, hoping his secrets weren't written all over his face. "You know how Kate and I met."

"It just seems crazy. She wandered around in the dark after escaping a kidnapping and landed at *your* door, and that chance meeting led to … what y'all have." Ben shrugged. "I'm happy for you."

"I'm just glad our paths crossed." Alex gazed at the house, the windows aglow from the lights on inside. "I can't imagine life without her."

Ben shifted, almost as if he were nervous about something. "Listen, DJ's already inside. I just stayed as a precaution."

Alex rubbed the cleft in his chin. "Can I ask you a question? In confidence?"

"Sure."

"If you thought someone was being abused by a boyfriend, what would you do?"

Ben chewed his lower lip. "Have you talked to her about it?" He blinked, as if deep in thought.

"You don't know this girl." Alex gave a humorless chuckle, shaking his head. "She's strong-willed and independent. Admitting she needs help isn't in her playbook."

He kept her name out of it, didn't even mention that it was his sister, not that it mattered much. Ben hadn't met his sister.

"What makes you think she's in trouble?"

"Her boyfriend rubs me the wrong way, but I know that's not a reason." Alex raked his fingers through his hair. "What has me concerned is—I talked to her earlier today, and I swear she was crying. When I asked her about it, she denied it."

Ben rubbed his buzz cut. "Have you seen any signs of abuse? Bruises?"

Alex swallowed the lump in his throat. The notion of someone hurting his baby sister set his blood boiling. "No black eyes or bruises that I've seen."

"Have you shown up unannounced at her house?" Ben, in his usual fashion, tried to help.

"She hasn't given me the address. I don't even know for sure there is a problem." Frustrated, Alex opened the door and stepped out of the car. "Forget I mentioned it. You coming in for a bit?"

"I'm gonna get going. I'll see ya later." Ben waved as Alex walked away from the car.

He took a deep breath, switching gears and shaking off the worry. As he reached for the doorknob, Kate opened the door.

"Howdy. You were gone a long time. I was getting lonely. Did you get the window fixed?" She closed the door and leaned back against the counter, a mischievous grin curling her lips.

"Yep. Good as new." His heart skipped a beat, and he hoped his face didn't give away his thoughts. His appointment had been successful. He wrapped his arms around her and tasted her lips.

She tasted like cookie dough. "Where else did you go? Did you start your own investigation?"

Ignoring both questions, he poked her in the side. "You're baking?"

The aroma of peanut butter and chocolate swirled around him.

"I am. You know me. With everything going on, I couldn't help myself. Now we'll have something to put in the cookie jar." She dropped her voice to a whisper. "Becca and I started making a list of suspects but didn't get very far. And I thought you didn't keep secrets."

He turned to walk down the hall. "Where's Becca?" Glancing back over his shoulder, he waited for an answer.

"I sent her home." Still at the counter, Kate slid the spatula on the cookie sheet moving cookies from the pan to the cooling rack, her back to him.

"*What?*" He rushed back over to her, frustration building. "Why? With everything going on?"

She spun around and flashed a wicked smile. "I'm kidding. She and DJ are in the den. They're watching a movie." She ran her finger down the front of his dress shirt, pausing briefly at each button.

He caught her hand as it reached the last visible button. "Don't tease."

Palm flat against his, she brought her other up and pressed it to his other hand. "Yes sir." Her tone and her eyes were still solidly in tease mode.

Interlacing fingers, he pulled her arms behind him, drawing her close. Brushing his clean-shaven cheek along her smooth jawline, he whispered in her ear. "I thought you were going to help me keep my promise. I want you more than whatever cookies you're baking. Please don't tease."

Her grin looked anything but contrite. "I'll be good."

"I'm going to change." He hurried down the hall.

Kate was sitting at the table dropping cookie dough onto a cookie sheet when he walked back into the kitchen. He sampled the dough.

He'd never tasted peanut butter chocolate chip cookies, but based on the bite he'd just eaten, he expected the finished product to be amazing.

He made himself a cup of coffee and joined her at the table. "Did you search without me?"

"Nope. Becca and I watched a movie."

"What movie?"

"Jane Eyre."

"Haven't seen it."

"Big surprise."

He tickled the toes sticking out of the end of her cast. "What else?"

"Meg visited, but you were here for that. DJ came over, we warmed leftovers, and I started baking." She shook off his tickles and stood up as the timer beeped.

"Let me get 'em for you." Alex pulled on an oven mitt and slid the cookies out. "These look awesome. May I have one?"

"Yes, but will you transfer them to the cooling rack first? Pretty please."

Alex did as she asked and then grabbed an extra cookie for his trouble. Before settling back at the table, he put another pan of cookies in the oven and set the timer.

He sank back into a chair and sipped his coffee. "We didn't have time to talk about Meg's visit. Anything I should know?"

Kate scrunched up her nose and closed one eye.

"That good, huh?"

"I understand that she's having trouble adjusting, but it's so maddening." She pulled on her hair.

"In all fairness, it is a big adjustment."

"She told me I should move in with her until I find a place in the city. And she says, 'the city' like it's some metropolis. What a joke. San Antonio is the biggest small town ever."

"That's part of its charm."

"Exactly. Anyway, I told her I had a house I liked already. That ended the conversation."

"Sorry."

"Next she's going to suggest that I sign up for a dating website, so I can find someone special."

"Ouch." Alex feigned a wounded heart. "Probably best not to let her meet Philip."

"You know what I mean. I'm not just ranting. If you have any ideas, I'd like to hear them."

"Does she understand that you are happy with your new reality, and that a close relationship is contingent on her accepting that reality too?"

"I've told her that. I stated that clearly months ago. She just doesn't get it."

"I'm sure it's hard for her." He set his mug down. "Aww, Katie, don't cry." He reached across the table and took her hand, kissing her knuckles. "We'll figure it out, okay?"

She nodded and wiped her tears. The timer beeped again, and he dutifully jumped up and pulled out another pan of hot gooey cookies. After transferring them to the cooling rack, he turned off the oven. "When is their movie going to be over?"

"I doubt they're even watching it. Those two love birds are constantly cuddling and kissing."

"Some people." He winked and poured himself another cup of coffee. "I need to sample this batch also."

Alex waved as DJ held Becca's car door open. "Goodnight."

Inside, Kate sat on the couch with the laptop open and ready. She grinned as Alex walked into the den. "Too late to start searching? I wasn't sure how early you had stuff in the morning."

"I have a mid-morning Skype meeting, but sure, let's search. But first, tell me about this investigation you and Becca started. I didn't want to talk about it with DJ here."

"We were trying to think of where I had been Monday and Tuesday. Someone seems to think I have something, but I don't know what that would be. I didn't even tell her about the locket. If I knew what they were looking for, it would help to narrow it down. Becca decided to start a list of suspects."

"Who did she put on the list?"

"Philip, Paul, and my nail tech. I didn't say we got very far."

"Philip did show up the night of the break-in, and he's been super attentive to my Kate." Alex winked. "Seriously though, do you think he could be behind this? What would be his motive?"

"Did he drop something secret or important when he visited that night and is now trying to get it back? Remember how he got so weird when you kicked that bead? Maybe he isn't who he seems to be. Could he be a spy? Is there a bug in the box of chocolates?" She opened the lid and chose one with a creamy caramel center. "Sorry. I got a bit carried away, but I suppose he could be trying to retrieve something he dropped. But would he really run me off the road to get it?"

"That's hard to believe, but we can't rule him out." Alex picked up the yellow pad and looked at the list. "I think you can safely remove your nail tech."

"Agreed. As I told Becca, she doesn't even know where I live. I feel bad even putting Paul on the list. What motive would he have?"

"I can't imagine anyone that knows you would run you into a tree. Think back. Was there any place you showed them your license? Someone could have gotten your address off that."

"I don't think so. The restaurant didn't ask for it when I bought the tee shirt. I can't remember if I showed it to the man at the antique shop."

Alex wondered out loud about a connection, but the doorbell ringing cut him off. "Be right back." He pulled open the front door and was met by a smiling Philip, all decked out in running shorts and a tank top.

"Mind if I come in for a moment?"

Alex stepped aside and pointed to the den. "Kate's on the sofa."

"Hey, Philip. Thanks for the chocolates. I've been making good use of them." Kate pointed at the half-empty box.

"Great. I don't have but a minute. I'm just headed out for a run, but I wanted to check on you."

"I'm good. Alex has been a big help."

"I noticed he was hanging around more." Philip winked as if he and Kate shared a secret. "Well, I gotta run, literally. Call if you need me for anything." He let himself out the front door and took off jogging down the street.

Kate rolled her eyes once Alex strolled back into the den. "He's like a puppy, but not in a good way."

"Maybe he is the one behind all this. Why does he keep coming around?"

"Really, Alex? Really?" She gave him one of those looks.

"I know what he said, but what if he's lying? Maybe we can go over there, and I can snoop around to see if he is on the up and up."

"Not tonight."

"Oh no, not tonight. I wasn't suggesting we break in or anything." He leaned back and plonked his feet on the coffee table. "Let's focus on Grace's family." Spiral in hand, he recapped where they'd left off last night. "What do we search now?"

"Let me make a list of where each family member is buried." Her fingers danced across the keyboard, her fingernails clicking on each letter. "Ruth died in Bexar County, Texas."

"Can we view the original? Will it give us any information?"

"Yes, and yes." She entered her username and password, and the image popped up on the screen. "The informant was George Cooper, and it notes the name of the cemetery—the burial park down near the missions."

"Want to drive into *the city* tomorrow and visit the cemetery?" He tried to keep a straight face.

She elbowed him in the ribs. "I'd love to drive into town. But I can't tomorrow. I have a doctor's appointment, remember? The next day?"

He laughed, glad that she found him funny.

Feb 12, 1836

Settlers from San Antonio de Bexar came through town. They are retreating toward the Sabine River. Panic set in when they learned Santa Ana crossed into Texas. Father says we will be safe as far east as we are.

Reuben is in San Antonio de Bexar to help defend the Alamo. His wife just gave birth, and we are trying to keep her calm. Father will stay here with us rather than leave to fight.

Thankfully my house is near my parents. I am trying to maintain things while Nathaniel is away. I think Mother guesses my secret but hasn't spoken of it. I want to be excited. I need the war to be over and my beloved Nathaniel home.

~*~

March 5, 1836

Days ago, they declared an independent Texas. Father says that is the best option. Mother wonders if we will live long enough to see it. There has been no word from Reuben. I understand Rebekah's worry. I've had no news from Nathaniel, but reports say that General Houston has not engaged the Mexicans in battle.

I am trying to be brave.

CHAPTER TWENTY

April 13th – 1:47 am

I awoke to the clap of a thunderbolt and pulled the covers up to my chin. I hadn't gotten used to Texas storms. The room lit up, and for an instant it was as bright as the middle of the day. Awake, I listened to the wind and pelting rain. In the dark with all the noise, my mind toyed with me. I imagined a wizard rising to full height as he drew in strength, flashes emanating from the wand. Like a conductor, he cued the rumbles and flashes, then lifted his hand and the wind obeyed by slamming against the house.

I closed my eyes. Hopefully, it would blow over soon. Lightning sparked through the night, and I felt its electricity dance on my skin. The house rattled again as gale force winds bombarded my quiet. I huddled under the covers, a little frightened, but feeling childish, while Alex slept soundly across the hall. The barrage of noise made it easy to imagine someone lurked outside, plotting my demise.

Storms had a way of making me feel small and alone. My fear wanted company—negative emotions seemed to travel in packs like girls to restrooms—so fear invited disappointment to hang around. *Eventually.* Every time I pulled the word out of my memory bank, it sounded more discouraging. I replayed what Becca said over breakfast. *He loves you, but it's too soon for him.*

My phone lit up and vibrated across the nightstand.

Alex texted: *You okay?* He could apparently read minds and see through walls.

I tapped out a quick reply: *I don't like the storm.*

His response made me love him more: *Hot cocoa in the den until it passes?*

Thunder pounded the air just as lightning illuminated the night. A second later, the house plunged into darkness, the power knocked out.

I sent him another text: *I guess hot cocoa is out of the question.*

The light from his phone announced his entry into my bedroom. "We can still wait out the storm on the couch. Be careful in the dark. I don't want you to trip."

We shuffled into the den, his arm around my waist. The sectional became our fortress while the wind and rain raged outside.

He tucked a blanket around me. "So, what's your plan for figuring out who Madeline's father is?"

"Not sure yet. I'm going to mull it over and hope an idea pops."

"Or you could take a break from searching for a day."

"I've already lost time because of my hospital stay, but maybe you're right."

He wrapped his arms around me. "Could you repeat that last part you said? Maybe put it in writing?"

"Very funny."

The power came back on, and the winds died down. Like a wizard sapped of his strength, the storm moved on, leaving only sobbing clouds in its wake.

"I need more sleep. I'm going to crawl back in bed." I pushed up off the sectional.

"As you wish." His movie reference warmed my heart like spiced cider on a snowy night.

"Love you." I shuffled down the hall with Alex close behind.

He stopped at my door and waited until I tucked back in bed. "Night." He double tapped the frame before walking away.

With my eyes closed, I listened as the rain sang a lullaby, and I drifted off, afloat on my dreams.

I woke to the sound of kibble clattering in the bowl. Bureau meowed as he jumped off my bed. I breathed in the aroma of coffee and sat up. I hated the cast, but there were upsides to being waited on. The benefits were easier to appreciate when I wasn't letting the irritability blind me.

I limped down the hall and dropped into a chair. "I'm glad you were here last night." I snatched a slice of bacon from the platter and folded it into a pancake.

When he'd cooked the other morning, he'd made enough breakfast to feed a few armies. We'd be eating pancakes and bacon for days.

"When I heard the storm coming, I checked the radar. I've seen storms like that take down trees and knock out power. They can get rough." He copied my breakfast idea.

"How did you know I was awake?"

"You texted me back." He refilled his coffee cup. "What time is your appointment?"

"One, but I don't want to talk about it. He's only going to tell me how much longer he thinks I'll get to wear the cast. The best I can hope for is a new color. I'm tired of purple."

"But you'll lose Philip's number."

"Someone doodled all over his number. Now it looks like a garden of robots."

"They were supposed to be flowers."

"I wonder what Gram thinks about you staying here." I made myself another pancake taco.

"Do you care?" He eyed me over the rim of his mug.

"A little." I did care, more than a little, but I wasn't completely sure why.

Reclining on the couch with my foot propped on pillows, I scanned the recent additions to Netflix. Alex was right. I needed a break from research, and binge watching something sounded appealing. Finding something to watch proved difficult, not because of the lack of variety but because there was so much. Too many shows looked interesting.

Alex tapped away at his laptop. He'd moved from the dining room to the other length of the sectional, but he was a million miles away, buried in code.

"I thought you had a meeting."

"Rescheduled."

"Oh. What are you working on now?"

He looked at me sideways. "You really want me to explain it?"

"Not really."

"Watch your show." He patted my cast.

Settling on a series about a cowboy sheriff—who wouldn't want to watch that?—I started the first episode. When it ended, the next one started without me even clicking a button. *Auto play is the greatest feature ever.* As the third episode ended, Alex spoke up.

"We don't have time for another one, unfortunately." He closed his laptop and set it aside. "Want a hand?"

There was that word again, want.

"Sure." I shifted and used his arm as a grab bar to pull up off the couch.

The lunch rush had ended by the time we arrived at the restaurant, the perfect time to enjoy a quiet meal in a tourist town. My appointment unfolded just as I'd expected. The doctor gushed about how well it was healing, then put on another cast. A beautiful burgundy color now covered my lower leg. Technically, I think the name of the color was black cherry. I was just happy it wasn't purple or pink. The doctor said I'd probably have it on only another week or so, as if I'd be happy with that news. Stasis had to be better than getting around on crutches. Maybe that would be a viable business idea. I could offer stasis to people waiting on bones to heal or ankles to mend.

Sitting at a table in a local brewery—a table we would easily wait an hour for on a busy weekend—we scanned the menu.

"Oh, hi." I snapped to at the sound of the waitress flipping open her order pad.

"What can I get for you two?"

"Salmon for me." I closed my menu and waited for Alex to decide.

"The schnitzel, please."

"Be right out." Her shoes squeaked as she padded along the stained concrete floor.

"Must be new." He reached across the table and rubbed his thumb along my knuckles. "Sorry it's another week. I know you were hoping to get it off today."

"I'll live, I think." I rested my chin in my free hand. "He encouraged me to put weight on it. You don't have to be my constant companion. I'm not rushing you off, just releasing you from any obligation."

"I'm not leaving you alone. Besides, obligation is an ugly word." He was quieter than normal, and it made me wonder what he was mulling in that brain of his.

"Penny for your thoughts."

"I feel bad even saying it out loud." His voice tight, he lined up his silverware.

"What's wrong?"

"That restaurant and Marisa seem to be the only things that connect two of the incidents. The thought that Marisa could..."

"Just stop. You know that's not true." My voice came out shrill, pained. I'd had the same thought, but it didn't make sense. "What about the waiter? Maybe he was there when we went back. I didn't even think of him before."

"The waiter doesn't know where you live. And before you say anything about Paul, I've already considered him. I don't like him, but that doesn't make him a criminal. Besides, he wasn't at lunch with us when the truck was broken into. Only Marisa. I'm going to call her."

"And say what? Excuse me. Did you run my girlfriend off the road? Alex, she's your sister."

He squeezed my hand. "But it's the only thing that makes sense."

"To what end? Is she trying to scare me away from you? We can see how well that has worked." I tugged at his hand and hoped that he'd look up.

"But what if that is exactly what's going on?" The question landed on the table with a thud, but finally he lifted his gaze. "She—"

"And here ya go. The salmon for the lady, and the schnitzel over here. Anything else I can get for you?" The waitress smiled, unaware she'd interrupted our conversation.

"Everything looks delicious. Thank you." I turned my attention back to Alex.

The waitress squeaked away, off to serve other patrons. I waited to see if he'd finish what he started to say. His unfinished sentences were starting to make me crazy.

"Alex, I'm sure that's not what's going on. I really think she likes me." While some of the pieces fit, motive left a gaping hole. Marisa didn't have one. Surely, she didn't think me such a poor match for her brother that she would break the law or try to hurt me.

Alex poked at his food.

"Who wouldn't like me?"

His clenched jaw relaxed into a smile.

Chapter Twenty-one

April 13th – 6:15 pm

The kitchen door slammed after Alex pushed it closed with his foot.

Kate sat at the table and watched as he carried in the twelve bags of groceries. "Why did you carry all of them at once?"

"Because I can." He dropped the bags on the table.

She separated the perishables from the pantry items, and he transferred the cold stuff to the refrigerator.

"After our late lunch, I'm not very hungry, but if I put chili on now, it won't be ready for hours. We'll be eating pretty late."

"Sounds good to me. I haven't had your chili in a while."

Once he had the ingredients simmering in the pot, he suggested they continue the series she'd watched that morning. They sprawled on the sofa and picked up where Kate stopped watching.

During the intro of each episode, Alex did a quick stir. Many episodes later, the chili had simmered long enough for the spices to permeate the entire pot, and they were hungry again.

His favorite dish to make, topped with avocado, chips, onion, and cheese, his chili was some of the best around. At least, that's what he'd been told. The savory meat filled the senses, then dissolved to a mild heat.

By the time they'd consumed the food, it was well past midnight.

"I know it's very late, but I was thinking we could watch another episode or two." He loaded their bowls into the dishwasher.

"Sure." She limped into the den and dropped onto the couch. "This dang blasted cast."

He sat down in the corner of the sectional. "Here, lean back against me." With his legs resting on the coffee table, he was turned just enough that she could lean back onto his chest, her casted leg stretched out. Bureau joined them and curled up near Kate's feet.

"Want to elevate it with a pillow?"

"Nah. It's perfect just like this." She ran her fingers along the veins on his hand. "We've spent a lot of time snuggled on this couch since the accident. What changed?"

"You might laugh." He pointed at her cast. "That'd just be in the way, or I might get whapped with it."

She grinned. "What was different about the other night?"

"I almost forgot you were wearing it." There was so much more to that answer, but he didn't say more.

"You're a magician."

"How's that?"

"With only a few words, you made me like my cast." She kissed his hand.

Alex started the show and wrapped his arms around Kate. For the time being, this was as close to perfect as he could imagine—to have Kate in his arms and to inhale the scent of her herbal shampoo. Catching the person who ran her into a tree would be the cherry on top.

As the credits rolled after two episodes, she whispered, "I like it when you call me Katie."

Alex kissed her on the top of her head. If there was a choice to make regarding his sister, there wasn't any doubt who he'd choose.

March 13, 1836

Mrs. Dickinson, who had gone to Bexar to be near her husband, returned to town. The news Susanna brings is hopeless. All the men at the Alamo were slain. How she speaks so calmly of her dead husband is outside my understanding. She is a braver woman than I am.

The grief of the town is nearly unbearable. Mother and Rebekah are inconsolable, but the news is even worse. Santa Ana is headed this way. We must flee or face death.

~*~

March 14, 1836

I loaded what I could in our wagon. I pray that Nathaniel forgives me. They set fire to our home. As we left town, flames danced toward the sky. There is no home for Nathaniel to return to, only me and soon, our child.

Chapter Twenty-two

April 14, 2016 – 9:32 am

The buzz of an incoming text woke me. I yawned as I read it. Marisa asked about my ankle and offered to show me the house on the property if I felt up to it. I replied: *Yes! I want to see it. I'll be ready when you get here.*

Quietly, I slipped out of bed, not wanting to wake Alex. We'd stayed up way too late the night before. He needed rest. I wanted him to see the house, but with everything he'd been doing to take care of me, rest ranked a higher priority.

After getting dressed, I slipped outside and waited on the porch.

Marisa pulled up just a few minutes later. "Alex isn't coming?"

"I'm letting him sleep. We were up really late." I hobbled out to the security guard. "I'm going to look at that property next door. You can stay parked here. You can almost see the gate from where you are parked."

The guy glanced where I pointed. "You sure?"

"Yep." I waited as Marisa pulled up behind the security guard.

"You didn't even tell Alex you left?" She didn't hide her dismay.

"Your brother has spent almost every waking hour taking care of me. He needs rest. If he knew I'd left the house, he wouldn't sleep."

"That's true." Marisa helped me into her car. "The house on the property isn't in great shape, but I don't get the idea it's the house you're interested in."

"I have a house. It's the land that intrigues me, but I still want to see it."

We went through the same routine of opening the gate, but given everything that had been happening, Marisa locked it behind us.

"Have you, uh, had any more trouble?" Marisa cringed when the car hit a washed-out spot in the road.

"They broke the window on Alex's truck. Not sure if you knew that part. I keep thinking of the warning in the note about people getting hurt."

"A note? You saw the guy?"

"I wish. He had on a mask. Dropped a threatening note in my car." I stared out the window, trying to forget the accident and falling in love with the land around me.

"Kate, I'm so sorry."

"You don't need to apologize. You didn't do anything wrong." I grinned as she parked near the house. "I wonder how old this place is."

"I'm not sure." She glanced at the paperwork. "Let me unlock it, then I'll help you out."

"I can manage." Keys jingled as I made my way up the steps. When the door creaked eerily, I was happy that the sun was shining bright. "No ghosts listed in residence?"

"No, but I can't promise there aren't any in the family cemetery."

I laughed as I clunked my way into the house. Shuffling through the two-room house, I scanned the time capsule, enthralled by the strong sense of the past that remained within the old walls. Pictures on the wall caught my attention. "I'd love to know their stories. This place is amazing."

Marisa disappeared around the corner. "Looks like this bedroom was updated aft—Ack!" A thud followed her scream.

"Marisa? Are you okay?" I hobbled as fast as I could to the other room.

She lay sprawled on the floor. "I'm okay. Be careful. One of the floorboards is loose." She pushed up off the floor, biting her lip.

"You're hurt. Let me call Alex."

"Absolutely not. I don't need any help." She leaned against the wall and rubbed her hip. "I'll be fine. I'm sure it's just a bruise."

"Can you get back to the car? We should head back." I made my way to the front door but stopped in front of a sampler hanging on the wall. "I need to find out who lived here."

"Don't hurry because of me. Take your time. I'm fine." Marisa flashed a smile. "You take this genealogy stuff seriously."

"I think it would be so interesting to find out the history of who lived here."

"That would be amazing."

I wandered through the rooms again before heading to the door. "Want to drive around the property a little before we head back?"

"Absolutely." Marisa locked up as I made my way off the porch.

CHAPTER TWENTY-THREE

April 14th – 11:07 am

A few minutes after 11 am, Alex slipped out of the bedroom and stopped outside Kate's closed door. He didn't remember her closing it last night, but as tired as he'd been when they finally went to bed, he'd likely forgotten. It wasn't a big surprise that she'd slept so late. Wanting to let her rest, he tiptoed down the hallway and brewed a pot of coffee before dropping two slices of bread into the toaster. He glanced at his phone and saw that he had a message. After listening to the voicemail, he stepped out to the porch to return the call. It rang and rang before going to voicemail.

"Hi. I just got your message. I can't make it over there today, but I'll come by tomorrow if that works for you. I can't wait to see it." He hoped he could sneak away again without too many questions.

By noon, he started to wonder if Kate was going to sleep the day away. He tiptoed down the hall, stopped outside her door and listened. Not a sound emanated from her room. He wandered back to the kitchen, determined not to be concerned.

Coffee sloshed out of his mug as he carried his third cup of coffee to the table. When the back door opened, Alex shook his head, biting his tongue. Marisa held it open as Kate maneuvered through.

Anger flared, but he fought to control his temper. "Kate, I thought you were asleep. When did you leave?" His jaw clenched, he tried to keep the edge out of his voice.

"Marisa texted, and we went to look at the house next door. How late did you sleep?"

"I've been up about an hour. Remember what I said about not leaving the house without me?"

"I was with her." Marisa put her hands on her hips. "Don't worry so much. The security guy could see the gate."

Ignoring his sister, he focused on Kate. "Please don't do that again." He wanted her to understand his concern. "Please."

"I'm sorry. I didn't think it was a bad idea." Kate leaned her crutches against the counter.

"What did you think of the place?" He didn't want to be angry with either of them. "And why are *you* limping, Marisa?"

"She fell at the house but says she's okay." Kate dropped into Alex's lap. "I love the place. I want you to see it soon." She fluttered her eyelashes. "You forgive me?"

He tucked her hair behind her ears. "Yes. I just don't want to take any chances."

"I'll catch y'all later." Marisa pulled open the door.

Kate stood up, using the table for balance. "Don't leave!"

"I really do need to go. I have to get back to the office." Marisa laughed, hands raised in defense.

"As long as we aren't chasing you off."

"Not at all. Talk to y'all later." She waved.

"I'll walk her out." Alex followed her. He closed the back door and leaned in Marisa's driver's side window. "Are you okay, Marisa?"

"Oh, yeah. I'm fine."

"Don't give me the *I'm fine*, please. And I'm not talking just about the fall."

She rolled her eyes. "You worry too much. I really need to go."

He backed away from the car, and she pulled out of the driveway. Her responses didn't settle his fears about what might be going on, but he reconsidered the idea she might be somehow responsible. If she'd wanted to hurt Kate, Marisa had the perfect opportunity to do harm, but she didn't. Thinking of his sister as a suspect didn't sit right anyway.

Taking advantage of his moment of privacy, he pulled out his phone and called Becca. "Hey. You free tomorrow? I have an appointment, but I won't go unless Kate has someone else here with her."

Becca laughed. "You mean in case Philip decides to stop by?"

Alex rolled his eyes. "Can you come or not?"

"I'll come. An appointment again? You gonna say where you are going?"

"No."

"I hope you know what you're doing. Please don't break her heart." Her serious tone surprised him.

"Becca, it's me." He ran his fingers through his hair. If Becca thought he was up to no good, Kate probably did too.

The implication stung, but setting her right would tip his hand and give away the surprise.

"I'll be there by nine. Maybe I'll take her to breakfast."

Alex shook his head, as if it emphasized his point. "Please stay here. That's why Travis hired security. And I've arranged for Maddox to park out front too."

"We'll stay put. See ya in the morning." She ended the call.

As he walked inside, Kate limped toward the den. "Mind if we don't go to the cemetery today?"

"Fine with me. Everything all right?"

"I'm sore. Maybe we can go another day."

"Are you going to work on the family tree?"

"Yes. I just need to find the story aspect, if that makes sense. And I need to call Bruce about scheduling the birthday surprise."

After his conversation with Becca, he worried that Kate was upset but not saying anything. "Will I be in the way if I sit with you while you work?"

"I expected that you'd sit with me. You're being weird." She dropped onto her favorite spot on the sectional.

Alex carried his coffee into the den and sat down next to her.

When she draped her legs over his lap, he relaxed. "I'm sorry I snapped at you."

"I forgive you, and I'm sorry." She kissed him again.

Alex handed her the phone. "Why don't you call Bruce Jackson now?"

She dialed the number and waited. "Mr. Jackson, this is Kate Bentley.... Yes, I've managed to find quite a lot of information. I was hoping we could schedule her surprise...Thursday? Um..."

Alex shook his head, and Kate grinned.

"I can't meet then. I have another engagement that evening."

Alex focused his attention on Bureau, sure that his expression would give away too much of the surprise.

"What about Wednesday?... Great." Kate scratched at her cast. "Yes, just text me the name and address of the restaurant. See you then." She ended the call and interlaced her fingers with Alex's, bringing his hand to her lips and kissing his hand. "Thank you."

"For what? This is all your doing."

"For indulging me. For helping me believe I could do this."

There were a hundred ways he could've responded. The lengths he would go to indulge her were far beyond driving her around and helping her search genealogy records. "You underestimate yourself."

She kissed his hand again. "I need to put together a family tree, a chart. I bet Becca can help me with that. She has great design sense. Have you seen her drawings?"

"I haven't."

"I want to get one created for the birthday surprise, then after we meet, I'll have one professionally printed."

"Sounds like a good plan. I know it will be a wonderful evening." He squeezed her hand.

CHAPTER TWENTY-FOUR

April14th – 2:00 pm

I scratched at my cast, frustrated by the itching. "Taking a break was a great idea. I just had a thought about how to figure out who Madeline's father is."

Alex jumped up and grabbed my laptop and notes. "What will you search?"

"I honestly can't believe I didn't search this already." I scanned my notes as the laptop booted up. "I'm going to search for Madeline, only listing a mother's name."

"Because you haven't found a birth certificate or marriage license for a prior marriage for Tabitha."

"Right." I entered the search parameters and watched the screen, willing it to load faster. "I think this might be it."

"Madeline Hughes?"

"Uh huh. Look her mom is Tabitha Miller, and her dad is Nathaniel Hughes."

"What happened to Nathaniel Hughes? Were he and Tabitha married?"

"I haven't found a marriage, but that doesn't mean they didn't marry. Let me search his name."

I scrolled through pages of Google results looking for anything relating to early Texas. "I can't find anything that tells me what happened to him. I've already searched the genealogy websites."

"Maybe while you sleep, your brain will figure something out." He leaned back and rested his feet on the coffee table.

I limped over to my office corner and dug through the basket that held my office supplies. I really needed a new system of organization. The tape dispenser found my finger, and I got nicked by the serrated edge. "Ouch." Finger in my mouth, I tossed the tape on the table. Grabbing a stack of paper from the printer tray, I shuffled back to the coffee table.

"Can I help you with anything?" Alex eyed me as I hobbled back and forth.

"Sure. I want to empty the coffee table, so I can spread out these pages and tape them together. That way I can sketch out the family tree."

Alex sprang up off the couch, moved my research and laptop to the corner nook, and wiped down the coffee table after carrying mugs back to the kitchen. Sitting on the floor by the coffee table, I laid out the blank pages. Alex handed me strips of tape, and I connected the sheets. With all the edges and corners fastened, I flipped over the spread of pages.

"I'll call Becca later and see if she'll help me with a prettier tree, but this at least give a visual."

"Want me to read you names, so you can write it out?"

"That'd be great. You sure I'm not keeping you from work?"

"I'm all yours."

"No projects?"

"Finished everything. I have a few requests, but I'm not taking on anything new this week."

I wrote Grace's name at the bottom center of the sheet. "Ready when you are."

"Father: George Cooper. Mother: Ruth Whittaker." He watched

as I wrote the names and matched his pace to the speed of my writing. "Do you want the dates and locations for birth and death?"

"Yes. That should be on the chart."

I added the information for George and Ruth and then moved up the paternal line. Alex fed me the information one person at a time. We worked well together.

"Finally done." I dropped the pencil and rubbed my hand.

"What now?"

"Back to my Texas History lesson. I want to grab notecards and put a timeline together."

"Where are the notecards? I'll get 'em."

"In my bedroom, on the shelves near the door."

"After this, we should watch the older version of The Alamo. The one with John Wayne." Alex padded out of the room, his boots lying near the coffee table.

"How can I say no to John Wayne? Or you?"

"I'll remember you said that." He winked at me as he dropped back onto the couch. "You tell me the event, and I'll write them out. What are you going to do with them?"

"Write out a narrative to include in the file I give the client. I want to pick one particular person or family line to spotlight for each client. At least that's what I envision." I grabbed the copied stack of papers and my spiral. "1825 DeWitt Colony Established."

Alex printed the date and event on a yellow card.

In no time at all, we had the timeline mapped out and transferred to note cards.

"Okay. I think that's it." I tossed the papers and notecards on the coffee table. "Thank you for all your help."

"Sure."

"Ready to watch the movie?"

"As soon as I make us some popcorn."

The credits rolled up the screen, and my thoughts wandered back to the family tree.

"Oh, I never called Becca." Still snuggled against Alex, I dialed.

"Hey Becca, it's Kate. Would you be free to help me create a family tree poster for my client? I need your creativity."

"Sure. I was planning on being at your house tomorrow morning because Alex has another appointment. Would he be able to drop you off in town? My mom's place would be perfect for this kind of project. The security guy could park on her street, and DJ can be there."

"I'll ask him." Trying to maintain my smile, I sat up and turned to Alex. "Could you drop me off on the way to your appointment?"

"At Becca's?"

"Her mom's house in San Antonio. You could make arrangements with the security company. She said DJ would go too."

"Yeah. I can do that."

"Thanks." I tried to be casual, but I was disappointed and curious, curious about where he was going and disappointed that I didn't already know he had plans. *I don't like the secret-keeping.* Although we'd spent many hours together in the last three months, I hadn't met any of his family until recently, and even then, I mistook his sister for his love interest. *Major fail.*

"Becca, that works. See you there in the morning. Just text me the address."

I shifted away from Alex, dropped my feet on the coffee table, and grabbed my spiral. Flipping to a clean page, I stared at the empty space between the lines. *Focus on writing the narrative.* I wrote out an opening sentence, then scratched through it. I wanted to tell a story, not write a history lesson.

Imagine crossing the Sabine River into Texas or landing in Matagorda Bay after sailing from New Orleans. In 1825, Green DeWitt persuaded families from Missouri, Tennessee, and other states to leave their homesteads and venture into Texas.

Disappointment morphed into irritation, but channeled anger proved helpful.

The Miller family made that journey and arrived in Texas

sometime before 1835.

Wishing I had more mundane detail about life in early Texas, I continued, trying to make the narrative more than a string of dates. Alex scooted closer to me. Word choice became of utmost importance as I crossed out words and rewrote sentences.

"You writing the narrative?"

"Yep." I didn't look up from the page.

In September 1835, Corporal deLeon and five soldiers marched to Gonzales, requesting the return of the cannon. The men of the town answered by taking them prisoner.

Imagine the fear as families hid by the river, while the men surrounded the cannon. Come and Take It was their cry.

I already used the word imagine. I need to find a different word. I marked through the word, then through the whole sentence.

Women and children huddled by the river in fear as Mexican troops approached. The cannon, once buried in a peach orchard, was now mounted and ready for battle. A flag flew over it, cut from a wedding dress, and it displayed their battle cry: Come and Take It.

History seemed interesting when it felt like events happened to real people. I scanned my notes looking for the name of the Mexican officer in charge of the unit and tried to ignore Alex's quiet attention. It was easier to relive the Revolution with anger and irritation burning in my gut.

Ordered not to engage in open conflict, Castañeda left—

My pen quit working. Scribbling circles in the margin, I silently begged ink to appear.

"Need me to get you another pen?"

"No." I jumped up and limped over to my table. I couldn't find any pens in my cluttered supplies basket, so I hobbled to the kitchen and pulled open my junk drawer. I grabbed three pens.

Picking up my spiral, I dropped onto the other end of the couch, far from Alex.

Ordered not to engage in open conflict, Castañeda left without the cannon, but the dispute kicked off the fight for liberty.

Awkwardness hung around us like body odor after a workout. *He lied. He is keeping secrets.* Seeds of doubt took root as I remembered how I felt when I saw him hugging Marisa at the cabin. I didn't like that he was sneaking around, but I couldn't imagine him cheating on me. Of course, then I remembered Meg's comment. The more I thought about it, the harder I fought back tears. *Do* not *cry.* I reread what I'd written in the narrative.

By all the accounts I'd seen, Castañeda was a likeable fellow that followed orders even though he disagreed with General Santa Ana. The General distrusted the Anglo settlers and sent troops after the cannon in a show of force. *Is this my show of force?* I decided to leave Santa Ana out of that part of the narrative. The notecards lay on the coffee table right in front of Alex. I needed them to know what happened next. With a knee on the table, I leaned over and picked them up. I could feel Alex watching me.

Stirred to action by the orders of Santa Ana, an army of volunteer Texans marched to San Antonio de Bexar. From October to December, the Mexican army fought skirmishes against the Texan army, which was now larger and no longer only Anglos fighting for independence.

The narrative sounded more and more like a textbook. And I was in danger of losing my personal battle with tears. *The narrative. Think about the narrative.* I blinked and rubbed my eyes.

Back home, women and children tried to carry on while the men were away. Messages were delivered on horseback. How often were they updated about skirmishes, the wounded, or those slain in battle?

Concentrating on the words was difficult when I knew full well my actions set off my own skirmish. Alex wasn't stupid, he understood the implication of my one-word answers, yet he hadn't said a word.

By the end of December, San Antonio was in the hands of the Texans, and volunteers were headed home.

I glanced at my phone. I'd been writing for a half hour, and I hadn't even written about the fall of the Alamo. At this rate, it would take me years before Sam Houston made it to Washington on the Brazos. Alex still sat, gazing at me from the other end of the couch.

A breath caught in my throat when he moved the notecards across the table. I wanted him to notice my irritation, but I wasn't sure I wanted to talk about it.

At the beginning of 1836, an angry Santa Ana, marched his troops across the Rio Grande, determined to make an example of the Texan army.

I scribbled words so illegibly, I wasn't sure I'd be able to read it after the fact. Alex sat on the coffee table, his knees on each side of mine.

In fear, Texans ran from their homes, some in wagons and some on foot, headed toward the Sabine River.

My client wouldn't care about all this. I wrote about the Texans, but I needed to write about her family.

Just give up.

I slipped the pen into the coils of the spiral notebook and set it on the couch next to me. Silent, I pushed the cuticle back on my thumbnail, then my index finger. After giving attention to my middle finger, ring finger, and pinky, I moved on to my right hand, anything to avoid Alex's gaze.

He reached out his hands, leaving them open in front of me. "Is this about my appointment?"

I nodded, staring at his hands.

His hands still open in invitation, he asked, "Do you trust me, Katie?" His hot-cocoa voice made the minefield of a question seem inviting, but it also seemed superbly unfair.

What kind of a question is that?

He remained quiet, as if he actually expected me to answer him.

I touched my fingertips to his. "You haven't given me any reason, which I know of, not to trust you."

"But do you trust me?" He leaned toward me, and I could smell the Mountain Rain scent of his detergent.

"I do. With my life."

"What about your heart? Trust me with that?"

A silence hung in the air, but he waited. My heartbeat pounded in my ears, and I inched my hands into his. "Yes." Inconvenient tears filled my eyes as I made eye contact. "But the secrets make me uncomfortable." Somewhere inside me a curtain opened a little more, and my focus drifted to the floor.

He leaned down until he looked me in the eye. "If I promise to tell you about them soon, is that enough?"

"You're giving me a choice?"

"Yes. If you'd rather I tell you exactly what I've been doing when I disappear, I will tell you right now. But if you trust me, please wait."

Harbored hurts peeked out of the deep recesses of my heart and trickled down my cheeks. He tossed the notebook aside and sat down next to me. I buried my face in my hands, determined not to dissolve into a puddle of tears. He pulled me into his lap.

"I do trust you, it's just that I worry that I'm not, I don't know… enough, deserving…name your adjective."

He tightened his embrace.

"I see all my own faults, and there is a nagging voice whispering it will end when you realize I'm not good enough, pretty enough, or whatever. The secret errands make the voices louder." My honesty leaked out, but thankfully, not in wails and sobs.

He stroked my hair without interrupting.

"Then I question the idea of trust. How do I trust anyone after all that happened? And my sister hardly speaks to me." I wiped my face on his tee shirt. "I act like everything is fine, and it doesn't matter. But I think about it all the time."

He rested his chin on my head and rocked gently.

"When you keep things to yourself, I fill in those silent places with my own ideas." I buried my face in the curve of his neck. "I don't like not knowing things."

He exhaled slowly, like a young child mourning his favorite Matchbox car as he prepared to hand it to a friend just to avoid a fight. "I—"

'Don't explain." I wiped my eyes. "I trust you, even though I can't say it without crying."

A soft laugh echoed in his chest, and he kissed the top of my head.

"I love you, Alex." I gripped his tee shirt with my fist and rubbed the cotton between my thumb and index finger.

When I looked up at him, his green eyes sparkled. "I love you too, Katie."

I'd just handed him a key to the places that were all my own, and it terrified me. As long as I was being brutally honest, I decided to lay all my cards on the table, short of proposing to him. "I want to add your name to the deed for the land."

He buried his face in my hair for several seconds before running his knuckles along my jaw and lifting my chin. "I'm not sure what to say. You've kind of caught me off guard."

"I'm sorry. If you don't want to, I understand."

He brushed his thumb on my lips. "I want to. I wasn't saying no, not at all."

I gathered the courage to spring my next idea. "Maybe you could build a cabin on the land. The house that's there isn't in great shape."

"Living right next door? I think I could handle that."

"It would be almost perfect."

"Almost." Hc pulled me to his lips.

May 5, 1836

Only Mother and I have made it home. The whole town is burned.

~*~

May 7, 1836

It pains me, but I need to write what happened.

We left home in such haste because we feared Santa Ana was at our doorstep. As we passed the river, we saw them sinking the cannons. What a heartbreak. It seemed there was no defense, and our only hope was to reach Louisiana. The rains made travel difficult.

Father left us to join with Sam Houston. A wheel on Mother's wagon broke, so we tried to salvage as much as possible by adding it to my load. When my wagon landed in a large rut, the axle broke. From that point on, we were on foot. Rebekah and her tiny one separated from us after two weeks, and later we heard she fell from hunger. Her baby perished in her arms long before she fell.

The muddy landscape and high water did more to destroy our family than the Mexican army. It was all I could do to bring Mother home alive. She has not spoken since Amos drowned trying to cross a river. Oh, the horrors we suffered.

Rumors met our ears, tempting us to return, but then we heard of the massacre at Goliad. Many men joined us, having left the Texas Army. "Sam Houston will not fight," they say. When horsemen ran through our encampment saying that the Mexicans were defeated and Santa Ana had been captured, we didn't believe it at first. When others arrived with the same news, cheers went up, and we all turned for home.

Jeremiah ran to meet up with Father and Nathaniel. They were fighting with General Houston at San Jacinto. I pray my brother returns, even if he is the only one. Mother and I wait at home in silence. I jump at every footstep and hoof beat.

The baby inside me still moves, so not all news is dreadful.

Chapter Twenty-Five

April 15th – 9:18 am

The next morning when Alex walked down the hall in his spiffy clothes, I smiled calmly, although my pulse raced, but not because worry or distrust needled me. He skipped breakfast, and we headed to Becca's mom's house. Alex smiled the entire way to San Antonio, but the small beads of sweat on his brow made him look almost nervous. I didn't ask. I wouldn't ask, not after last night.

When we passed the Fair Oaks exit, I entered the address into my map app. My phone gave Alex directions. A few miles down the road, he exited and followed surface streets until we came to a small neighborhood with older homes and massive lots. Each house sat on at least an acre. Around them were newer neighborhoods with houses butted up to each other. If we ever moved to San Antonio, I'd want to live near the area. *What? If we?* That was an unexpected tangent, on the far side of until. Thankful that thought bubbles didn't appear above my head, I scanned the mailboxes for the house number. "There it is, on the right."

He turned down the long driveway and pulled to a stop near the side door. "Wait right there."

I always waited for him. Landing on one foot without help had proven painful more than once. When he opened the door I turned, ready to get out as always. He held my waist, but instead of helping me down, he kissed me, kissed me like he had that night on the couch. When he pulled back, his eyes danced.

I rested my forehead against his. "Um, wow."

"Security showed up right on time."

"I didn't realize we had an audience."

He lifted me out of the seat. "I'll be back as soon as I can."

"Okay." I waved as I stepped inside.

Becca's mom greeted me with a huge smile. "Hi. You can call me Diane. So pleased to have you." She fussed over me, telling me to just ask for whatever I needed and served me a glass of tea before ushering me into her craft room.

Becca grinned as I walked in. "Great space, isn't it?"

Like a kid admiring Christmas lights, I gaped at the large room with built-in shelves along one wall. They were stocked with fabric, bead trays, decorative paper, and paper crafting supplies. Against the opposite wall sat a sewing table with a thread rack mounted to the wall above it. Bulletin boards, family photos, and art covered the other exposed walls. A large table surrounded by barstools occupied the center of the room. "Beyond amazing. This is a dream room."

No sooner had I gotten situated at the table, my phone buzzed.

Alex texted me: *Love you. Be back as soon as I can.*

I replied with a kissing emoji, not caring if it seemed silly. My daydreams were interrupted when Becca dropped a stack of sketches in front of me.

"I drew a few ideas for us to play with." She seemed just as excited about Grace's gift as I was.

"She was up half the night. I think you've created a monster." DJ walked up behind her and tickled her in the ribs, then waved and laughed as he shuffled out of the room. "Call me if you need anything. I'm happy to critique."

Becca giggled, and I pulled out my taped-together family tree. Flipping through her sketches, we decided on a layout. Becca pulled out a long length of extra-wide butcher paper and started penciling a tree.

"Becca, is there anything you can't do?" I never ceased to be surprised by my friend's talents.

She laughed. "Lots, but this kind of stuff is fun." She sketched branches leaving places for names and dates. "Names and dates will be on leaves. We'll attach those to these branches."

I cut out leaves in several shades of green, using a pattern Becca created. After she finished sketching the tree, she shaded the trunk and branches with a sponge and brown ink. Within two hours, pencil lines morphed into a life-like tree. She started writing names and dates on leaves and asked me to sponge the bottom edge of the chart.

"I'm almost afraid to touch it."

"You'll do fine. Just think of it like you are antiquing it or tea staining it."

"Just the bottom edge?"

"Start with that. We'll go up the sides a little, but then use blues and greys along the top."

I set to work, and another hour evaporated. Becca stretched and said she needed a break. She wandered off to talk to DJ, and I heard Alex's voice in the kitchen. I stared at the door, knowing he'd come find me.

He smiled as he sauntered into the craft room. "I'd never see you if you had a room like this."

Somehow in those three and a half hours, I'd forgotten how amazing he looked all dressed up.

He walked up behind me and wrapped his arms around me.

I leaned into him and breathed in deeply. "We're nearly finished." I pointed at the chart.

As he read over it, his eyes twinkled. "Your client will love it." He rested his chin on my shoulder. "Come on into the kitchen. I brought lunch."

DJ, Becca, and Diane were already seated at the table as I limped into the kitchen. "Start eating. Don't wait on me."

They all dug into the burgers and fries. Alex pulled out my chair, then sat next to me. I watched as he flipped his tie over his shoulder.

After picking the onions off my burger, I took a bite. "So good. I didn't realize how hungry I was."

Over lunch, Becca filled her mom in on our project.

Diane beamed. "You are both welcome to use my craft room anytime."

"Thank you." I dunked a fry in ketchup.

Becca rubbed her stomach. "Kate, do you think you could finish up the last few leaves? I have a pounding headache, and I just don't feel great."

"No problem."

When Alex and I got back into the truck, I may have glanced around looking for evidence of where he might have been. It wasn't because I didn't trust him, but curiosity ate at me.

May 7, 1836

Father and Jeremiah are home.

He recounted the last battle to us shouting "Remember the Alamo! Remember Goliad!" That was what General Houston told them as they attacked the Mexicans during their siesta. In only eighteen minutes, the Texans defeated an army. Texas had won its independence.

He looked to me with tears in his eyes. "But for us, the price was too great. We lost nine men." After rubbing his face, he continued. "One of them was your Nathaniel."

I must force my chest to breathe. How will I live without Nathaniel? How will I raise our child alone? He will never benefit from the Texas he fought for. Grief overwhelms me, but I remember to eat, only because another depends on me for life.

Mine is not the only heartache. The cries of victory mix with the wails of despair as families return to their homes and grieve the loss of fathers and brothers, mothers and sisters.

~*~

May 9, 1836

Jeremiah ran into the house, a wide grin spread across his face. "I saved our treasures." The words sounded hollow echoing off charred remains of the house. When we returned, our chickens were gone, and the pig had been slaughtered. The idea of treasure seemed laughable given our current condition.

"What have you saved?" Father, always ready to see the bright side, seemed excited.

"Mother's pin and a few other things. I buried them in the barn." In a handkerchief he had her brooch, a locket, and a small ornamented box.

"Well done!" Father slapped him on the back. "Mother, look!"

A hint of a smile tried to escape, but it was washed away by her tears.

CHAPTER TWENTY-SIX

April 15th – 3:33 pm

Alex unlocked the door and held it open while Kate shuffled through. Inside, he wrangled off his tie and started toward the extra room.

"Alex?" She sang out his name in a playful tone.

He stopped near the hall. "Yeeeees?"

"What should we do with our afternoon and evening?" She limped up in front of him.

"Please don't be upset." Alex wrapped his arms around her. "I meant to tell you earlier. I called Travis and asked him to come over. I have dinner plans."

"You are going to dinner with Ellie's parents without me?" That little dimple appeared between her eyebrows.

"No. I told them we'd get together after your cast came off." He kissed her on the forehead. "Allow me another secret, please."

It was so hard to try and surprise her. With her birthday in less than a week, planning the evening stretched her trust and maybe her patience to its limit. But the scheduled dinner he couldn't miss, and if it didn't go the way he hoped, the less she knew, the better.

She traced her finger through the cleft in his chin. "I'm not mad."

"Thank you." He untucked his shirt.

She grabbed his hand. "Do we have time to talk?" Her tone suddenly serious, the playfulness disappeared.

He smiled, but his muscles tensed. "Aren't we talking now?"

"Please." An intensity burned in her eyes.

Sensing where the conversation was headed, in a direction he wasn't ready to take it, he cradled her face in his hands. "Let me change, then we can chat about whatever you want, even chick flicks." He planted a quick peck on her lips.

Her brown eyes puddled with tears. "Sure, yeah."

He plodded down the hall. When he closed the door, the sound echoed. He hadn't intended to slam it. He forked his fingers through his hair. A tightrope looked like a highway compared to the line he was walking.

Thunder rumbled. He undressed and put the slacks and dress shirt back on hangers. After yanking on a pair of jeans and a Henley, he fell back on the bed and closed his eyes. Avoiding the conversation meant avoiding her, which he hated.

When lightning flashed a few minutes later, Alex ventured out of the room, unsure of what he wanted to say or how he'd handle what he thought she planned to say. Kate's bedroom door hung open, the room vacant. He walked into an empty kitchen, and his pulse quickened. He ran to the den—also vacant. Room to room, he quickly searched the house. *Where is she?* His truck was still parked where he'd left it. A quick peek out the window verified that the security guard was still parked outside.

He dropped into a chair at the kitchen table. A soft creak caught his attention. Racing out the front door, he stopped just beyond the threshold.

She met his gaze and flashed a hesitant smile, her brown eyes still misty. Scooting to the side, she tapped the swing. The pitter patter of the rain cast a melancholy spell. Kate drew her favorite quilt—the one made by his grandmother—up to her chin. The muddled questions in her eyes pleaded with him to join her.

Alex sighed as he trusted his weight to the swing. "Sorry I took so long."

She shrugged. "I didn't mean to make you feel cornered." She wiped her face with the quilt.

"Cornered?" He shot her a sideways glance. His mind raced, trying to navigate the landmine of her implication.

"It's okay." She stared at the stitching on the quilt. "I can't believe we've only known each other a few months. It seems longer."

The wind stilled, and his heartbeat echoed in his ears. "It does."

Her jaw fell open. "Really?"

"My hermit existence seems like a lifetime ago." His boots scuffed against the porch in rhythm to the swings movement.

She slipped her hand out from under the blanket and laced her fingers with his. "I love you, Alex."

He nodded, forming a coherent sentence in his head. "That only begins to describe how I feel."

She leaned her head on his shoulder, and her hand, still tangled with his, shook. "I want…"

He held his breath, but she left the sentence unfinished and squeezed his hand.

"Kate—" After a deep breath, he relaxed.

"I know. You need time." She focused on her fingernails.

He lifted her chin and brushed his thumb along her lips. "You know I love you, right?"

She pulled his arm around her and snuggled close. "I do."

He hid a smile. Whether her word choice was carefully chosen, he wasn't sure, but he filed it away as a sign they were on the right path. The rains picked up, gusting and spraying them with drops. Nestled on the bench, they swung in silence until the storm blew over.

Precisely at the scheduled time, Travis knocked at the back door.

Alex pulled it open. "Come on in."

"Hi." Travis glanced around then lifted his eyebrows. "Where's Kate?"

"Back in her room. She'll be right out." Alex nodded toward the den.

Travis sat take-out containers on the counter.

"You stopped at the Thai restaurant she likes?"

"Of course." He followed Alex into the den. "I appreciate you calling me. How are preparations coming along?"

Alex sat so that he could see the doorway. "So far, so good." He rubbed his hands on his face. "Keeping secrets from her is really difficult."

Travis chuckled. "Y'all want the same thing."

Alex snapped his head up. "Has she said anything to you?"

"That she loves you is clear, but you know that."

He stared at the coffee table and nodded slowly. "Today, I think she almost—"

Travis cleared his throat.

Kate stood in the doorway. "Am I interrupting?"

"Hi, sweetheart. Thanks for inviting me. I brought Thai food."

She hugged him, but watched Alex over his shoulder. "Yum. I'm starved."

Alex retreated to the back to grab his wallet and keys. He listened as Kate described the family tree she and Becca created. As he walked down the hall, she watched him and smiled as he stepped up next to her.

He leaned down and planted a kiss on her cheek. "I'll be back after while."

She put her hand on his arm and whispered in his ear. "I love you."

After another quick peck, he walked out the door.

Alex walked up to the restaurant, scanning the waiting area for Tom and Meg. When he pulled open the door, Tom waved.

"Hi. It's good to see you again." He patted Alex on the back.

Meg hung back and flashed a tight, forced smile.

Hope she thaws. They followed the hostess to a table and slid into a booth.

The waiter hurried over. "What can I get you to drink?"

Tom perused the list of beer options. "What's on tap that you would recommend?"

"The Shiner is a popular choice."

"I'll take that, and she'd like a frozen margarita."

Meg patted Tom's hand.

"I'll have a Dr Pepper." Alex took a deep breath as the waiter hurried away. "How was Colorado?"

"Cold. I'm not sure how people actually live there." Tom shook his head and laughed.

"It was great being back home." Meg enunciated each word.

Alex tried to keep the conversation going, in spite of the chill from the ice queen. "Looks like you've healed nicely."

"Good as new." Tom tapped his shoulder.

Alex hadn't seen him since right after he'd been released from the hospital months before. Injured in the ordeal surrounding Kate's kidnapping, they'd been distant, entirely because of Meg. Alex had managed to get Tom's number and asked him about meeting for dinner. Since they'd both come, Alex held onto a glimmer of hope.

The waiter passed out drinks. "Have you decided?"

As Tom and Meg ordered food, Alex thought about what he wanted to say.

"And you, sir?"

"A bacon cheeseburger, please."

As soon as the waiter walked out of earshot, Alex launched into his explanation. "I know things have been a little weird since Kate's kidnapping. It was obvious then that she loved you, Meg, and I know she still feels that way." He sipped his drink. "She misses seeing you."

Meg remained silent.

Alex met her gaze. "I care about Kate immensely. More than anything in the world, I want her to be happy."

She clutched her drink. "We want that for her too."

"And that brings me to my point. Kate's birthday is coming up in less than a week. I apologize for the late notice, but I'm throwing her a surprise party at my cabin. I hope that the two of you will be there to surprise her and celebrate with us." He smiled, hoping the invitation would be well-received.

"Sounds great! Meg was just talking about Kate's birthday." Tom glanced at his wife.

She drew a long sip of her margarita and smiled. "I feel so honored that you asked us to be there. But I'm not sure why."

"You are her sister, and you are important to her. I hoped you'd be there on her birthday." He curled the straw wrapper into a small circle. "I'm not trying to come between you."

"Maybe you aren't so bad." She dabbed her eyes with her napkin. "With everything that's happened, it has been weird, but I love Kate."

"I know you do." Despite her tantrums, Alex never doubted that she cared for Kate.

Meg clutched Tom's hand. "We would love to attend, wouldn't we, Tom?"

"Of course. Sounds like a lot of fun. What can we bring?" He smiled back at her with a look of relief.

Excited by how well the evening had gone, Alex wasn't sure how he'd keep the party a secret from Kate. "Just yourselves. I've been meeting with caterers and sneaking around planning this shindig. Kate is not an easy person to surprise."

Meg laughed, a melodious sound that reminded Alex of Kate's laughter. "You are right about that. Kate and her curiosity make it almost impossible to surprise her."

Shortly after 9 pm, Alex settled the bill on the sly when he walked away from the table. Although Tom and Meg sounded like they could talk for another four hours, Alex wanted to go back to Kate's. As they said goodbye, Tom shook hands and thanked Alex for dinner.

Meg surprised him by hugging him. "I know you make Kate happy. It's clear she loves you. I can't wait until her birthday. Mums the word!"

If Alex had known that a little buttering up was all Meg needed, he'd have done it weeks ago. The evening had gone even better than he hoped, and he'd learned a little more about Kate from Meg's stories.

On the way home, he mentally ran through the list of people he wanted to invite to the party. *Travis knows. Meg and Tom know.* He'd called Kate's friend, LeAnn, in Colorado, who had gleefully accepted the invitation.

He'd called Marisa, but his calls had been declined every time, so he sent Marisa a text about the party, sure to mention that it was a surprise. Ben knew about the surprise, but Alex called him anyway.

Ben answered on the first ring. "Alex? Everything okay?"

"My sister hasn't answered her phone all day. I've called three times. It isn't like her to ignore my calls." Alex didn't share these worries with Kate, but the situation with his sister concerned him. He only vented to Ben, who didn't know Marisa but could give rational advice.

"Is this the one you were asking about the other night?"

Alex nodded to no one. "Uh-huh, but I really don't know if there is anything like that happening."

"She's not answering or she's ignoring?"

"After one ring, it goes to voicemail." Alex couldn't imagine his sister purposefully declining all of his calls.

"And you don't know where she lives?"

"With that boyfriend, but I don't know where that is." Worry strained Alex's voice. "That makes me a horrible big brother. I let her down after Ellie died, and now—she doesn't even ask for my help. I don't know what to do. I can't talk to Kate about it. She'll only worry."

Ben remained quiet a minute before responding. "Have you tried asking Maddox? He talked to her after the break-in, didn't he?"

"Good idea. I'll do that." Alex needed to invite Maddox and Beth also, so he'd work the question about Marisa into the conversation.

After a short call with Maddox, he had two more confirmed guests for the party, but no more information about Marisa. Alex hadn't yet decided if he should invite Philip. But DJ and Becca and Gram still needed to be invited. Alex called DJ.

He answered after two rings. "Hey, Alex."

"Is Becca there? Can you put me on speaker phone?"

"Sure. Done. What's up?"

"Anybody else there?"

"What's with the cloak and dagger routine? No one else is here."

"I'm planning a surprise party for Kate. Her birthday is on Thursday."

"So that's what you've been up to." Becca sounded pleased.

"Gram is invited also. I haven't had a chance to speak with her alone, so please convey my invitation to her."

"She'll be tickled."

"And I have a big favor to ask. Could you be at my cabin at five that night to let in the caterers and other guests? I'll arrive about six thirty with Kate."

"Of course. I'm so excited."

"Becca, you can't tell her. I know it will be difficult, but please. I've worked so hard to surprise her."

"Alex, we won't spill the beans." Becca giggled.

Alex parked next to the house and closed his eyes. Everyone who Kate would want at the party had been invited. If they could just solve the mystery of who broke into her house and ran her off the road, life would be almost perfect. He slid out of the truck, anticipating the gleam in her dark brown eyes.

As Alex pushed open the back door, she shuffled across the room. "Hey."

"Y'all have a nice evening?"

"We did." Travis shook Alex's hand. "Kate told me about the land she wants to buy."

"It's a nice place." Alex motioned toward the den. "Let's sit."

Travis shook his head. "Thanks, but I have an early meeting, so I'm gonna run."

"Don't leave on my account." Alex hoped they'd moved past that awkwardness.

Travis chuckled and patted Alex's arm. "You aren't running me off." He hugged Kate, then left through the back door.

Alex dropped into the corner of the sectional and held open his arms. "Come sit with me, please."

She snuggled up next to him. "You look tired."

"I am."

"Go get some sleep."

"Not yet." Alex tilted his head back. Keeping secrets, even temporarily, exhausted him.

Kate shifted into his lap. "Please talk to me."

"What do you want me to say?"

"You're just so quiet. It seems like brooding."

"I'm drained and a little worried about all that's happened and about my sister. I just want to hold you and unwind before bed. Is that okay?"

She relaxed against him. "Want to watch something?"

"Sure." He grabbed the remote and started a show.

Sometime during the episode, he dozed, but his eyes snapped open when Kate kissed him.

"Goodnight. I'm headed to bed." She pushed off the sofa.

He held her hand until distance separated their fingers. "Night. Love you."

She shuffled down the hall.

He glanced at the time and frowned as the warning came to mind. The evening had gone so well, but he couldn't think of anything else but the note. He waited until Kate settled into bed before making himself coffee and turning on a war documentary.

May 12, 1836

Again today, I heard Susanna recount the events of the battle at the Alamo, and I'm embarrassed to admit jealousy burned in my chest. Her husband ran to her when the Mexican army broke through the walls, when they were being overrun, knowing all hope of victory was gone. He kissed her goodbye, asked her to save their child, and left to return to the artillery. She never saw him again.

Why am I jealous of such a tragic tale? Oh, to have had but a minute with Nathaniel to tell him of the life we created and the treasure of one last kiss.

~*~

May 24, 1836

Barely a month has gone by since I learned that my Nathaniel would not return to me. Father has built us a small house. It is sufficient for the four of us.

The news of a raid on Fort Parker has dampened the excitement of our victory. The descriptions of terror suffered by the families are too brutal to recount here. If only I could erase the words from my ears. Children were taken as captives.

CHAPTER TWENTY-SEVEN

April 16th – 4:44 am

I shuffled down the hall at some crazy early hour. The face I couldn't remember haunted my dreams as did the sound of glass breaking. The terrors always ended with the note. The words ran through my head, and my sleep ended.

I wandered out to the kitchen, and the light from the television caught my attention. Alex lay sprawled on the sectional, sound asleep.

As I tucked the quilt around him, he opened his eyes and grabbed my wrist.

"It's just me. Go back to sleep."

"Sorry." He rolled over and buried his face in the back cushions. Soft snores made it seem like he slept peacefully, but based on his reaction moments ago, I knew otherwise.

I tiptoed into the kitchen. Quietly, I pulled out my muffin tins. If I understood the therapeutic power of mixing flour, eggs, and sugar, I'd make millions with a self-help recipe book, but I didn't. I only knew it helped to ease my tension.

While the sun worked its way up toward the horizon, I blended the batter and filled muffin cups. With only two muffin tins, the process trudged along. Five dozen muffins sat on the counter when he wrapped his arms around me and ran his hands over the ruffles on my apron. "Smells like cinnamon muffins."

"One more dozen in the oven." I pointed to the basket on the counter. "Help yourself."

He snagged a muffin and poured himself a cup of coffee. "Everything okay?"

I sat across from him cradling my coffee mug. "Mostly. I was just thinking about the warning note and decided to bake a few dozen muffins."

"I was thinking that maybe…"

I rested my elbows on the table and leaned forward. "I'm listening."

"I'd rather not sit around here all day. We can take our muffins to go, drive to San Antonio, and visit the cemetery. Afterward, I can show you where I grew up and went to school. If you want."

I clapped my hands together, thrilled at the suggestion. "I love that idea. Oh. Oh. Oh. What's the date?" I was in danger of pulling a muscle in my face, my smile stretched so wide.

Alex chuckled. "It's the sixteenth."

"I think it's Ruth's birthday. That's kinda a neat coincidence." I limped around behind him and draped my arms around his neck. "Thank you. I'm excited to see where you grew up."

He pulled me into his lap. "I would feel much better if they caught the creep that ran you into a tree. Speaking of… want to take a few minutes and pop in on Philip?"

"For real?"

"We can just stop by and while you chat, I'll have a look around."

"But what if he is lying to us?"

"Good point. You stay here. I'll be back in a few minutes."

The timer beeped, and I popped up out of his lap. "I'm going to get ready while you play private investigator." I pulled the muffins out of the oven, and set them on the cooling rack.

"If I'm not back in a half-hour, call the police." He laughed as he walked out the back door.

Alex returned before I needed to call in the troops, but he didn't say anything about his visit with Philip. We loaded into the truck, and he nonchalantly checked his rearview mirror multiple times on the way into town.

"Think it's a coincidence that the car you thought might be following us that day was light-colored, just like the one that hit me?"

"Nope. But I don't want you to worry." He planned to do that part all on his own.

"I can't promise that, but I'm glad you are with me."

He reached over and squeezed my hand. "Do you know where in the cemetery we'll find the grave? It's a big place."

"I don't. We'll have to stop at the office."

As he navigated the narrow, paved roads through the tree-covered burial park, I scanned the headstones. Some were very old.

At the office, I hobbled in with Alex at my side. I glanced up at him, and he smiled down at me. A burning desire to explain myself and maybe even propose sparked inside me. He loved me, of that I had no question, but what if the idea of marrying again seemed too big a risk for him. I wasn't content with the current circumstances beyond a temporary arrangement. I wanted to be, but no amount of wanting granted the contentment I hoped would overshadow my desire to marry him.

I snapped to, worried what look was plastered on my face, when the lady behind the counter cleared her throat.

"We were hoping to get the location of a grave." Alex laid his warm hand in the small of my back.

"What's the name, hun?"

"Ruth Whittaker Cooper. She died in 1955." I shifted on the crutches and leaned on Alex.

"Give me just a minute." The lady pulled open a card file drawer and fingered through cards until she found what she needed. "Found it."

She gave Alex directions, drawing arrows and circling the location on the map. I half-listened and let my thoughts return to want I wanted to say.

"You ready?" He folded the map.

"Uh huh." I turned to the lady who'd helped us. "Thank you so much."

She nodded and returned to her work.

Alex pushed open the door and stayed beside me until we got to the truck. "Everything okay? You seemed a million miles away in there."

"I'm fine. Really."

Armed with the map, he headed for the grave. He continued down the road in front of the office a short distance, then glanced down at the map on the center console. He turned left onto a tree-lined road. At the fork, he stayed to the right following the red line she'd drawn for him, then took a left. After passing two cross streets, he slowed and looked around. "She mentioned a cluster of trees. It should be around here somewhere."

"I think maybe she meant those." I pointed to the left, and Alex pulled to the side of the road.

He helped me out of the truck, but I opted to leave my crutches. I didn't feel confident in my ability to use them in the grass. I limped toward the trees and read each headstone.

"Over there." I stopped when I saw the headstone.

"Why did you stop?"

"Bruce said that Grace knew nothing about her mother. He certainly didn't mention anything about her grave."

"Okay?"

"There are fresh flowers on it. And today is her birthday. Someone else has been here." I hurried to the plot as fast as my cast allowed.

"Who could have left them?"

I snapped a few photos. "Please save the map. I want to give it to Grace." I tucked my phone back in my pocket. "I'm not sure who left it, but I have an idea about where to start my hunt."

"You going to make me guess?"

"Ruth didn't have any other children, but she had siblings. Maybe a niece or nephew left her flowers."

"Who would be Grace's cousin, right?"

"How cool would that be? Here's your family tree, and, by the way, I found your cousin."

"Want to head straight home and skip the detour?"

"Absolutely not. I can't tell you what it means—" I turned back to the truck. "I want to see where you grew up."

Twenty minutes later, Alex and I were parked along the street in front of a pale-yellow bungalow.

He rolled down the windows and the smell of fresh cut grass wafted in. "Think someone cut that with scissors?"

"Manicured definitely describes it." I pointed at the flower beds. "The pansies are pretty."

"This is where my parents lived when I was born. We moved before my brother was born, but this is where I spent the first year of my life." He squeezed my hand, and I tangled my fingers with his.

"This is really sweet."

"It didn't look like this when we lived here. The neighborhood has rebounded." Alex grabbed a third muffin from the bag. "We should move on. I don't want people to think we're casing the place."

"Where to?" I couldn't wait for the next stop.

"Next, the house where I lived until I left for college." Alex drove for several miles, crossing outside Loop 410. He pulled up in front of a two-story house on a corner in a neighborhood only a couple miles from Becca's mom's house. "This is it. That window up there on the right was my bedroom." He leaned in front of me, smelling wonderful as he always did, and pointed out the window. "And back here—" He pulled around to the side of the house. "—is the large oak tree that I spent hours in and under."

I ran my fingers up and down his arm. "Is it hard being here?"

"A little. I haven't been by here since we cleaned it out and put it on the market."

"What happened to all the stuff?"

"I have it in storage." He kissed me, just a quick peck. "One of these days you can help me sort through it."

"Just say when." I hovered between tearful and giddy.

"Next stop, my high school." Alex winked, clearly happy with my reaction to his tour.

After a ten-minute drive, he pulled into a parking lot across from the high school. "They added buildings since I was here, but this is it."

The fence along the street had cups stuck in it spelling out *Go Rams.*

"I want to see pictures of you in high school." I flashed him my most persuasive grin.

"Let's not be rash. We need to come to some agreements before I show you potentially damaging photos." He rubbed his thumb on the back of my hand and gazed at me, the gears in his brain spinning. His smile fell away, jaw set. He pulled out of the parking lot and drove without saying where we were headed.

I held his hand and quietly looked out the window but didn't ask. Everything about his body language said not to. He turned into a neighborhood that couldn't be more than maybe five to ten years old, just outside the loop. Trees covered the landscape, and large homes filled the neighborhood.

In a cul-de-sac, he pulled to the curb and stopped. He stared at the steering wheel and tightened his grip on my hand. I knew then where we were. I pulled his hand to my lips. He looked at me, tears pooled in his eyes.

I only managed a quick glance at the house. "I'm so sorry, Alex."

He squeezed his eyes closed and nodded. Before releasing my hand and throwing the truck in gear, he planted a quick kiss on my fingers. "Scars and all?"

CHAPTER TWENTY-EIGHT

April 16th – 2:30 pm

He drove to the interstate in silence. When he needed both hands on the wheel, she leaned over and rested her hand on his leg. He hoped she didn't ask why he'd included the last stop because he couldn't explain it. Until they stopped at the high school, he'd never thought to take her there.

"We can pick up pizza rolls and snuggle up and watch more of that cowboy sheriff show." She pulled her hand away and wiped her eyes.

"Don't you have some cousins to research?"

"Yes, but it can wait."

"I'm okay, Kate. Really." He reached across the cab and clasped her hand. "Besides, I'm interested in discovering who left the flowers."

Her head whipped to the right, and she pointed at the antique place just off the highway. "Do you think we should stop at the antique store and see if anyone asked about the locket?"

"No. I called Maddox about that days ago. We'll let him take care of it." He'd decided to let Maddox do what he'd been trained to do and let him handle the investigation.

"You ever going to tell me about your visit to Philip's?"

"Not too much to tell. He seemed thrilled that I stopped by. He gave me the grand tour and explained about the knotty pine floors and how they'd been refinished. I got to hear all about the period appropriate colors he'd chosen for each room and the antiques he planned to purchase to furnish the house."

"So, no indication that he's not on the up and up."

"I don't think he's responsible, but maybe you shouldn't have him around when I'm not there." He gripped the wheel a bit too tight remembering Philip's smug smile.

"What did he say to you?"

"He said that he thought you'd really like his place. Then added, 'Maybe if things don't work out ...' like he expected me to step out of the picture at some point."

Philip was guilty, maybe not of breaking into Kate's house or smashing her into a tree, but he'd achieved felony stupid. Alex unclenched his fist.

"What did you tell him?" Her expression danced somewhere between shock and amusement.

Multiple possible answers tumbled through his head, but he opted for a non-answer. "What do you think I told him?" He exited the freeway. "Only odd thing was when I reached down to open an old trunk, he shrieked. 'Don't open that. It's over a hundred years old.' That was strange."

"Think he's hiding something?"

"I think the chest is really old. But what's the point of having it if you can't open it?" He did think Phillip was hiding something, just a gut feeling, but the last thing Alex wanted to do was worry Kate, so he kept that observation quiet.

"Well, cousin hunter, where do we start?" Alex set two Cokes and her bag of notes on the coffee table.

Kate looked up from her laptop and laughed. "Cousin hunter?"

"I was trying it out. Doesn't sound right." He dropped down next to her and lifted his arms so she could swing her legs across his lap. "How do we figure out who left the flowers?"

"I'm feeling my way through the dark on this, but this is my idea. Ruth had siblings. What if some of those siblings are still alive? Or maybe a niece or nephew left them."

"Makes sense. What can I do?"

"Grab my notebook, and we'll work down the list of her siblings."

"My money's on the sister or one of her kids."

"What's the name of the oldest child?"

"Arthur Whittaker."

"When was he born?"

"1923."

Kate's fingertips danced across the keyboard, then a list names and dates filled the screen. "Looks like he died in 1945 in France. Who's next?"

Alex noted the year of death. "Did he ever marry? Any kids?"

"Great question." She ran her finger down the screen reading the information on the digitized death certificate. "Never married."

Alex read off the next name.

Kate repeated the search with a new name. "Edward died in 1972. His wife is listed as Mildred. Let me see if they had any children."

He watched over her shoulder as she searched the birth index with the parents' names entered.

"Two kids. Both boys. Jack and Frank."

He jotted the names and birth dates as she read them off. As she searched, she stopped the small talk. A quiet hand-off of information filled the next hour as they searched each of Ruth's brothers and their children.

"There is no death certificate for this brother, but let me do a quick Google search."

"What will that find you?"

"Sometimes I'll stumble on an obituary, like now, maybe. A Henry Whittaker died last year. Let's see if it's the one we are looking for."

He read over her shoulder. "Preceded in death by brothers, Arthur, Edward, William, Richard, Charles, and sister, Ruth."

"His sister, Shirley, is listed as a survivor. So she was alive last year. Let me google her."

"I told you it was the sister."

"We don't know that yet. I can't find any obituary listed. Let me see if she had any children."

"She must've married because her last name isn't listed as Whittaker in her brother's obit. Is her husband still alive?"

"Oh, let me check. Hmmm. I can't find an obit for him, either. She had three children, two sons and a daughter."

"So how do we contact any of these people?"

Kate navigated to a phone number lookup website and entered Shirley Johnston's name. "Hopefully I can find a phone number."

"I think you just did. This is kinda exciting. Call her."

Kate glanced at the time. "Here goes."

He called out the number, and she dialed. He listened as Kate introduced herself and asked to speak with Shirley Johnston.

"Okay, well, I wanted to speak with her about her sister Ruth. I'm helping a descendant of hers research their family tree." Kate left her number, then hung up, her expression rather grim. "Not sure they'll call back. The daughter answered. Her parents' house is on the market, and all the family tree information is in storage. She said she'd mention it to her mother when she was available."

"You didn't ask about the flowers."

"I didn't want to sound creepy or stalkerish. Besides, even if they didn't leave the flowers, I would love to talk with them."

"What do we do now?"

"We snuggle, eat chocolate, watch *Longmire*, and wait."

"I like everything except the last part." He stood up and stretched. "But if I'm going to eat chocolate, I want coffee. You want anything?"

"Just a glass of water."

The credits scrolled up the screen, and Kate shuffled down the hall. "I'll be back out in a minute."

Her phone rang just as the bedroom door closed. He recognized the number he'd read out to Kate and answered it. "Howdy. Kate's phone."

"Hi, this is Kathleen Hernandez. I spoke with Kate about an hour ago. She wanted to talk to my mom."

"Yes. She stepped away from the phone. May I take a message?"

"My mom almost did a cartwheel when I told her that Kate was helping a descendant of Ruth find her family. Mom would very much like to meet with Kate. Please have her call me so that we can arrange a time. Tomorrow is pretty busy for us, but maybe the next day if she's free."

"She'll be thrilled to hear that. I'll have her call you." He paced in the hallway until Kate emerged from her bedroom.

"You miss me that much?"

"Kathleen called back. Her mom wants to meet with you."

"Seriously? You aren't pulling my leg?"

"How cruel do you think I am? Your leg is in a cast." He handed her the phone. "Call her."

Kate returned the call and arranged to meet on Monday. Back in search mode, she ended the call. "Earlier she said her parents had their house on the market. The address is listed in the online directory. Want to see it?"

"Sure, I guess."

She opened a tab and pulled up a realty site. "Here it is. What a small world."

"What?"

"Your sister is their realtor."

When the sun sank low in the sky, Alex wandered into the kitchen, hoping to find easy fixings for dinner.

"I think I know why Becca isn't feeling well!" Kate rested her cast on an extra chair.

"Okay? I didn't realize it was a guessing game."

"Think about it! She's tired and nauseous. You think maybe...?

"Oh, wow. Maybe you're right." He pulled out the assorted leftovers. "Do you want kids?" He looked back over his shoulder.

Kate blinked several times. "Yes." She opened her mouth to say more, but then closed it.

"How many?" He could feel her curiosity boring holes into his back.

"Well, when I was younger, I would've said three."

"And now?" He clicked start on the microwave.

She shrugged. "I'm not sure."

"What changed?" He turned to face her.

"That window is closing." She stared into her glass of water.

Nothing came to mind as a follow-up to that comment.

She rescued them from awkward silence. "What about you? Do you want kids?"

"Uh huh."

"How many?"

He shrugged.

Kate let her phone ring, waiting for Alex to expand on his response, but when he didn't, she answered at the last minute. "Hello… Sounds wonderful. We don't want to impose.… Ok, great. What can I bring?…Can't wait."

Alex set her plate in front of her.

"Becca and DJ want to have us over for an early dinner tomorrow."

"You going to ask her?"

"No." She shot him a look. "Of course not."

"When is your next appointment?" He tapped her cast.

"One week from yesterday. I'm tired of this cast." She twirled her fork in the Pad Thai.

"Well I hope for your sake it gets removed."

Alex sat at the edge of the bed. He had no idea how he'd sleep. The day had been uneventful as far as the warning Kate had been given, but he couldn't shake the thought. The longer they went with nothing happening, the more his worry piled up.

He sat down on the floor, just outside the extra room where the hall turned toward the master bedroom. When his backside fell asleep, he wandered into the front of the house and checked all the locks. Again. A quick peek out the front window assured him the security guard hadn't left or been taken captive. Parked across the street sat the nondescript car. The driver gave a quick nod.

As Alex ambled back toward his post in the hall, his phone lit up when Kate texted: *Please go to sleep. I will scream your name if I need you. I promise.*

That set his mind racing in a completely different direction.

July 18, 1836

Father said to set an extra place for dinner. I am tending to the house now. Mother went to bed, and rarely rises. The death of her sons and grandchild are too much to bear. She rarely eats.

As for me, my heart has bled for Texas, I will not see it fail.

Our dinner guest was a man who fought alongside Father during the revolution, Mr. Wesley Kent. I remember him from our journey to Texas. In six years' time, he has aged more than ten. He returned from San Jacinto wounded, only to discover that his wife and young child perished fleeing their home. His once young face is now etched with lines of pain and grief. The air of sadness about him, I understand. But, it is good to have him at the house. He is good company for Father.

~*~

August 1, 1836

Madeline Cora Hughes came into the world, her eyes bright. I am all that she has. I hope it is enough.

~*~

August 17, 1836

Mr. Kent has been a frequent visitor. Tonight, when he arrived for dinner, I didn't hear him enter over the cries of the baby. I hurried to finish preparing dinner, while Father and Jeremiah were outside tending to the animals.

When Madeline fell suddenly silent, panic gripped me. The worry that she, too, will be ripped from my life, like her father, haunts me.

Wesley, I mean Mr. Kent, cradled her, smiling into her chubby, red face, his smile so broad it pressed dimples into his cheeks. His countenance stirred hope and sadness. Maybe there is an end to this wandering of grief.

The last time I remember seeing that smile, it was directed at Reuben as we neared Gonzales after our long, tiring journey. So much has changed.

~*~

August 20, 1836

Father convinced Mother to get out of bed. He acquired some fabric and thread. She sews clothes for the baby. Nary a word does she speak, but at least she is taking food.

Mr. Kent was a guest at our table again tonight. He stayed until late, discussing the future of Texas with Father. His leg is mostly healed, and he rarely uses his cane.

Busy with the baby, I didn't hear Mr. Kent's question the first time. When I asked him to repeat it, he queried what I thought of moving west to Bexar or even beyond. I declared my ignorance of the landscape or climate of that area. Father chuckled at my answer. The baby's cries interrupted further conversation.

Chapter Twenty-nine

April 17th – 4:12 pm

Alex turned off the lights and joined Kate near the back door. "Where are your crutches?"

She slung her purse over her shoulder. "I don't need them."

"Indulge me and take them, please." Alex scanned the room.

She sighed. "They're in the den."

Once they were on the road, she listed all the little things she'd noticed that convinced her Becca might be expecting. "Remember DJ carried her to the table from the front door."

"I guess I don't see how that is proof."

"Guys behave strangely, more romantically when they are excited about something in the relationship, right? Don't they?"

He chewed his bottom lip, contemplating his answer. "You read that in a magazine?" Answering a question with a question would hopefully work as an avoidance tactic.

"If DJ knows she's pregnant, he might be—I don't know—more attentive. What was he like just before he proposed to Becca? Was he all sweet like he's been these last few days? They cuddled during the entire movie in the den."

"I didn't know DJ when he met Becca, so I can't really answer that. But I guess a guy might let his excitement spill out in sweet, romantic gestures." He chose his words carefully, never taking his eyes off the road. *Is this about DJ and Becca or just a cover for a different conversation?*

"I bet I'm right. Wait and see. In fact, since Maddox followed up on the locket and assured us that's not what the guy was after, I wrapped it up and tucked it in my purse, just in case."

"If she announces, you're going to give it to her?"

"Yep, to celebrate the little heart beating inside her."

"Don't get too excited, though. They could be getting a puppy."

"Just stop it." Kate looked down when her phone beeped. She grinned and replied to the text.

"Something funny?"

"No. It's Marisa. She's asking about Becca's jewelry."

His sister spent more time texting and talking with Kate since the two of them had met than talking to him. Overjoyed that they got along so splendidly, he didn't complain.

When Alex pulled up in front, Becca opened the door.

Kate hobbled up the walk. "Are you feeling okay?"

"Yes, come on in. Sorry, DJ ran to the store. I'm hoping he'll be back soon."

"Can I help with anything?" Kate pointed to the kitchen.

"Absolutely not. Sit. Besides, there isn't much to do until he gets back." Becca sat in the arm chair and tucked her feet underneath her.

Alex dropped down next to Kate at the end of the sofa.

"I forgot a few things I needed for dinner, like pasta and salad. DJ left just before you got here."

"No worries. I can't wait to show the chart to Grace. And, I located one of her aunts. I meet with that lady tomorrow." Kate scratched at her cast.

Alex stepped to the entryway when his phone rang. "Marisa?"

Sniffles echoed through the phone. It wasn't like her to be emotional.

His heart rate increased. "Everything okay?"

"I'm on my way to your place. I need to talk to you ASAP."

"I'm not home." He looked around at Kate and Becca. "Kate and I—"

"It's important, and I'd rather talk to just you. Alone. *Please.*"

His thoughts whirring, he scrambled to think of a meeting place. "I can be at the burger place just off the highway in Kerrville in a matter of minutes."

"I'm ten minutes out." She hung up.

Alex rubbed his face. "That was Marisa. She's upset, really upset. But I don't want to leave y'all alone."

"Alex, go. Security is parked out front. We'll be fine."

"And our neighbor, Brady, is right next door if we need anything." Becca waved her hand, motioning him out the door.

"Are you sure?"

"Yes. Go!" The ladies answered in unison.

He ran out the door and relaxed a bit when he spotted the neighbor on his porch. Alex drove to the restaurant, speeding most of the way. When he pulled into the lot, Marisa jumped out of her car.

"What's wrong?"

"Let's talk in your truck." Tears streaked down her face.

He ran his thumb through the cleft in his chin while she climbed into the passenger seat. "You've got me worried."

She pulled a tissue out of her pocket and wiped her eyes. "Paul and I have been dating on and off for eight months. It took me a long while to see his true colors, too long." She touched Alex's hand. "When he asked me to move to San Antonio with him, I was overjoyed. I didn't say anything to you because I thought you wouldn't approve of us living together, especially because he's so much older."

Alex didn't respond. If he remained quiet, she might arrive at her point more quickly.

"About two months ago, I saw something that made me a little suspicious. After a bit more snooping around, I realized that he wasn't exactly who I thought he was. I discovered he was a thief."

"What?" He kneaded his temples. "Ay, Marisa."

"Honestly I had no idea before then. And—please don't hate me—I think he's the one that broke into Kate's and the one that ran her off the road."

Though his cheeks burned with anger, he maintained a calm façade. "Why do you think that?"

"Because of the car accident. His car was messed up that day. I reported it but didn't want to say anything to you until I was sure."

"He went after Kate?"

"I think so."

Alex slammed the steering wheel. "She could have been killed."

"I didn't know until after. Honest."

"Why didn't you say something, Marisa?"

"I didn't want you to hate me, and I didn't want him to be suspicious, so I stayed with him."

"So why are you telling me all this now?" His words sounded sharp and cold, but he couldn't help that.

"He used my phone to text Kate and find out Becca's address. I'm worried."

"What is he looking for? What does he want?"

"I don't know, Alex. When I saw the texts, I worried because I couldn't live with myself if…if, you know…something happened to Kate…or Becca."

Alex threw the truck in reverse. "Buckle up."

"Where are we going?"

"To Becca's. Kate and Becca are there now. Alone."

"I'm so sorry. I shouldn't have rambled."

He reached over and patted her hand before clicking his Bluetooth. He listened to it ring until it rolled to voicemail. "Hey, DJ, meet me at your house ASAP. I mean as soon as you get this message. I think someone is planning to break in to your place. Kate and Becca are there."

Alex hung up and handed Marisa his phone. "Call Maddox."

"I already did. I left a message with him before calling you."

"Marisa, why did you show up at the cabin a few weeks ago?" Alex stopped abruptly as a light turned red.

"I suspected Paul was a thief and wanted to talk to you. I didn't know what to do."

"So why didn't you say anything?"

"Kate showed up, and I didn't want her to think badly of you because I was dating a thief."

"She wouldn't have cared, Marisa." He tapped the steering wheel until the light turned green.

"I know that now, Alex. But I'd only just met her, and you are so in love. Are you going to—?"

"Don't change the subject."

They drove the last mile to Becca's in silence.

September 12, 1836

Mr. Kent showed up to dinner with flowers and handed them to me. Until he greeted me with wishes, I scarcely remembered it was my birthday. I welcome his visits, and not just because it is good for Father. I enjoy his company. During the last few weeks, he has asked my opinion more than once on things I'd never before considered. I've listened and asked questions to be able to engage him with any knowledge.

~*~

September 14, 1836

Mr. Kent has been to dinner almost every night this week. Without a family, I know he appreciates the meal and conversation. The last few nights, Father has left us at the table talking while he attended to Mother. I hadn't given it much thought until tonight when Mr. Kent laid his hand on mine.

The sadness that so marked his frame and countenance on his first visit has faded over the months of visits. His words, so tender, caught me off-guard. "Marry me, Tabitha. Will you do me that kindness? When your heart is mended enough to feel again, can it ever feel for me?"

I stared at my hand tucked under his. It felt small under his rough and leathered palm. A timidity I'd never felt with him rushed over me and colored my cheeks. A smile signaled my answer before my eyes met his. "It does even now. Yes, I will be your wife."

~*~

September 15, 1836

It warms my heart to see Mother smile again. News of our engagement infused her with happiness. My only hesitation is leaving her in such a condition, but Father insists they will be fine.

236

Wesley and I chose not to delay our wedding. In three days, we'll marry.

~*~

September 18, 1836

Mother pinned her favorite brooch to my collar. "A wedding gift" she called it. The cameo that Jeremiah saved had long been my favorite.

Wearing my finest dress and bonnet and with little Madeline on my hip, I sit to write one last time as Tabitha Hughes.

Chapter Thirty

April 17th – 5:38 pm

Becca and I wandered into her craft room to pass the time. She strung a necklace while I laid out a combination of beads on a tray.

"I love what you pulled together."

"Thanks. You must be rubbing off on me."

The back door creaked open. Becca dropped her necklace and ran to the kitchen. "Hey, DJ. Alex left to—"

I slipped off the barstool, intending to head into the kitchen. Becca's shriek stopped me cold. A thud echoed through the house, and I froze.

"Please don't hurt me, Paul." Becca's voice sounded thin, panicked.

Paul? Anger burned my eyes. I didn't have the option of being too chicken to investigate. Before stepping into the hall, I shot off a quick text to DJ: *Come home now! Becca's in trouble.*

"Where is it?" Paul's sugar-coated voice had been replaced with a rough, angry snarl. "It is worth a small fortune. Give it to me."

My mind raced. I grabbed one of my crutches and used it to limp as quietly as I could. Thankful the hall and living room were carpeted, I made my way toward the kitchen, making almost no noise.

The sneer in Paul's tone made his intentions clear. "I told Kate that keeping it would end up with someone getting hurt. Do you really want it to be you?"

"I don't know what you're talking about." Becca sounded scared.

I worried he'd really hurt her. Plastered against the wall, I peeked around the door frame into the kitchen. Becca lay curled up on the floor holding her head. Paul squatted next to her. *I can't let him hurt her.* If I'd been alone, I would've found a place to hide and wait for help to arrive, but I wasn't alone. I had to get him away from Becca.

Conscious of keeping my breathing quiet, I tried to focus. I didn't doubt Paul would hurt her. She'd announced that Alex had left, and I wasn't much of a threat, especially not in a cast. There had to be some way to get him away from her.

I gauged the distance between me and Marisa's creepy boyfriend. I'd never take him by surprise in this cast. I leaned back against the wall, trying to think of a plan. Luring him to me seemed my best chance of getting the drop on him. *What can I use?* I rested on my crutch and glanced around the room.

I cringed when Becca yelped and almost gave away my location by calling out to her. I bit my tongue, drawing blood.

"Where's your husband?" Paul's voice was a swirl of rage and desperation.

Becca whimpered her answer. "He'll be home soon."

"Then you best tell me where it is quick." He never bothered to tell her what he wanted.

Near panic, I breathed in deep. The bookshelves a few steps away prompted an idea. I hobbled over and silently slid a small book off the shelf. Positioning myself just outside the kitchen door, I flung the book toward the opposite side of the room. I waited with my crutch raised high.

"Who else is here?" Worry echoed in Paul's voice.

Becca didn't answer.

"Tell me!" Footsteps thudded across the kitchen floor.

As soon as he cleared the doorway, I brought down the crutch with all the strength I could muster.

Paul cried out in pain as he tumbled to the floor. I blinked, shocked my plan actually worked. He grabbed his head and moaned. I raised my crutch above my head, ready to bring it down again but stopped when Brady came into view. He barreled toward Paul, knocking him back to the floor.

"I was on my porch when I heard a scream." He knelt down with a knee in the small of Paul's back. "Have any duct tape?"

Becca ran out of the kitchen holding two rolls of paisley printed duct tape.

"How incredibly embarrassing to be bound with paisley tape." Humor seemed the best way to avoid melting into a puddle of tears. Confident that kicking Paul a few times would help also, I somehow managed to keep away from him.

Brady bound his hands, and Becca wrapped his feet.

"What hit me?" Paul looked back over his shoulder.

"Who hit you might be a better question." Brady pointed at me, chuckling.

"With this." I raised my crutch off the floor.

"You?" Paul let loose a string of profanities, and Brady slapped a piece of tape over his mouth.

"I'll call the police." He disappeared into the kitchen. His cowboy boots scuffed against the floor as he paced.

Suddenly aware she hadn't said a word, I limped over to her. "Becca, are you okay?"

"Uh huh. I need to call DJ." She stared at her phone a moment before touching the screen.

As it rang, DJ ran in the back door, calling her name.

"In the living room." Her voice didn't even crack, but that changed as soon as he came into view.

Stepping over the guy on the ground, DJ gathered her into his arms. "Are you okay? Really?"

Through tears, she assured him over and over she wasn't hurt.

"And?" He laid his hand on her belly.

"I think everything is fine." She leaned against him, and he wrapped both arms around her.

Watching their interaction brought me to tears. My suspicions had been confirmed. The doorknob rattled, interrupting the tender moment.

DJ moved closer to the door. "Who is it?"

"Please let me in. Are they okay?" Alex's voice wavered.

As soon as DJ opened the door, Alex nearly tackled me with a hug. "Marisa said Paul might—" He stopped mid-sentence and stared at Paul writhing on the floor.

"I couldn't hide. I had to help Becca." I buried my face in his chest.

Planting kisses on the top of my head, he whispered, "I'm sorry I wasn't here."

Brady walked back into the living room. "Police are on their way."

DJ kept one arm around Becca but extended his hand to Brady. "Thank you. I cannot say that enough."

"These two had it well in hand." Brady seemed winded yet relaxed, despite the ordeal.

I didn't leave Alex's arms, but turned to face him. "Thank you."

"I'm glad I could be of help. I'm going to run along, but, DJ, you tell the police to just come next door if they need a statement from me." He disappeared as quickly as he arrived.

"What happened?" DJ looked down at Becca, his voice dripping with tenderness.

"I heard the door in the kitchen and thought it was you. But when I ran in, he tackled me." She wiped her eyes. "I was so scared. He wanted to know where *it* was, but I didn't know what he was talking about."

We waited while she blew her nose and swiped at tears.

"Kate was the one that saved the day. She made a noise, so he ran to the living room. Next thing I knew, he was on the floor. Even in her cast, she came to my rescue." Becca inhaled like she was pulling herself together. "Then Brady came running in, and we taped him up."

Paul grunted through the tape.

She ran to the kitchen and returned holding a sleeve of saltines. Munching and wiping crumbs from the side of her mouth, she moved close to us and away from Paul. DJ planted himself right behind her, and she leaned back onto his chest. He put his arms around her.

She whispered, "There's a Baby Crawford on the way, but we aren't ready to make it public. We were going to tell y'all during dinner."

I hugged her. "I am so excited for you." I motioned to my purse, and Alex grabbed it. I fished out the gift and handed her the small box wrapped in pretty paper. "I was hoping that's what you were going to tell us today. Just not like this."

Alex's phone rang, and he stepped outside to talk. A minute later, he walked back in and put his arm around me. "I need to run. DJ, are you staying? I can't say much for today's security guard."

"In his defense, Paul and Brady both came through the back door." I squeezed Alex's hand.

"You can go." DJ pulled Becca back into his arms.

Alex leaned down, kissed me on the cheek, and whispered. "Maddox needs to talk to Marisa. I'll explain it all later, but I figured you'd be more comfortable here."

I nodded. "Is she okay?"

"I think so." He slipped out the door.

Becca and I finally sat down again after the cruiser left with Paul in the backseat. DJ followed them to the station after Becca and I assured him that we were fine. We both knew he needed to see Paul behind bars. Sleep didn't seem possible otherwise.

"I've wanted to tell you for days. We only kept it a secret because it's still early." Becca cradled a mug of tea.

I rested my cast on the coffee table. "I get to babysit."

"Of course."

Alex returned a while later, his brow etched with concern. He pulled me aside. "Marisa needs to move out of that apartment tonight. I didn't know if you wanted to stay here or go back to The Castle."

"Becca and DJ need some time. Mind taking me home?"

"Sure. I'll just—"

"I'll lock myself in and won't answer the door. Please don't call anyone to stay with me." Relieved that the drama was over, I wanted to be home, but I didn't want to entertain anyone.

"I may call you a hundred times."

"And I'll answer every time."

My phone rang as he pulled out of the driveway. "Yes?"

"I said I'd call a lot." He hadn't relaxed enough to pull off the humor. "I'm not sure how long I'll be. Don't know how much stuff she has."

"Call Torres. He'll help you."

"I might." That was code for 'I have no intention of asking for help.'

We chatted while he drove into town. I hoped maybe bridges would be rebuilt between Alex and Marisa while they worked side by side. I opened the laptop and began organizing the information I wanted to give to my client.

After a couple hours, the phone rang again and startled me out of my genealogy search.

"Kate, Marisa might be headed your way. I gave her a key to the cabin, but told her she could go to your place if she didn't want to be alone."

"I hope she does come by. She doesn't think we're mad at her, does she?"

"Not sure. And Ben is coming to help with the rest of this stuff. I'll be late."

"Love you."

A short while later, Marisa parked in the driveway.

Surprised at her lack of tears, I opened the door and hugged her. "I'm glad you stopped by."

"Alex wouldn't let me help anymore. I was just in the way. Thought I'd check on you before heading to the cabin."

"Well, I'm glad you came over. And Alex has help. I don't think you've met Torres."

Marisa stopped. "Who?"

"He's a detective friend of Alex's. Great guy."

"That's good of him to help." She pulled a strand of hair into her mouth. "I'm not even sure how to begin an apology for all that happened."

I shook my head. "You didn't do it, Marisa. I'm sorry Paul turned out to be such a rat."

"Yeah. Let's not talk about him." She dropped onto the end of the couch. "If I never hear his name again, I'll be a whole lot happier."

"Then while you're here, let's talk about Alex." I had dozens of questions I wanted to ask.

When Alex got back to the house, it was late. Marisa had left when he'd texted that he was on his way home, and I guessed the choice was intentional. If she wasn't at the house, she wouldn't have to see him. I unlocked the door, and he headed straight for the den after flipping the bolt. His brow wrinkled, he dropped onto the couch and rubbed the cleft in his chin.

I hopped over to the couch and sat down. "Everything okay?"

"Yep. Want coffee or cocoa or something?"

"No. I want you to sit down and talk to me."

He wrapped his arm around me. "I'm rattled. You were in trouble. Marisa was in trouble. How could I not see that it was Paul?"

"You did see it. You've been worried about her since you met him."

"I didn't say anything to you about that."

"You didn't have to. Neither of us liked him, but assuming he was up to no good was a leap you didn't want to take because of Marisa."

"The day she talked to you at the hospital was the day she started piecing things together. When we met her for lunch that day, she realized all that he'd done."

"But she didn't say anything."

"She reported it to Maddox, but I guess she was afraid to tell me."

"Don't beat yourself up."

"I don't want people to think badly of Marisa. I'm just so glad everything is okay with the baby."

"I don't think badly of Marisa, neither does Becca or DJ."

"She was in the truck when I was at Becca's."

"Which is why the fragrance of perfume lingered in your truck."

He nodded, a partial grin lighting up his bronze cheeks. "I hadn't noticed that. When I left the house so quickly, it was to meet with Maddox. He'd been working the case since Marisa reported her suspicions."

"He never said a thing."

"She begged him not to. He met with Marisa and took her statement. Paul was somehow figuring out what to steal from the houses she had listed. She saw one of the stolen items in his drawer but didn't want to believe him capable of theft. Then he went after you."

"What did Paul steal?"

"She's not sure. Her clients mentioned break-ins, but not all of them said what was taken." Alex leaned his chin on my shoulder. "I feel horrible. How could I have thought Marisa would do those things to you?"

"You were putting the pieces together, but we were missing a piece. A big piece. I promise not to tell her."

"Thanks. I'm just glad it's finally over."

"This has been a busy few weeks. We've solved the mystery of who broke in; although, we still don't know what he thinks I have. I successfully researched a family tree for my first client. There is one more thing to solve."

"What's that?"

"The case of the disappearing Alex."

"Oh, but Katie, some mysteries are not so easily solved."

November 12, 1836

My writing has been sorely neglected. As a mother and a wife, I stay busy from sunrise to sundown. I continue to help Father and Mother as much as possible, but she is greatly improved. The moments I have to spare, I spend with Wesley.

~*~

July 22, 1837

Yesterday we welcomed little William Reuben Kent into the world. Wesley is a proud Papa. There is little time to write, but happiness fills my days.

~*~

November 15, 1838

Wesley stormed into the house, his face red. It took him a long minute to calm down enough to relay what he heard. Homes upriver away from town, had been raided. They stole away the children, children that we knew. This attack was brutal. Friends were killed.

I'm glad for our house in town. It offers protection from the raids, but my heart breaks for the families that have been torn apart by the Comanche raids.

~*~

April 21, 1841

Wesley brought me flowers today. Every year on this day, he brings them as a remembrance for our victories and all we lost.

Soon another little one will be added to our house.

~*~

April 30, 1841

Matilda Elizabeth Kent was born two days ago. To see Wesley with his children expands my heart with love that has no end. It is good to see him smile.

The economy of Texas is not faring well. Wesley and I pray for better days for our children.

Chapter Thirty-One

April 18th – 11:20 am

When Alex glanced at me the third time, I realized my repetitive tapping bothered him.

"Why are you nervous?"

"I'm not. Just excited." I uncrossed my legs and tucked a foot underneath me. "If this goes well, Grace gets more than a family tree."

"I'm sure it'll go just fine. Why wouldn't it?"

"Don't make me think about what could go wrong, please."

Alex laughed and pulled into a parking space.

"How many?" The hostess cradled menus in her arm ready to lead us to a table.

"We are meeting people."

"Right this way." She darted off but slowed her pace when she noticed my cast. She pointed to a table. "Here ya go."

Kathleen stood as we approached and helped her mother up. "It's very nice to meet you."

Shirley wrapped me in a hug. "Thank you for finding me. I can't wait to hear about my sister." She wiped her eyes and eased back into her chair.

Alex helped me get settled before taking a seat next to me. "Kate's pretty good at finding family."

"Thank you for meeting with me." I took a deep breath and tried to focus on all I wanted to say. "I just started working as a genealogist. My first client hired me to research his wife's family tree as a birthday surprise."

Shirley dabbed her eyes. "What a romantic idea."

"While researching, I visited Ruth's burial plot and noticed the fresh flowers there on her birthday. I went home and after some digging, found your name and number."

"Charlie—that's my husband—drove me out there early that morning. In recent years, I've visited her grave on her birthday. She died so young, but I'm not sure I miss her any less now than I did the day I learned she'd passed."

Kathleen patted her mom on the shoulder. "You mentioned a descendant of Ruth's. Mom was under the impression she died without children."

"She died in childbirth. The baby lived."

"George kept that important fact from us." Shirley's shoulders bounced gently, and she buried her face in a napkin. "Can't blame him much. Ma and Pa behaved horridly when Ruth married George. When she died, they blamed him. Ma convinced herself that he killed Ruth. I should have reached out to George."

"Hindsight is a difficult thing." I patted her hand. "I'm guessing Ruth's daughter might be a bit excited to know she has an aunt."

Shirley's eyes lit up, and she clapped her hands to her chest.

"Yesterday, I dug through the storage unit on mom's orders." Kathleen laid an envelope on the table. "This is a letter mom received from her sister."

Shirley nodded, and I slipped out the folded pages. I angled them so that Alex could read along with me.

Shirley –

I miss you. Marrying George may not be the smartest thing I've ever done, but I love him. Given the choice, I'd do it all over again. Please understand that. Mother and father's reaction broke my heart. It's still hard to believe that they don't want to see me. It's worse than being orphaned—living in the same town and being cut-off.

Will you visit me? I have a surprise. If you can arrange it, send a return letter, letting me know when and where.

With all my love, Ruth

"I did write back, but never heard from her. I even went to the arranged place, but she never showed. Maybe she didn't receive my reply. The surprise must've been that she was expecting, but she never got to tell me."

I wiped my eyes and shook my head at the black smudges on my fingers. I needed to find a new brand of waterproof mascara.

"There's more." Kathleen handed me another envelope. "George sent this to mom when Ruth died."

"I was so crushed, I never even answered the letter." Shirley shook her head.

Shirley-

Ruthie died. I wanted you to know.

-George

"I think all the ancestors I dug up will pale in comparison to her learning her own life story." I squeezed Alex's hand.

"Well, family, ancestors—all of that is important in my family. My mother's maternal line has roots in Texas back to the fight for independence. Our family has keepsakes and treasures that have been passed down." Shirley choked out the last words.

"Forgive my mom. Recently we lost one of those keepsakes. But we have a diary written by Tabitha Miller who came to Texas in the 1830s. It's very old, but I made a copy for you." Kathleen handed me the copy.

"Thank you. Excuse me just a minute. I want to make a quick phone call." I hopped up from the table and hobbled outside.

Alex followed me out. "Everything all right?"

"I want to call Bruce. They need to meet Grace. She can't truly learn about her family unless they are there."

"Good thinking." He found a shady spot on a nearby bench.

"Mr. Jackson. This is Kate. As I mentioned before, I found information about Grace's family tree. But I turned up an aunt and a cousin who live here in town."

A gasped echoed through the phone. "I hardly know what to say. Please invite them to her party. What a surprise that would be!"

"I was hoping you'd want me to invite them. I'll let you know what they say." She hung up and clasped Alex's offered arm. "He was a *little* excited."

"I imagine so. You've knocked it out of the park." Alex held open the door, and I hobbled through.

Kathleen and Shirley smiled as Alex and I took our seats.

I rubbed my hands together, deciding how to word the invitation. "My client invited you, your spouses, and whatever other family in town that would like to join us to attend his wife's surprise birthday party Wednesday night. That's where we'll give the big reveal about her family tree."

"This is all so exciting." Shirley fanned herself. "I'd love that."

Kathleen ran her finger along her lower lids, but her makeup still looked perfect. "There are quite a few of us."

"Give me a rough head count when you know so that we can have enough seating. He'll be thrilled."

We finished up lunch, and I soaked in all the stories Shirley shared about her family and history.

Alex checked the time. "We need to be headed out soon."

"I'd love to stay for hours, but I'm closing on some property." I clutched Alex's offered hand and stood. "I'll text all the information about Wednesday."

When we parked outside the title office, Marisa waited near the door. She apologized again.

I wanted to steer the conversation in a different direction. "Did you set up the paperwork with Alex's name on it also?"

"I did." She glanced at her brother, who purposefully ignored her.

Once we were seated at a long conference table, Alex and I signed page after page. A short while later, after the paperwork had all been signed and the check had been handed over, we owned property. Together. That little tidbit made eventually seem a wee bit closer.

Much to my disappointment, we left the title office, without the keys. Marisa promised that as soon as the out-of-town owners signed tomorrow, she'd run the keys out to us.

I grinned all the way home. So much had happened in such a short time. Starting a business, buying land—it still didn't seem like my life. I shot off a text to Travis, letting him know that I'd signed on the dotted line.

"Telling your dad?"

"Uh huh. The inheritance is the only reason I was able to do this."

"Does he know you put my name on the deed?"

"I didn't mention it, but he wouldn't have a problem with it."

After parking, Alex hesitated before climbing out of the truck. "Kate, what do you say we snuggle on the sofa and watch television until really late? Unless you have other stuff you need to do?" Clearly, he'd forgotten about the diary.

"That sounds perfect." I needed to unwind, and though I wanted to read about the life of Tabitha Miller, enjoying time with Alex took precedence, at least in my book.

November 24, 1841

Santa Ana has attacked again. Never have I been so thankful that Wesley's leg never fully healed. His wound may keep him with me. The rumors of battle cause him grief, but he doesn't speak to me about it. We talk of everything else.

~*~

November 27, 1841

I woke in the night to the sound of Wesley's tears, a heavy sadness I haven't seen in him in years. He is worried he cannot protect us if the Mexican army pushes this far. I clutched him to my chest, whispering hope that war and loss are behind us and will not return. What more can I do? I pray that a second love is not wrenched from my heart.

~*~

July 15, 1843

News of an armistice with Mexico reached town. Sam Houston has managed a peace, but there are still problems yet to be solved.

~*~

September 12, 1845

Texans are calling to join the Union, to become a state. Wesley says it offers security from Mexico and financial stability. Many are excited to be a part of the United States. It seems so long ago that we left.

~*~

December 31, 1845

Two days ago, we joined the union. Texas is now a state. Men on horseback are spreading the news which is receiving great cheers. Wesley has a twinkle in his eye and the children are asleep, so I will end my writing.

Chapter Thirty-Two

April 19th – 7:30 am

When Alex wandered down the hall, he found Kate propped up on the couch in the den, clutching the diary. She looked up at him, her eyes red, the small trashcan next to her full of wadded tissues.

"Kate. What's wrong? Why didn't you wake me?" He sat down next to her and rubbed her arm. "How long have you been up?"

She shook her head. "Hours. I didn't want to wake you. I tried to sleep, but then I got up to read the diary."

He sat down and bundled her into his arms.

"It's been slow reading because the crying makes the words so blurry I can't see."

He stroked her hair. "You need to sleep."

"I don't know if I can now."

"Is it really *that* sad?"

"Parts of it." She wiped her eyes with her sleeve. "She was married to Nathaniel, but he died."

"Let me get you something to eat and make you a cup of tea."

Alex put the kettle on the stove and rummaged through the tea stash until he found a bag of chamomile. While the water heated, the coffee pot sputtered and grumbled. After adding a drizzle of honey to her tea cup, he poured the boiling water over the teabag and let it steep. He warmed up a couple cinnamon muffins, then carried everything into the den.

He sat down in the corner of the sectional. "Slide over this way. Curl up against me while you sip your tea." He propped his feet on the coffee table, and she did as he suggested. The diary found a new spot on the cushion next to him, and he handed her a muffin.

She nibbled it and sipped her tea. When she finished eating, she buried her head in his shoulder. "I might just fall asleep right here."

He grabbed a throw pillow from the other end of the sofa and laid it in his lap. "Here."

She reached for the diary. "You read. I'll sleep."

He tucked the diary next to him and chuckled when Bureau jumped up. Purring, the cat nestled by her feet and, after several circles settled down for another cat nap. Alex rubbed Kate's back, and it wasn't long before the rhythm of her breathing changed. She didn't even react when he moved his hand.

He opened the diary.

He started at the sound of his phone ringing. Silencing it quickly to avoid waking Kate, he texted Ben: *What's up?*

He replied within a second: *You free?*

Alex rubbed his eyes and tapped out a response: *At Kate's. You coming over?*

Bubbles danced while Ben typed an answer: *I'll bring pizza rolls. What time?*

Alex glanced at the time. She'd been asleep for a couple hours. He answered: *Anytime*

Looking at the curls draped in his lap, he remembered that night in front of the fireplace during the first week he'd known her. As he reminisced, she stirred. He known her months, but it felt like years.

She blinked and rolled onto her back. Her lips curled into a sleepy smile. "I slept a long time, didn't I?"

"Uh huh." He ran his fingers through her hair.

"It's just like that night in your cabin."

"Yep, except no one is outside hunting you. Not anymore."

She shifted upward so that she was sitting in his lap and nuzzled her face into the curve of his neck. "How much of the diary did you read?" She peppered his neck with kisses.

"Mmm." He tilted his head back and closed his eyes. "All of it."

"Just tell me if you want me to stop." She continued along his jaw line and around to the other side of his neck.

"Kate."

"Yes?"

"Do you want to talk about why you were crying?"

"No." She ran her finger down the cleft in his chin.

He sat up and rested his forehead against hers. "I love you."

"I know." She leaned back, her eyes dark and dilated, and traced him with her gaze.

"And there's nothing you could do that would make me not love you." He pulled her closer, barely touching his lips to hers when her phone buzzed. "My sister only texts *you* now?"

"It's probably about the keys."

She held up the phone, so he could read the text: *I've got the keys! Place is all yours. You home now?*

Kate replied: *Yes! COME RIGHT NOW please.*

He kissed her forehead, and her sparkling eyes tempted him to spoil her birthday surprise. "All caps? Excited a bit?"

"I can't wait. You'll finally get to see inside that house."

"Maybe I could just live in that one for a while." He scratched Bureau, who nuzzled Alex's hand wanting attention, and a message popped up on his screen. "Torres is on his way over."

"We won't be here."

"I'll just tell him to let himself in."

When Marisa arrived, Alex moved her car into the garage so there'd be room for both the truck and Ben's car in the driveway. She opted to stay at the house, and he failed to mention that Ben was headed over. After all that she had been through, Alex wasn't about to set her up, but he wanted her to meet Ben. *And what better place than at Kate's?*

Alex scooped Kate into his arms and carried her to the truck.

Between exclamations of excitement, she dropped kisses on his neck. He held her an extra minute before sitting her in the truck. "It's fun to see you so happy."

"Oh, we forgot to warn Marisa that Torres is coming."

"Darn. That's a real shame."

"You want her to be surprised?"

"Maybe." He winked and hurried around to his side. He drove to the gate, unlocked it, and jumped back in the driver's seat. "House first?"

"We just have to be careful. Marisa fell last time we were there."

Alex shot her a look that showed his displeasure. "That was the day y'all snuck over here."

"I wonder who lived here. The owner left all the stuff."

"Are you planning to just dig through what they left?"

"Maybe. Is that problematic?" She leaned forward as he drove through the gate and bumped down the dirt road. "Over there."

He parked in front. "Wait here a sec."

She handed him the keys, and he unlocked the front door.

He opened the passenger door and helped her out. "I see what you mean about needing a new cabin."

"It's just old." She hobbled through the house, opening cabinets and drawers. She squealed when she discovered a box of photos tucked away in a drawer. "I found pictures. The owners must not know that these were here."

"Kate, not everyone cares about that kind of stuff."

She perched on the dusty old bed, laying out photos. "There are names on the back. This is a goldmine!" Hurriedly flipping through pictures, she didn't even stop to read names.

"And now you have another family to hunt down." Alex riffled through the papers in the box. "Look here's a handwritten family tree." He carefully unfolded a yellowed sheet. "Didn't you mention the name Kent?"

Kate stared at an old tintype photo. "What?" She blinked at him as if she hadn't heard the question.

"You okay?"

She showed Alex the picture. "In this picture it is tiny, but that looks like the brooch Becca found."

"Kate, look. Isn't Kent one of the names you were researching?"

"Wesley Kent. Why?"

"He was married to Tabitha?"

Her eyes went wide. "Yes."

"They're on the tree."

She brushed the tears off her cheek before they fell on the priceless pages and photos. "I wonder if this photo is of Wesley and Tabitha? This is crazy."

"You've got quite a story to tell Grace."

"Oh. Oh. Oh. I need to text Becca." Kates fingers flew across the keypad. A second later she held up a photo of the brooch. "What if they are the same brooch? Maybe that's what Paul stole from Marisa's client. He must've dropped it in her bag at lunch thinking it was Marisa's bag."

"Text Maddox. Tell him we'll meet him at the house." Alex gathered the photos and papers back into the box.

When he pushed open the back door, Ben and Marisa stood face to face. Alex hoped the chance meeting went well, but he knew better than to ask.

Kate announced her discovery. "Paul stole the brooch from Shirley Johnston and tossed it in Becca's bag. It's the only thing that makes sense."

Marisa cocked her head, a puzzled look on her face. "The Shirley Johnston that had her house for sale?"

"Yes. Can you believe it?" Kate hobbled toward the table.

Ben shook his head. "I'm not sure whether you have the best luck in the world of the worst? Tell Maddox yet?"

She grinned sheepishly "I just texted him. He's on his way over."

"Thanks for bringing food." Alex dropped paper plates onto the table. "They smell good. Let's eat."

"What brings you to the house?" Kate's words spilled out in a rush as she jumped topics.

"I need a reason?" Ben handed Marisa a plate and stepped back to let her get food.

Kate popped the top on a Coke. "I should have put the pieces together sooner."

Alex watched Ben walk a wide circle around Marisa and wondered what they'd talked about. "Kate was busy saving people, so you can't hold it against her that she hadn't sorted it all out."

Ben piled on four pizza rolls. "Like when you had the gun pointed at you?"

"Yes, and when Becca had an intruder in her house," Alex said.

Kate turned red. "Okay, that's enough. Stop teasing me."

Ben held up his hands. "I wasn't teasing. Promise."

Alex jumped up when someone knocked. "Must be Maddox."

As expected, Kate's uncle stood at the door. "You solved my case?"

Ben laughed. "Seems so."

Kate flipped open her laptop. "When I met with the burglary victim, Kathleen, she mentioned that a keepsake was taken."

Maddox shook his head. "Wait just a minute. Why were you meeting with the victim?"

"I didn't know she was a victim until after we met. She's related to my client's wife," Kate said.

Maddox pointed at Marisa. "And you were their realtor?"

She shot Ben a sideways glance as she took a seat at the table. "Yes."

"Let me get this straight." Maddox ran through the story making sure he understood what all had happened.

"When was the break-in?" Alex handed Maddox a paper plate and pointed to the pizza rolls.

"Tuesday morning." He piled a couple on his plate.

Alex leaned back, trying to let go of the alternative ways it could have ended. "Just before you met for lunch." He glanced from Kate to Marisa.

"Paul tried to use you to get the brooch back home after stealing it." Ben focused on Marisa, rubbing his buzzed head.

"And then he used Marisa again to show him where Kate lived by showing up unannounced that night." Alex set his plate down.

"Becca had her jewelry spread out all over the dining room table, remember?" Kate looked at Marisa. "Paul took so long to walk to the front door. It was weird, but I just thought he was creepy. Sorry."

"You don't have to apologize. He was rotten. I'm not sure why I couldn't see it sooner."

"I'd left by the time you arrived." Ben's gaze riveted to Marisa.

She jumped out of her chair and slipped down the hall, surprising Alex. He stood to go after her, but Ben shook his head.

"Let me. I must've said something to upset her." He disappeared into the extra room.

Kate shot Alex a concerned look. "I shouldn't have said that."

"She'll be okay." He hadn't seen his sister react that way in a long time. Even under stress, Marisa stayed measured, and what Ben said hadn't seemed the least bit upsetting, though it sounded more personal than a comment shared by two people who'd only just met.

Maddox pushed back from the table. "Anyone want to tell me where I can find this stolen brooch?"

May 15, 1851

The promise of adventure has put a twinkle in Wesley's eyes. He reminds me now of the young man walking with Rueben on our way to Texas. The wagon is nearly packed. In the morning, we head west.

When he'd asked about moving so many years ago—the day my Father chuckled at my flustered answer—I had responded, thinking Wesley might leave. I was careful not to give him encouragement to go. Though I never expected anything more than conversation, I enjoyed his company.

After he proposed and we married, nary a word was spoken about moving west. I thought the subject was dropped. I was wrong. Somewhere on the other side of San Antonio, our new home awaits our arrival.

~*~

June 11, 1851

William and Wesley have worked tirelessly to construct a home. Two rooms on each side of the breezeway made the new place seem a luxury. A separate kitchen, a few paces from the house helped keep the living quarters cool.

A month of living out of the wagon has worn on the entire family, but the end is in sight.

~*~

November 7, 1851

The air here is cooler, less humid than back home. To be with Wesley, to see him happy, I would have gone anywhere, but I am enjoying our new adventure. Sheep graze around the house, kept out of the garden by a sturdy fence.

Madeline misses home. Gracious, she has not complained about the move, but she misses her beau, Charlie Wilson. Before we left, I brought the budding relationship to Wesley's attention. He laughed, saying that if Mr. Wilson loves our little girl, he will come find her at her new home.

That seems unlikely, and I ached for Madeline.

~*~

February 20, 1852

I am learning to speak German. It helps when visiting with new settlers in the area. I love hearing the stories they bring of life across the ocean. The sausages and cheeses they've gifted us are wonderful.

~*~

July 12, 1853

Wesley brought home an unexpected dinner guest, and Madeline dropped the bowl of peas. Mr. Wilson smiled wide. Coming all this way, there is little doubt about his intentions.

Wesley was right.

~*~

August 9, 1854

Wesley, Charlie, and William have started construction on a house.

After Charlie proposed, Wesley granted him ten acres near the back of the property. Charlie's been working night and day, clearing the land and prepping a site for a home. Relieved that my girl will stay close to me, I am excited for her future. Charlie Wilson is a hard worker and loves her more than anything.

~*~

September 23, 1854

I snuggled close to Wesley even though the night was warm. Watching our little girl—for he was a papa to her all these years—marry and leave home left us emotional and sentimental. His arms around me, I listened to the rhythm of his heart. I couldn't imagine loving anyone more, but I had loved Nathaniel with all my heart. But that seemed a lifetime ago. Was it possible that I loved Wesley more because of Nathaniel? Do hearts, once broken, have more capacity to love?

~*~

June 25, 1856

I am a grandmother.

CHAPTER THIRTY-THREE

April 20th – 5:42 pm

Alex stood in front of the hall mirror knotting his tie. "Kate, she is going to love it, all of it."

Kate gathered the items she needed for the surprise. Her hands shook as she laid the diary, notes, and copies of documentation in a decorative box emblazoned with the word FAMILY across the top. Next to it sat the old box from the house next door.

"I hope so. Did Maddox get the brooch back to them?"

"He did."

She scanned her checklist for the party. "Becca was sad to see it go, I bet."

"DJ was happy to get stolen goods out of his house."

She closed the box and cocked her head like she couldn't decide whether to say something or not.

"What?" Alex hoped prompting would hurry the thought.

She straightened the collar on his dress shirt. "You look smashing, my love."

"And you look fabulous." He picked up her boxes and offered his arm. "Shall we?"

Kate and Alex were the first to arrive at the restaurant. Within a few minutes, Shirley and fifteen other family members arrived. Kate texted Bruce. "Everything is ready."

When the waitress gave the signal, Kate and Alex unrolled the chart. Shirley and company ducked behind it. Well, most did. A few had to slip through the other door and wait.

Bruce walked in, smiling and holding hands with Grace. "Happy Birthday, love." He pointed to the chart. "I hired Kate to trace your family tree as a birthday gift."

Grace clapped her hand to her mouth, and tears rimmed her eyes. "Oh my. I don't even know what to say." She walked up to the chart and ran her fingers along the lines. "Thank you." She hugged Kate, and then embraced her husband.

"Bruce said that you grew up not knowing anything about your mother's family. We wanted to remedy that." Kate rolled up her end of the chart just enough so that Shirley and her husband were visible. "Grace, meet your aunt and uncle."

Grace grabbed her husband's arm. "Really?"

"Shirley is your mom's sister." Kate's smile could've lit a small city.

Shirley clung to Grace. While they cried happy tears, the rest of the family joined the group. "And as you can see, you have a few cousins."

"This is more than I could have dreamed." She hugged her husband again.

"Same for me. I didn't even know Ruth gave birth before she died. I have so many stories to share about my sister, about our family." Shirley pointed to the chart. "Our family has been in Texas a long time."

Grace clapped her hands together. "This is all so exciting."

As they all finished dessert, Kate clinked her glass and asked for everyone's attention. "Grace, there is more, just a little bit." She handed her the box. "In the box are the records of your family and a copy of a diary written by Tabitha Miller Hughes Kent. Shirley and Kathleen had a copy made for you."

"Thank you. I'm a little overwhelmed."

Kate cleared her throat. "Your great great great grandmother, on the day she married Wesley Kent, received a brooch from her mother."

Shirley pulled a small bag out of her purse.

"We thought you might like to see it." Kate nodded toward Shirley.

She opened the velvet pouch and laid the brooch in front of Grace. "Kate recovered it this week. It was stolen from our house a short time ago."

Grace gushed about the surprises.

"And I have one more surprise, for all of you." Kate picked up the other box. "Yesterday, I stumbled on these treasures." She pulled out the old tintype and the handwritten family tree.

Shirley gasped. "We have a photo just like that. Where did you find it? That's Tabitha and Wesley Kent."

"It was in the house I just bought."

"In Kendall County?" Shirley wiped her eyes.

"Yes." Kate caught Alex's hand when he stepped close. "We bought their old homestead, but I didn't know until after the papers were signed."

The rest of the evening Alex watched as Kate lived out her dream, sharing history with families, giving them a glimpse of their ancestors' lives. Her birthday couldn't arrive fast enough.

She smiled all the way back to the house.

Once they were home and settled in the den, he handed her a glass of wine. "To a great start to your business."

She took a sip and draped her legs across his lap, smoothing out her dress. "I decided on a name for my business."

"The Amazing Kate?"

"No." She rolled her eyes. "Finding Treasure. Finding Treasure Genealogical Services."

"That's perfect." He kissed her.

Somewhere in the house, a clock dinged midnight. Kate pulled Bureau into her lap. "It's so late, but I'm too wound up to sleep."

"I get to be the first to wish you a happy birthday." Alex brushed a knuckle along her cheek. "How would you like to celebrate?" Giving her the option risked not doing as she asked since he'd already planned the entire evening. He guessed that she'd figured that out. But not asking didn't seem right.

She flopped back onto the throw pillows behind her and eyed him, a sparkle dancing in the dark brown pools. "Surprise me."

Chapter Thirty-four

April 21th – 8:38 am

When I woke up, the house smelled of coffee and bacon. Alex whistled a tune in the kitchen. The day was off to a great start. As I hobbled down the hall, he changed his tune to Happy Birthday.

Too silly to even say out loud, I relished the fun of having a boyfriend on my birthday, a first in my thirty-two years of life.

Alex kissed me on the cheek when I got to the table, then whistled another bar of "Happy Birthday."

"I can't wait until tonight."

Alex winked. "What time is Travis picking you up?"

"About noon. I think he's more excited about my birthday than I am."

"He's excited to share it with you."

"You can come with us. He invited you too." Kate eased herself into a chair.

"Nah, it is definitely a dad and daughter lunch."

He sat bacon and pancakes on the table.

I skipped the syrup and folded my pancake around a slice of bacon. "Torres is a nice guy. I wonder if he has a girlfriend."

Alex shook his head. "I can't believe you."

I tapped his hand. "It's not that I'm interested, obviously, but he just seems like a great guy. And the thing that happened with Marisa, when she ran down the hall—it made me wonder."

"You make me laugh." He drizzled syrup on his pancakes. "And I'm glad you aren't interested in Ben."

"You seemed to hit it off with him. You going to spend more time together?"

"Girls spend time together."

"You know what I mean."

Alex kissed me on the way to refill his coffee. I wasn't getting more of an answer.

Travis took me to lunch at a quaint place in a small town not far from Schatzenburg. Commemorative plates covered the walls of the dining room.

Once we were seated and food had been ordered, Travis teared up as he sat two small boxes on the table. Pushing one of the boxes my direction, he wiped his eyes. "Your mom and I bought this for you on your twenty-first birthday. This was one gift we held onto, praying that you'd one day return to us."

I pulled on one tail of the ribbon and watched it slip off the box. Ripping away the paper revealed a small velvet box. I lifted the lid. "It's stunning. You picked this out, didn't you? Mom mentioned that in the letter."

Travis nodded. "Here let me help you."

I lifted the necklace with the teardrop shaped pendant—a Swiss Blue Topaz surrounded by tiny diamonds—out of the box. The fine white gold chain felt almost weightless on my neck. I lifted my hair out of the way as he fastened it.

"Thank you, Dad." I threw my arms around his neck. Calling him dad became easier every time I said it, and the twinkle in his eye signaled that it meant the world to him to hear it.

He handed me the other box. "And this is from me."

I unwrapped another small velvet box and snapped it open. "Oh my! These are beautiful." I quickly took off my silver hoops and put on the diamond stud earrings. "You are spoiling me."

"It's about time I got the chance to spoil my little girl."

I, of course, responded with tears. Surrounded in happiness, I tried not to give voice to the inkling of disappointment buried inside. I loved the jewelry from Travis, but I wanted a velvet box with something else inside, not from him.

"Everything okay?"

I dabbed at my eyes. "Mostly."

"I'm willing to listen."

"I'm sure you don't want to hear about my relationship woes."

"You and Alex are having issues?" He turned his coffee cup in a circle, focusing on the coffee that sloshed near the edges.

"Not exactly. I just … I don't know."

Travis laid his hand over mine. "You want my dad advice?"

I chuckled at how foreign it sounded. "Sure."

"He cares about you, a lot. I think you should talk to him. Be honest with him, Kate."

I sighed. "I will, but after tonight. He's planned a surprise. Won't admit anything, though. I don't even know where he made reservations."

"I hope the two of you have a wonderful evening." Travis leaned back as the waitress set plates of food on the table. "I can't wait to hear about it."

Alex wasn't at the house when I got home, which disappointed me, but I didn't have much time to wallow before Becca showed up. I'd asked her to come and help me choose a dress, secretly hoping that if she knew something, I might get a hint.

I wanted to wear something that made me feel attractive in spite of the big, clunky cast. Jeans wouldn't fit over it, not that I'd wear them for the special occasion. The destination remained a mystery. Alex only said he'd made plans, and he only admitted to that when I walked out the door for lunch.

As Becca and I talked about what I should wear, I decided that either she didn't know anything, or she was impressively secretive.

She looked through my dresses one at a time, pausing now and then. I didn't have that many, but she took her time going through them.

When she saw my burgundy dress, she stopped and held it up. "This one, I think. Try it on."

I pulled off my shorts and tee shirt, and pulled the dress over my head. I would've twirled, but I couldn't move fast enough to make it look like a twirl. The sweetheart neckline framed my new pendant. The form fitted dress hugged my waist, then flared away at my hips. If I stood just the right distance from the dresser mirror, I could see the dress but not the cast.

"What do you think?" I liked it and hoped she thought it worked well for the occasion.

"It's perfect. And it matches your cast." She clapped. "I'd love to stay and see the finished result, but I'm meeting DJ and Gram for dinner. Gotta run. Call me later and tell me about the evening." She gave me a quick hug before running out of the room.

She knows something!

"Becca!"

A laugh was her only response.

I didn't have time to ponder what she didn't tell me.

Alex whistled a tune in the other room.

I texted him: *Doing my hair and makeup. I'll be ready soon.*

A thumbs-up popped up in response.

I wrapped my hair around hot rollers and pulled out my makeup bag. After digging out colors that accented my dress, I applied powder foundation, eye shadow, lip liner, and lipstick.

After staring at my reflection, I wiped off the lipstick and chose a different color. Butterflies danced the conga through my stomach. I pulled the wand out of the mascara and then twisted the cap back on. Seconds later, I opened it again and bounced the wand up and down. *Might as well go all out.* I slid the brush along my lashes with my mouth hanging open. *Is it true that it helps you not to blink?*

I smiled at my reflection and pulled the clip off the first hot roller. A ringlet danced. As I released each curl, I stuck the rollers back in their case. Sleek, straight hair was such a great look, but I'd tried getting my hair to lay flat and failed. I needed to embrace my curl. With my hair in large ringlets—not the look I wanted—I flipped my head upside down and ran a pick through the curls. Then I held my breath as I returned my head to the upright position. I closed one eye and glanced at the mirror. I grinned. A little conditioning spray tamed the puffiness.

I was assessing myself in the mirror when a knock sounded. "Alex?"

He didn't open the door. "You about ready?"

"Let me just put my shoe on." Unable to wear any sort of heel, I opted for my cutest canvas tennis shoe, a floral print that matched the dress perfectly.

I opened the bedroom door, and the look on his face lit up my insides.

His admiring gaze warmed my cheeks. "You look amazing."

I ran a finger down his raspberry-colored dress shirt. "People will think we coordinated on purpose."

He offered me his arm. "Twinkies."

"You are so handsome." I looped my arm around the charcoal-colored jacket sleeve and hobbled beside him out to the truck. He helped me in like always, but I took extra caution with my skirt.

He unbuttoned his jacket before climbing into his seat. "I love you, Katie."

"I'm glad because I love you too."

"How was lunch with your dad?" Alex fiddled with something in his pocket.

I fanned my face trying to dry my misty lashes before my makeup started to run. "Wonderful. He brought me a gift that he and my mom bought for my twenty-first birthday." I pointed at my pendant. "And Travis, I mean, Dad bought me these." I pulled my hair away from my ears.

"They're beautiful. You look good in diamonds." He nodded toward the pendant. "What is the blue stone?"

"Blue Topaz." I fingered the blue teardrop, wondering what was in his pocket.

"I've worked really hard to surprise you." He pulled out a blindfold. "Will you wear this?" His voice cracked with uncertainty.

I nodded.

Hopefully my mascara wouldn't smudge before we even got to

our destination. If he was trying to build my anticipation, it worked. He tied on the blindfold and then backed out of the driveway. He held my hand most of the way to wherever we were headed. I wanted to listen to every sound and note every turn, trying to determine where we were going, but I was too easily distracted. His thumb caressed my hand, and with just that slight touch, Alex dominated my thoughts. Excitement danced like sugar plum fairies inside me.

He stopped the truck, and I waited in my seat until the passenger side door opened. When I felt the warmth of his hands on my waist, I reached out and clutched the lapel of his jacket. Sliding my hands up the coat, I wrapped my arms around his neck.

"I got you." His voice came out in a husky whisper.

"Is this one of those trust exercises?"

He laughed and slipped his arm around my waist. "Lean on me. I'll bring in your crutches in a few minutes."

I gripped his hand that rested on my hip and took a deep breath.

"It's just a few steps. You okay?"

I nodded and leaned into him. *Are we at the cabin?* Trees rustled, and birds chirped. Dirt deadened the sound of my steps. We stopped, and I heard him push open a door. *He didn't use a key.* It probably wasn't the cabin.

He moved behind me, and a wall of cool air greeted me. The aroma of food beckoned me in. Alex fiddled with the knot, then as the blindfold fell away, light accosted me. A chorus of people shouted, "Surprise!"

The cabin, decked out with balloons and flowers, was filled with my smiling friends, their faces blurred by my tears. I blinked, conscious of my mascara. Meg bounced up and down her hands clutched to her chest. Tom, with his hand on Meg's shoulder, lifted his drink in greeting. *What magic did Alex conjure up to get them to come?*

Marisa, her green eyes wide with delight, clapped and smiled. Detective Torres, Ben rather—I needed to remember that—stood at her side and tilted his longneck bottle.

LeAnn hugged Jeff and wiped at happy tears. "We flew in this morning. Didn't want to miss your surprise." The ring on her finger glinted in the light.

Jeff had proposed days after the ordeal in January, and they'd married the following month.

Aunt Beth and Uncle Pat beamed, their hands clasped like teenagers. Philip gave a polite nod.

Becca's face glowed. She lifted her eyebrows and mouthed "Sorry." She knew how to keep a secret. When DJ called out, "Happy Birthday," the rest of the group echoed his sentiment.

Gram waved from a chair at the table. "I hope this is the best birthday yet."

Travis stepped up and wrapped me in a bear hug. "Happy Birthday, sweetheart."

"Thank you, Dad." I kissed him on the cheek. I wiped off my lipstick mark and realized his face was covered in tears.

I swallowed back a surge of emotion. "Meg, I'm so happy you came. Thank you all for coming. This is a wonderful birthday surprise." Holding onto the doorframe, I turned to face Alex. "Thank y—"

When I saw him, I immediately regretted wearing mascara. A collective gasp went up from the guests. I wasn't the only one he'd managed to surprise.

Alex was on one knee.

He held out a small box, the lid flipped open. "Will you marry me?"

"Yes." Tears spilled down my face as laughter bubbled up. "Yes. Yes. Yes." I threw my arms around him. "On the porch swing that day, I almost … well, I thought about …"

He winked. "I'd have said yes." After kissing my neck, he whispered, "I almost slipped up that day in the kitchen and ruined the whole surprise."

"When you said, 'I want …'?"

He rested his head against my forehead. "I want you to be my wife, to kiss you goodnight instead of saying goodbye at the end of every day."

"It's all so romantic. And at the door."

Stepping forward, he swung it closed with his foot, like he'd done that first night. "Where we met." He pulled the ring from its cushion.

My hand shook as he slipped the platinum ring, set with a single white diamond, onto my finger. "It fits perfectly. How did you …?"

He pulled his fist out of his pocket and spread open his hand. The circled twist tie lay in the middle of his palm. "Surprised?"

I answered with a kiss. "All the appointments…"

"Only Travis knew."

"Dad knew?" I glanced back at my dad, who grinned like a kid who'd just been served a triple-scoop ice cream cone with sprinkles.

"I asked him for your hand. At the hospital, while you were sleeping."

With my hands on Alex's chest, I smiled as the light refracted through the diamond into a million sparkles. "I can't wait to be Mrs. Alejandro Ramirez."

"I know, and I love that. I wasn't nervous about tonight. I knew what your answer would be. Containing my excitement, that was hard." He pulled me closer. "Anticipating this look—the one that's dancing in your eyes—made it difficult to sleep at night."

"I don't want a long engagement."

"That makes two of us." He kissed me in a way that made my knees buckle and my heart race. Desire and happiness swirled in his green eyes. "If you don't mind, I'm not going to build a cabin on your land."

"Our land." I inched up on my toes and pulled him down to meet my kiss. "I wanted you close. I like your plan better."

Acknowledgments

Special thanks go to Pamela, Glenda, Rennie, and all the members of the Schatzenburg, TX group on Facebook for listening and giving feedback when it was needed. And I have to mention the 10 Minute Novelists group on Facebook, a fantastic writing group.

I want to send a huge thank you to my husband and boys for allowing me to do what I love.

About the Author

Pamela Humphrey was inspired to write after researching her genealogy. Intending to create a booklet for her mom and immediate family, she set about gathering stories and pictures of the Ramirez family. She ended up writing her first book, *Researching Ramirez: On the Trail of the Jesus Ramirez Family*, a family history of her great great grandfather's family. During that research, she found a christening record that ignited her imagination. Using the documentation she'd found as a backbone for the story, she imagined what life was like for her ancestors and wrote *The Blue Rebozo*, a fictional account of her great grand aunt's life.

On a road trip, when driving through the Texas Hill Country, the landscape sparked the idea for a romantic suspense series. Weaving mystery, genealogy, and romance, she wrote *Finding Claire* (Book One) and *Finding Kate* (Book Two). She is currently writing the next installments in the Hill Country Secrets series.

Pamela is a stay-at-home, homeschooling mom who enjoys many creative outlets: sewing, paper-crafting, jewelry-making, reading, and conversing with imaginary characters (what most call writing). She lives in San Antonio, Texas, with her husband, sons, black cats, and leopard gecko.

Connect Online

Website: www.phreypress.com
Facebook: http://www.facebook.com/phreypress
Twitter: @phreypress

If you want to read more about the town of Schatzenburg, TX, or the characters who frequent that little town, check out the website for extras and short stories.

Interested in reading more about Detective Ben Torres and Marisa Ramirez? *The Chase*, a romantic suspense novel, tells their story. Look for it Summer 2018.

www.ingramcontent.com/pod-product-compliance
Lightning Source LLC
Chambersburg PA
CBHW050600190726
48283CB00007B/2226